ONE
NIGHT
ONLY

ONE NIGHT ONLY

a novel

SAUMYAA VOHRA

PAN

First published 2023 by Pan
an imprint of Pan Macmillan Publishing India Private Limited
707 Kailash Building
26 K. G. Marg, New Delhi 110001
www.panmacmillan.co.in

Pan Macmillan, The Smithson, 6 Briset Street, Farringdon, London EC1M 5NR
Associated companies throughout the world
www.panmacmillan.com

ISBN 978-93-95624-51-0

Typeset in ITC Giovanni Std by R. Ajith Kumar, New Delhi
Printed and bound in India by Thomson Press India Ltd.

To Dadi and Nani,
the original cool girls

ONE

THE CACOPHONY OF this crowded cafe had become music to her ears. The bustling of the tray-laden waiters, with their tight smiles and limited patience for the one-coffee loiterers who commandeered the best tables. The unabating stream of city traffic right beyond the bay windows that did nothing to cushion the noise from outside. The giggles of girly lunches at which that one extra house cocktail would always be ordered, tipping the group over into raucous territory. It was a mixture of sounds that had become deliciously familiar to Natasha Joshi over her frequent visits. Right now, though, she was running far too late to take it all in.

'I know, I know, you're always on time and I'm awful. Very sorry, madam. Your weird diet coffee is on me,' Natasha said, sliding her bag onto the raised shoulder of the chair opposite her foot-tapping friend, Faiza.

Faiza Haider, her ex-colleague and now impossibly close friend, had a bemused expression on her face. She was used to Natasha's ways after years of picking her up for work and having to spend a daily fifteen minutes scrolling through Instagram, before Natasha finally came running up to the car in a flurry of apologies, her Sunsilk-straight hair flying behind her.

'It *is* on you, because forty-five minutes is fucking shameful.' Faiza grinned, her faux chagrin fading. 'And it's not "weird diet coffee", you asshole. It's a nitro cold brew. It's pretty good, and healthy – try it.' She slid the glass across to Natasha.

'Yeugh, no, it looks like a bad Coke float,' Natasha declared, pulling her empirically pretty, lightly freckled face into a cartoon-esque version. 'I'm getting my sorbet spritzer.' She waved her hand wildly, trying to get an uncaring waiter's attention.

'It's 2 p.m., you alcoholic.' Faiza shook her head. She'd renounced alcohol (for the most part) about five years ago when she'd decided to start a fitness handle on Instagram – no small feat for the day-drinking habitué she had become during her advertising years. Four-pack abs and toned legs were her currency, though, according to Faiza's publicist, her 'beautiful bronze skin and high cheekbones' helped. She'd have a tequila or two on special occasions, but mid-afternoon on a Thursday failed to qualify.

'Whatever! I'm getting cheese fries,' Natasha said, and they both grinned at the reference to *Mean Girls*, a movie they'd watched obsessively during those early post-pitch sleepovers.

Orders placed, they turned to each other in anticipation.

'So? Tell me,' Natasha prodded. Faiza had been texting her about a client all day, ending her barrage of messages with 'I'll tell you when we meet.'

'Okay, so, Cliff notes is that he's a *chomu*,' Faiza summarized, pushing stray strands of her dark, choppy bob out of her face.

'But the long story is he's been turning up for *every* goddamn shoot. Like, four out of five – and we haven't even shot the fifth.' She slurped around the ice in her coffee with her straw.

'I mean, *technically*, it's his brand, so shouldn't he be there?' Natasha asked.

'Umm, he has a bloody comms manager! She is paid a *lot* of money to do exactly this. She needs to supervise the shoots and, *technically*, he should just give the final approvals. But no.' Faiza rolled her eyes. 'He is *always* there, Nattu. And super-casually asks me if I want to get a coffee every single time. Like, how many ways to tell you *fuck off, sir?*'

'Ay yai. Show me what he looks like, na? Is he very uncle-ish?' Natasha's face twisted.

'No, see, that's the thing – because he's decent-looking, his Delhi-boy brain can't handle that a girl can also be not interested.' Faiza handed Natasha her phone, thoughtfully opened to his Instagram profile. 'He's like, *I'm the whole package, bro.*'

Natasha flipped through his pictures, amused.

'Lots of gym "pix", I see.' She smirked. 'His captions are the best, by the way: "Blessed to have this body, treating it right is the least we can do. #blessed #eatright #fitnessmotivation."' The last hashtag brought forth a hearty snigger.

'See? He's the fucking worst,' Faiza said.

Natasha handed the phone back to her just as a waiter came bearing the cheese fries. She flashed her most disarming smile at him as a thank you, only to have him grunt in response as he pushed their glasses apart and wedged the small steel basket between them.

'So, he likes you.' Natasha turned back to Faiza, giving

up on the waiter. 'That could be a good thing ... unless he's being creepy.'

'I mean, sure, he's not groping me mid-shoot, but it's really irritating to have him there just ... *staring* while I'm trying to shoot, man. He doesn't *need* to be there. He doesn't *need* to watch me extra hard every time I do a hamstring stretch, or a lunge. I can't work or talk to the camera freely. Because of him!'

'Okay, yeah, I get that,' Natasha said, reaching for a cheddar-cloaked fry. Faiza watched her scarf it own, wondering if the Bermuda triangle swallowed calories before greasy food entered her friend's slim frame. 'He reminds me of Ritesh, from the third floor – remember?'

Faiza nodded, her mouth full of cold brew, catching a tiny dribble just in time before it ruined her red lipstick. She could instantly recollect the junior accountant at their old ad firm, Moksha. He was always finding reasons to linger on the creative floor – home to the art and copy departments. It had been one of the first things Faiza and Natasha had bonded over when they had met nearly eight years ago.

'Exactly. Like, you knew he'd never actually have the balls to do anything, but it still throws you off your game. That shady background-ogling is all it takes.'

'Hmm,' Natasha mused, patting the grease off her heart-shaped mouth. 'So, what can you do? I mean, complaining about him obviously isn't an option, na? Can you, like, gently tell the comms girl?'

'Not a chance. The ego on this guy is big; he'll pull the whole deal. They haven't paid me yet, and it's a fuck tonne of money, Nattu, so I'm not going to risk it.'

'Okay, then you basically have to make it tough for him to turn up, na? Can't you shoot at, like, a really inconvenient time? If he's not a morning type, just do a 6 a.m. shoot. I know *I* would never show up.'

'He's a morning person, man. My shoots are crack-of-dawn early,' Faiza said, as she took note of Natasha's horrified expression. 'What? It's fucking magic hour! You're such a philistine.' She scowled.

'Fine. What if it's somewhere far, out of his way?'

'I guess I could try that. But I *hate* this. Why should I have to tiptoe around the bastard's feelings?' Faiza protested. 'Isn't that unfai—'

She was cut off by a sudden shuddering of the table.

'What is that vibration?' Faiza asked, startled, as Natasha's phone buzzed with the intensity of a comic-relief vibrator in an ill-advised romcom. 'Can you not afford a dildo like the rest of us?'

Natasha held up a hand to Faiza's face, in a silencing motion, and answered, 'Hello?'

'Nattu, can you come over?' The voice on the other end belonged to Rubani Bawa, one of Natasha's closest friends since college. Right now, it was several octaves lower than even its usual soft sonority. She sounded … off.

'I'm out, baba; I'm with Faiza. But what happened?' Natasha asked.

'Kabir,' Rubani said, her voice an inch from breaking. 'He … we had a fight. He just … it was a small fight, wasn't even really about anything, and then he … he started packing his … I think he left, Nattu.' Her voice cracked as she finished her sentence. A silent sob followed.

'Oh fuck,' Natasha said slowly.

What happened? Faiza mouthed to Natasha with dramatic hand gestures.

'Kabir and Bani broke up,' Natasha mouthed back, covering the phone with her other hand. 'Henh?' Faiza asked aloud, not understanding.

Natasha waved her off and put a finger to her lips.

'Okay, Bani, we're coming over. We'll be there in thirty. You want us to get you anything? We're at Palm Tree – should I pack some chorizo tacos?'

'No,' Rubani replied, her voice as lacklustre as before.

'Okay, sweetie, we'll see you soon.'

That Rubani had turned down chorizo tacos – her staple order at the restaurant – set off an even louder alarm bell in Natasha's head. It was Bani who'd discovered this place on her first anniversary with her girlfriend at the time, bringing them all here promptly the same weekend for what she declared were 'the tacos that will change your life'. They hadn't, of course, but her obsession had stayed steadfast over the years, with Bani often making detours back from work to pack up a quick half dozen for herself and, well, whoever she was dating then, Natasha supposed. She couldn't remember the last time Rubani had been single, which is why her break-ups were always a Code Blue.

Natasha picked up her bag with one hand and raised the other to signal for the bill. 'Would I be a bad person if I asked them to pack the fries?' she asked sheepishly.

Faiza rolled her eyes. 'Yeah, yeah, pack the fries. And call Saira.'

'I feel like that connection has been lost, you know, – to our *roots*. To the soil of our motherland. I wanted this collection to reflect that reunion, you know? With our deeply Indian heart and soul. The fabrics, the detailing – *everything* is an homage to that Indianness.'

Saira Baruah pressed her lips together, nodding at the designer in front of her as he waxed eloquent about his new line. It was nothing particularly new; Saira had noted while perusing it, finding barely a few degrees of hues that distinguished it from his last ten. The spiel was clearly press-prepared, honed for him by a struggling PR firm trying to find a new way to sell his dated designs.

It was a jaded thought, but she had those moments. Most days she was as giddy about her job as an eighties' ballad about devoted love. Being Fashion Features Director for a world-renowned women's magazine was a joyride, a glamorous life replete with front-row seats to fashion weeks, gifts from designers and business trips to the most exciting parts of the globe. The perks were the uppers, meant to distract from the not-so-pretty parts of the job: late nights, working weekends and laughable pay – about a fourth of what she'd be making at an e-commerce company or luxury fashion house. On most days, it didn't bother Saira because she loved it all too much. Some days, however, waves of ennui overcame her, as did a sense of frivolity, that none of it mattered.

Today, as she listened to the notoriously arrogant designer spin buzzwords like 'homegrown' and 'sustainable' at her with oblivious alacrity, was one of those days. She scraped up her long, auburn hair, winding the curls into a thick bun and then let it drop, deciding against the look.

'Do you feel like you were inspired to go down this route as a counter to the cultural misappropriation some designers have been leaning towards? Not naming names, of course.' Saira smiled, rattling off the question without looking at her pre-prepared list. It was exactly that perceptiveness that Saira knew made her good at her job and had gained her a designation at thirty-one that most people barely got to in their early forties.

The designer, visibly kicked at the opportunity to take his contemporaries down a peg, launched into a monologue about 'the power of looking inwards'. Saira half-listened, knowing she'd run through the recording about five times before writing the piece from memory. She was starving and it was hard to focus, but at least this was the last work thing she had to do today, and then she would be free.

'... and the greatest textures are right *here,* you know?' the designer said with great fervour, just as Saira's phone began to ring.

'I'm so sorry,' she said, looking down at the screen. 'This'll only take a second,' she promised, answering the phone and, simultaneously, doing the awkward bow-out walk that customarily accompanied an ill-timed phone call.

Natasha calling in the middle of a workday was rare – unless it was an emergency. It was something she liked about her best friends; they all understood the concept of work hours, and that texting was always her preferred alternative to phone calls.

'I'm doing an interview,' Saira said, her tone strangled. 'Is it important?'

She smiled politely at the designer through the glass door of the balcony she'd stepped out to. He smiled back graciously, gesturing for her to take her time. *He might use a boatload of jargon, but at least he's a nice guy.* That would be a great opener for the piece, she mused, if only she could get away with it.

'... and she's sounding messed up,' Natasha said from the other side. Saira realized that she had zoned out and therefore missed the bullet points of the presentation.

'Sorry, um, signal here is crap, I lost you,' she said. 'Tell me again?'

She heard a heavy sigh. She was sure Natasha knew she'd tuned out but wouldn't say anything. She was accommodating like that.

'Kabir. Broke. Up. With. Rubani,' Natasha repeated, slowly and deliberately, causing Saira to roll her eyes. 'She's not sounding okay. Faiza and I are heading to hers now. Can you meet us there?'

Saira felt a slight twinge as she heard the phrase 'Faiza and I'. That meant they were together, hanging out, without her and Rubani. She had often told herself it was immature to be bothered by it — yes, the two were close, but *all* of them were close. Besides, Rubani and she had proprietary rights over Natasha's friendship for they had met her in college and literally grown up together. That meant *they* had the greater claim, didn't it?

'I have to finish this interview,' Saira said, snapping out of her reverie. 'But I can come after that. Want me to bring anything?'

'Bring some wine, if you can?' Natasha asked. 'I have cheese fries. I'm going to get some brownies also, but there's no booze shop on our way.'

'Wine, got it.' Saira made a mental note to get some Grenache rosé, Rubani's favourite, an after-effect of a pretentious ex that her friend had been doe-eyed about, which she'd forgotten to discard with the rest of his post-break-up leftovers. Rubani did that – kept her exes' preferences and tastes as souvenirs, blending them into her own personality over time. The only way to tell was to have known her long enough. She just hoped Kabir's unbearable taste in music or obsession with almond milk wouldn't leave a stain.

'Fuck, man, Nattu. I never liked that douche.'

'*Hai na*? I was just thinking that if we say it now, it'll sound like we're only saying it because he left her. Ugh.' She could practically hear Natasha grimace over the phone.

'Man, yes! Or, worse, she'll be like, *oh, if you thought that, why didn't you tell me earlier?* I actually did fucking tell her earlier, practically through a megaphone, but now she'll conveniently space out. Classic Bani. It's not like she ever says anything about our relationships.' Saira laughed, and heard Natasha chuckle in agreement.

'I mean, still. He was awful. She put so much time into him. The whole LA business. And forget that, it was still a bigger thing – remember the fuss he made about her going for that long weekend to Goa? Like, he can't handle her being away for one weekend?'

'Yeah, but that trip also got cancelled because Faiza had to work, and then what was the point ...' Saira recalled, adjusting her Proenza Schouler blazer. She was lucky she'd copped this from the fashion closet; everything they usually got was sample-size, but when they'd shot with a tall, 'curvy' model who matched Saira's frame – and accidentally got just enough eye glitter on it to return to the brand – she couldn't believe her luck.

'Ya, it keeps getting cancelled. That trip is cursed, I think.' Natasha sighed.

'It's just exhausting trying to get everyone together, man. Anyway, I'm digressing,' Saira said, clearing her throat. 'Kabir.'

'I don't know,' Natasha said with another long exhale. 'It's mean to think this is a good thing, but feels like it's better for her, no?'

'I think he was a bastard, so good riddance,' Saira heard Faiza's voice in the background and smiled. Trust Faiza not to mince words.

'I agree with Haider,' she said. 'He is a bastard. The problem is, unless someone is a cheating bastard, a wife-beating bastard or an alcoholic bastard, we don't really leave. We rationalize all the other kinds of bastards. Passive-aggressive bastard; emotional arm-twisting bastard; manipulative, controlling bastard – all that is "stuff we can work on", because it isn't the big three. I blame our mothers.'

'You *always* blame our mothers,' Natasha said, exasperated. 'You love blaming your mother. Just please don't blame mine – she did the best she could.'

There was an awkward pause. Mothers were a landmine subject with Natasha, and Saira kicked herself for bringing it up. She was normally extra-careful about it around Natasha, but Saira's disdain for Kabir had made her let that guard down momentarily.

'Sorry, Nattu, you know I didn't mean that,' Saira mumbled. There was a second's silence, which felt far longer to Saira.

'*Achha*, mother-blaming aside, I get your point. The bar is low; if the man's not a hundred per cent murderer, we tell ourselves we should learn to put up with his flaws. Come armed with that kind of thing, *theek hai*? We'll need it when she goes into hating-on-him mode,' Natasha said.

'Done and done,' said Saira. 'Seeing you in forty-five with wine. Now, will you gals please let me finish this interview?'

'Oh, yes, sorry, sorry, you go,' Natasha said. 'See you soon, babu.'

Hanging up, Saira slid open the balcony door. She was unkeen to waste a second more than necessary on this frou-frou interaction that had given her nothing to work with. There was little the man had said that hadn't been in the press kit she'd pored over in preparation and it seemed like a cursory last question would suffice to wrap things up.

'So, *so* sorry about that,' Saira said, her tone apologetic, apropos of disappearing for twelve minutes. 'Just a couple more questions and we're all done, I promise.'

'Oh, no, no, it's fine,' the designer said benevolently. 'Actually, I have a fitting in thirty at my Shahpur studio, so would you mind if we finished over the phone?'

'No worries at all, and since it's just the one question, I can simply shoot it over on email.' Saira grinned, delighted at her luck.

'Oh, excellent, I *always* prefer email.' The designer smiled. Doesn't like phone calls – another point in his favour. Now if only she could get past his repetitive use of exposed zippers.

'Great! Then I have what I need, and I'll see you at the show next week.' She gave him a hug – the industry was familiar like that – and opened Uber the second her back was turned. She punched in the details for the liquor store and the saved address for Rubani's house as final stop. Happier circumstances would have been preferable, but she was always up for an impromptu afternoon of drinking with her girlfriends.

TWO

RUBANI KEPT HITTING refresh almost maniacally on an Instagram profile that had nothing new to offer her. It was the same posts her boyfriend – now ex – Kabir had up yesterday; the same careful curation of low-angle beard selfies and gym-mirror shots mixed with just enough artsy pans of the evening sky to seem redemptive. She didn't know exactly what she was expecting – a champagne-popping boomerang announcing that he'd dumped her? A shout-out to 'all the single ladies'? It may have been a pointless exercise, but it had become a reflex for her now, like pushing back phantom locks after lopping off her long waves for an asymmetrical pixie. Every time she touched the razored side of her head where her thick tresses had once nestled, it came with a little pang of what used to be.

What could it be? Rubani thought miserably, lying listless on her bed. *What did I do? What did I not do?* Her eyes felt like they had been wrung dry before being hung on a clothing line. Her head pounded with the hangover-esque migraine that often followed a bout of serious sobbing. Her body felt like it had fused with the covers; they were holding her down in a state of inertia no force could break. Every single part of her was tired.

She'd expected the blow-up to be big when Kabir found the texts from her ex, but figured it wouldn't be worse than their usual screaming matches. Besides, the texts were perfectly innocuous – her ex had asked to be connected with a video editor and Rubani had suggested a few names, that was all; she had friends in the business who could use the extra cash. The simple query had turned into a general conversation about life and, soon, a few harmless reminiscences about their trip to Italy together. And that was when Kabir had discovered the thread.

'You had no business even going through my texts!' Rubani had shouted, shaken by the invasion of privacy that Kabir had sworn would never happen again. 'Those are my private conversations and it's not okay. I don't snoop through *your* stuff!'

'I wasn't snooping – don't you fucking do that,' Kabir's voice had gone low and angry. 'I unlocked your phone to pay the Netflix bill. I do it from your phone *every month*, you know that.'

'Oh, you just *accidentally* opened my WhatsApp thread with Devika instead? Because those apps look basically the same, right?'

'It popped up. A notification,' he had said through gritted teeth. 'And I clicked on it, I admit it. But the point isn't that, Rubani. The point is, I'm fucking sick of you and your gaslighting shit. You're in touch with all your exes because – what? Just in case you need a dick on a ripcord? Or a pussy, of course, because with you anyone is fair game, no?'

Her eyes stung with new tears at the memory of that comment, flung at her not even four hours ago in this very apartment. Two years of being together, *living* together, and he still thought that her sexuality was exactly the kind of cheap joke people made it out to be for comic relief. After that, there was no going back. It couldn't be de-escalated. Too much had been said.

The aftermath had seemed like montage from a Beyoncé video – the screaming, door-slamming, everything exaggerated for effect because there was something final about it that she didn't want to acknowledge. She was deploying every weapon in her arsenal, from begging words that didn't feel real, to tears that were.

It had all been for naught, as he had packed his small travel carryall, avoiding eye contact while she pleaded … and left. She had slumped desultorily on the bed and stayed that way for an hour. When she finally mustered the strength to wriggle to her left and grab her phone, a social media spiral caught hold and dragged her into a tempest. Old pictures, old videos, old texts. The old habit of waiting for him to call like he always did a couple of hours after a fight. The other old habit of caving and making the call herself.

'I'm sorry, baby,' she would coo, and he would coo back and come home.

This time, it just rang. And rang and rang.

Every time she was done crying, her eyes found a drop they could spare. As the freshest one rolled down her sodden cheeks, she finally navigated away from his name to Natasha's …

'Bani?' Her voice came sailing through the closed front door, followed by a light shuffle of bags. 'Let us in?'

Rubani willed herself up and met with a head rush of epic proportions, brought on by a ruthless cocktail of crying and staring at a screen from an angle she'd been warned against as a teen.

'Hi baby.' Natasha walked in, her thin cotton sundress swaying around her knees. Rubani was instantly comforted by her familiar fragrance: a mix of the rose sunscreen and floral perfume she always used. Faiza came in next, her faded bob in disarray. She leaned in and hugged Rubani tightly, and the scent of her friend's musky men's fragrance had a less visceral impact, but was reassuring still.

'I'm sorry,' Rubani said automatically, having said it on repeat a few hours ago. Her voice was almost robotic, making Natasha and Faiza exchange a worried glance.

Natasha took in Rubani's appearance for a second. Her bright, round eyes were lined with redness. Her generous mouth seemed like it was trembling a little, trying to hold back the next bout of tears. There was a tiny piece of tissue stuck in her nose piercing, presumably from blowing her nose on repeat. Her petite body – already tiny at barely five feet – was now slouched over so that she looked like a child. It was clear she'd been crying all day.

'There's nothing to be sorry about,' Faiza said, plonking down on Rubani's unmade bed. She looked around her friend's mammoth living room, the Lichtenstein and Warhol prints in a swirl of audacious fuschias and blues. It was a masterclass in how to turn pop art into anything, from coasters to quilts; she wondered if the unabating technicolour was what had driven Kabir away and hated herself instantly for thinking it.

'Absolutely,' Natasha said. 'And I'm glad you called. Have you eaten anything? I got you some cheese fries.'

Faiza narrowed her eyes at Natasha and she shrugged, looking over at Rubani to see if she had noticed the exchange.

Rubani was in no danger of noticing anything. She was staring zombie-like at her phone, affixed to the spot where she'd opened the door.

'Oho, Bani, can you just stop looking at that *abhi*?' Natasha chided.

'He hasn't blocked me. Do you think that means anything?' Rubani asked, her voice hoarse. She was the very picture of misery.

Faiza walked over and smacked the bottom of Rubani's hand, making the phone pop out of it and into hers.

'Hey,' Rubani protested weakly, extending her arms up as Faiza held the phone out of reach. Even on tiptoe, she was no match for Faiza, who towered over her five-foot-two frame.

'No,' Faiza's tone was firm. 'This is a disgusting road and I'm not letting you go down it. Think about how fucking pathetic it is, Bani.' She crossed the room and swiped to Rubani's call log. 'Eleven calls? Eleven? Bani, just *no* – have some self-esteem for fuck's sake!'

Rubani's eyes filled with tears again and Natasha quickly copped on to the fact that Faiza's freezer-burned brand of tough love – though well-intentioned – was not helping.

'Babu, listen,' Natasha said softly, guiding Rubani over to the couch. 'Right now, I think you just need to give yourself a break from him, okay? Maybe it's all a little too raw to think about *abhi*.'

Rubani, now properly crying, buried her head in Natasha's neck.

'Nattu, how can he *just* do this?' Rubani sobbed. 'Two full years. After every fight, I always said sorry to him. We built this home and this life and ... what is my mom going to say?'

Rubani's mother had been fond of Kabir; they would laugh about her obsession with teen dramas and he loved her *kadhi chawal*. Her parents had always been on the right side of Punjabi stereotypes – wealthy, warm and welcoming, without being conservative. She hadn't ever felt like 'coming out' to her parents because it just seemed such a strange announcement to have to make. Straight people didn't have to declare it with such fanfare, did they? So, one day, in the second summer of college, she'd casually mentioned to her mother that she was going on a date with a girl and would be home by eleven, as usual. After nearly two days of silence, her father made a joke about at least not having to worry that she would accidentally get pregnant. She then clarified that, sadly, that fear was not off the table; she liked men, too. 'Whatever makes you happy, *bachchey*,' her father had said, after only a brief pause. 'Just don't get pregnant.' She'd been grateful for the privilege of the matter ending there.

Natasha cricked her neck enough to make eye contact with Faiza and beckon her over. Faiza rolled her eyes but came and sat down on Rubani's left. She put her arm around her crying friend. She might be a blithering mess who didn't realize she'd just freed herself of a possessive, problematic man – but she *was* still one of her best friends.

'I love you, Bani; I'm sorry I was an asshole,' Faiza said, stroking Rubani's hair.

'I love you too, Faizoo,' Rubani managed between sobs. She switched her nesting position from Natasha's bare shoulders to Faiza's jersey-clad ones – a gesture of forgiveness, and easier to wipe tears on.

'Okay, so tell us what happened,' Natasha said, using her newfound freedom from Rubani's sopping cheek to go and politely wipe the snot off her collarbones. And heat those cheese fries.

Rubani painfully recounted the discovery of the texts, the detonation of the 'you'd sleep with anyone because you're bisexual' bomb, the pent-up anger from their last few fights and, finally, the packing up with a declaration to return for the rest when she wasn't home.

'I guess it had been building?' Rubani said, feeling like her eyes had been sucked dry of tears once again. 'I mean, I know it wasn't *only* this – he was pissed about having to turn down the Bombay job because I wouldn't move. And maybe that was part of it. I think he still wants to take it and was looking for a way to cut me out.'

'That is extremely unfair,' Faiza said, her outrage only too obvious. 'You turned down the gig in LA for him? Fucking LA! And he barely even acknowledged it.'

'I turned it down for many reasons,' Rubani protested, 'including you guys. I didn't want to have to move there, with no one and nothing. Like, out of all of us, only Saira does these things. She would do it, just go and start from scratch, but my life is *here*. You know you guys would've done the same thing.'

'No, you're right,' Natasha said. 'It's a nice thought, it's exciting, but I like my life here. Alex, you guys, OJ, my beautiful Safdarjung house – I'm *never* giving up that garden.'

'I would've moved in a fucking heartbeat,' Faiza grumbled, knowing she wouldn't. Her partner, Zaden, had three restaurants in the city that he needed to be here to run – and for the first time in her life, she was willing to put another person first. Especially since she could run her fitness handle from literally anywhere in the world.

'*Khair*,' Natasha said. 'The point she's making is valid, Bani. You *could* have moved if you wanted. He was pretty clear that he wasn't going to. He gave you a choice, and you can't deny that it factored into what you chose.'

'I hate how you always sound so fucking wise.' Faiza grinned. 'Even when you're literally just stealing my copy.'

'Please, what am I, Neha Verma?' Natasha scoffed, referencing a notorious plagiarist they'd both hated at Moksha. Faiza and Natasha shared a laugh, a moment that stung Rubani a little.

She knew Natasha was close to Faiza, possibly closer than she was to Saira and her, but it irked her when they made an exhibition of it. Though she'd never say it aloud, it bothered her that Natasha had chosen Faiza as her unspoken confidante when Rubani and Saira had been the ones who had done everything with her, from helping her cram for her psychology finals to holding her upright when she was too drunk to walk. How could working together for two years at a stupid ad firm be a stronger bonding experience than that?

'You know what, Nattu, I think you always hated him,' Rubani snapped with misdirected anger. 'You too,' she pointed at Faiza. 'And you're both just waiting to say "I told you so," aren't you?'

'I told you so,' said a muffled voice from behind the front door. It was Saira's.

'I just … can't.' Rubani sighed and slunk down on a bright pink bean bag as Natasha let Saira in.

'You know, y'all are fighting *damn* loudly,' Saira said, walking in and putting down a bottle of Jose Cuervo and Grenache rosé on the table with consecutive thunks.

'For us,' she pointed to the tequila, 'and only for you, Bani,' she said, blowing Rubani a kiss and gesturing at the rosé.

'For that, I'll forgive you for kicking me when I'm down,' Rubani said, sceptically, making a 'thank you' face at Natasha, who'd promptly sprung into action, pulling out flutes and coupes for the drinks.

'Okay, but listen, it's true. I'm the only one of these bitches that *ever* told you so. Remember when I saw him on Tinder six months after he'd moved in? Red fucking flag!'

Saira felt vindicated; she had always told Rubani that her boyfriend was a bad decision – at great risk to their thirteen-year-long friendship. She knew, via multiple Rubani-free conversations, that Faiza and Natasha had felt the same way; they'd just never dared bring it up.

But honesty had always been Saira's MO – she said what she felt, even if it had a fifty-fifty rate of success. Sometimes it made her come off as refreshing and real. Other times it landed her in some deeply uncomfortable silences, and even trouble.

Today, though, Saira felt a sense of redemption. She felt like the greatest judge of character that had ever lived. But one look at Rubani's puffy eyes and trembling mouth made her wish Kabir had proven her wrong.

'But, *but*, I'm not saying anything now. I wish it hadn't happened. All of us just want you to be happy, even if it *was* with that douchebag,' Saira said.

There was a flicker of a smile on Rubani's face. She'd had a 'rotisserie of assholes', according to Saira, and Jia, her closest friend outside of the foursome. As much as she wished she had better judgement to defer to, Rubani had always been drawn to men and women who weren't a hundred per cent present – as if daddy, mommy and self-esteem issues had rolled into one unforgiving snowball that relished knocking her down every time she found her footing. She still couldn't justify some of her romantic decisions, even to herself, the worst of which had been a marketing rep she'd dated for six months, who insisted she carry his luggage at airports and almost always 'forgot his wallet'. Rubani reached out and squeezed Saira's hand.

Saira furrowed her unusually thick brow. Ordinarily Rubani would've cracked a proper smile, even laughed. But seeing her like this was bothersome. Saira cast a glance at Natasha for reassurance, but caught a version of her own worried expression across her friend's pale features.

'Bani, you're staying the night at mine,' she decided. 'We all should. A sleepover.'

'I can't, my loves, I'm sorry,' Natasha said sheepishly. 'I have to be at Alex's office party.'

'Nor can I, sorry, S,' Faiza added. 'Zaden's coming back after three weeks, so we've had this dinner planned for a while.'

'You guys, bros before hoes, what the *fuck*, man?' Saira said, astounded.

'S, it's different, okay? Don't get into this. You can't keep shitting on other people's relationships just because you refuse to be in one,' Faiza snapped. It bothered her that simply because Saira didn't like commitment, she scoffed at everyone else's. She was supportive, until they chose dinner with their partner over girls' night, or a Sunday staying in with them over brunch with the girls. Then the Urban Dictionary phrases were bandied about, alleging what a crime had been committed by not choosing the ya-ya sisterhood over everything else.

'Okay, first,' Saira said, with a sharp intake of breath. 'I was with Sahil for almost a year. That's pretty long-term. I'm clearly capable of it.'

Faiza rolled her eyes exaggeratedly, but Saira ignored her and carried on.

'And secondly, whatever, fine. If you can't, you can't,' she said, her tone deliberately insincere. 'Bani, it's just us. But it'll be a blast. We'll watch movies and drink everything in my house. And we'll get food from the greasy Chinese cart on the way back.'

Rubani stared at the floor, nodding absently in assent.

The room quietened. Rubani may be mild-tempered, but she was never melancholic, and to see her like this was heartbreaking for the three.

'I could come over after ...?' Natasha volunteered weakly.

'Or,' Saira said, sitting up with alacrity, almost as if a light bulb had gone off behind her head, 'we could finally go to Goa.'

'This isn't *Dil Chahta Hai*, okay?' Faiza sighed. 'We're not unemployed. Or in college. We can't just take off tonight.'

'I'm not *saying* tonight, Haider.' Her brittle tone from their last interaction still lingered. 'I'm saying let's do it, man. Let's plan it and take the time off and *do* this finally! We keep talking about it – Nattu and I literally talked about it today! But we just never make it work. Let's just fucking make it *work*!'

Though the instinct was to push back, Faiza thought about it for a second. She missed the beach, and a vacation could actually be good for Rubani right now. She could even shoot some beach videos while they were there. And if Ishaan was around, she could meet him too; it had been a while, but the thought of seeing him again sent a little thrill down her body. It was worth considering.

She looked at Natasha who was also contemplating how nice it would be to finally use some of the leaves she had yet to take. Alex hated travelling; he only did it under duress for work. And Saira did have a point – they kept planning this trip but never took it. Maybe Rubani's break-up was the spur they needed.

'Yes?' Saira looked at them questioningly, batting her heavy lashes at them as if for comic effect. 'The guy who owns Paralía is an old friend; he'll give us a great discount and we will literally be right by the sea. He's always telling me to visit. Should I tell him we're going?'

Natasha and Faiza looked at each other and then at Rubani. Her eyes kept glazing over and filling with tears, which she kept wiping off with the sleeve of her shirt. She hadn't said a word.

'We'll have to figure out dates,' Natasha said and Saira's face broke into a grin. 'And it'll take some time,' she added quickly as Saira's expression shifted to visibly excited. 'But yeah, okay. I'm in.'

Saira got up, ran over and gave her a tight hug. While she was being squeezed, Natasha gasped out, 'Faizoo? Can you?'

Faiza scratched her head and frowned.

'I'll need to work,' she warned Saira.

'That's fine, don't care.' Saira brushed it off.

'*And* I'll need to take my equipment,' she added.

'I'll carry it,' she offered.

A slow smile spread across Faiza's face.

'Okay, yeah. Let's do this.'

'Eeeeeee!' Saira shrieked. 'I can't believe it. GOAAAA!'

THREE

AS THE SUN broke past the white voile curtains of their sea-facing room, it cast just enough of a mellow glow on Faiza's face to wake her up. Being a morning person and a light sleeper was usually why she was always the first one up on a holiday, a family vacation, or a girls'-night-spilled-into-sleepover morning. She looked at the queen bed next to her, where Natasha was tucked inside her white duvet, sleeping peacefully. *How does she always look like a fucking mattress commercial when she's sleeping?* Faiza thought fondly about her closest friend. Even her most irksome qualities were ones that Faiza had grown to love over the course of their eight-year-long friendship.

She did a lazy cat stretch and got out of bed, walking over to make herself her routine a.m. cup of black coffee. She took the steaming mug out onto the balcony and settled into one of Paralía's blue-and-white-striped deck chairs, tucking her legs beneath her. It was unseasonably warm for a November morning; the tenacious moisture in the air clung to her skin, causing just enough discomfort for Natasha to wake up and start cribbing – summer was not her season. But

Faiza didn't mind it. She preferred being by the sea to just about anywhere on earth.

She wondered if she had time for a run before the girls woke up; there was a lovely little road lined with palms behind this resort-y stretch that led to the nearby village, which would be perfect. But she decided against it. It was day one – she could give herself an unscheduled break day for once. Considering this trip had almost not happened, it seemed luxury enough just to be sipping coffee, staring out at the Aegean blue waters of Ozran beach with another nine full days of delicious nothingness stretched out in front of them. She hadn't felt that start-of-a-holiday delight in a long time. Thank god for that picture of Kabir and his friend!

After that initial burst of let's-do-this adrenaline, they'd all sort of forgotten about Goa and just taken turns staying with and checking in on Rubani. Saira, she had to admit, had done most of the heavy lifting. The crisis seemed averted; Rubani was slowly feeling better and needing them a little less. But then, this time last week, something had happened to undercut all that progress.

During her daily moment-of-weakness-Kabir-stalking on Instagram, she had found a picture of him looking too intimate for her comfort with a school friend who'd often been part of his birthday dinners and their group hangs. After some panicked digging online (and a few phone calls that involved casting aside her pride), Rubani managed to confirm that he was, in fact, seeing her.

The news had hit her like a trifecta combo-punch to the gut. The first punch brought with it the realization that Kabir was in a new relationship so soon after they had split.

The second that this woman was someone with history, who had likely known him longer and better than she had and fit in with his friends, most of whom were from school. The third — and this was the real kicker — was whether it was, in fact, new at all. She had been at their parties, group dinners; she had been in their home. Had it been going on all along?

The spiral happened quickly, and the girls had to lurch into action. They quickly revived the Goa trip — it was either distracting her with bonding time on a beach, or slitting the bastard's throat, and the latter seemed less legal. So research was done, tickets were booked, a cheery 'How are you, darling?' phone call was made to the 'old friend' at Paralía — and they were off.

'You're up early,' Rubani's voice called from the balcony next door. Her meek tone wasn't a patch on the chipper, often booming baritone Faiza associated with Rubani — it made her realize just how sad her friend really was. Kabir dating someone else might've been a 'good riddance' moment for them, but Rubani was probably going through more heartbreak than Faiza could imagine. She herself had only been heartbroken once before, and it wasn't even over a relationship — yet she wouldn't relive it for all of Bezos' billions.

'Morning, love.' She smiled, squinting at Rubani through the strong sun shine. 'You slept okay?'

'Pretty well,' Rubani replied. 'Mostly, I just feel like sleeping only. One of Saira's six alarms woke me up; otherwise, I would have slept in.' She smiled gently.

'Ugh, I keep forgetting. *Why* does she have six fucking alarms on holiday?' Faiza grumbled.

Rubani laughed. 'I think she forgets to turn them off. Anyway, I don't even understand why she has them. She slept through them all.'

Like a moment from a sitcom, Saira's seventh alarm, a string quartet version of 'Flowers' by Miley Cyrus, wafted softly but tirelessly out of Rubani's room. The two grinned at each other. They stared out at the beach for a moment together in silence. A beautiful young European-looking couple walked arm-around-waist. As they kissed, a family of four shuffled a few feet behind, looking aghast at the public display of affection.

'Let's just wake them up, no?' Faiza said, breaking the silence. 'It's a nice morning – let's go do a long, lazy brunch somewhere? I've heard that Grāma place is really nice.'

Rubani's eyes narrowed. 'I also heard it's vegan.' She was team steak-over-salad any day of the week.

'I don't think so,' Faiza said. She wasn't technically lying – it was about ninety per cent vegan, but for some reason they had salmon and tuna on the menu, so it wasn't not like the girls would die of starvation. It was just a healthy cafe – what was so wrong with that? 'Besides, it's in this beautiful, green place. You'll like it, Bani.'

'Okay,' Rubani conceded, sounding a little perked up. 'You go wake up Nattu and get her dressed – let her get a ten-minute head start on us.' It only made sense to factor in that Natasha took the longest to get ready; she was the only one who would bother to contour and highlight in the sticky climes of Goa. 'I'm going to change S's alarm so that it's noisy enough to wake her up.' She grinned. 'What's a loud song?'

'Anything by Cardi?' Faiza smirked. 'Or DJ Khaled?'

'DJ Khaled!' Rubani clapped her hands. 'That's genius.' She smiled.

Faiza laughed cheekily, standing up and collecting her coffee mug to head back inside. 'Just turn the volume *all* the way up, okay?'

An hour and a half later, the girls stared in dismay at the queue outside Grāma. What Faiza had described as a 'cute, tucked-away brunch place that's still relatively undiscovered by tourists' seemed, much to their chagrin, to have been discovered by tourists.

'There has to be something we can do,' Saira mumbled, pushing her way past the crowd indignantly. A near-decade of being treated like a royal because of her magazine job meant that waiting in line was now an outmoded concept to Saira – one she was never gracious about. The girls left her to it, leaning against their rental Kia parked under the shade of a cluster of palms.

'We should just go somewhere else; it's so hot, ya,' Natasha complained. Her pale skin, as susceptible to changing hues in the heat as bread in a toaster, had already tanned in the twenty minutes she'd been out in the sun. Her long, thick tresses had lost some of their frustratingly perky gloss to the heat, with stray strands, wet with sweat, stuck to her forehead. Faiza and Rubani, both ardent short-hair aficionados, were a lot less fazed by the afternoon sun.

'Why the fuck don't you carry a scrunchie, Nattu?' Faiza scolded. 'Just tie your hair in a stupid-ass bun and be done with it.'

'I forgot, okay?' Natasha seethed, frantically rummaging through her pastel Chloé bag that matched perfectly her rosebud-printed white minidress. Faiza wondered how she always ended up befriending women who saved up for designer accessories, her thoughts flashing back to her best friend from school. Natasha always spent wisely, but she bought designer bags when she could and looked after them with the meticulousness of a taxidermist.

'We're in!' Saira's head popped up, bobbing to beckon them over.

As they made their way down the winding, powdery, sandstone stairs of Grāma and into the brunchery, the wait suddenly seemed worth it. Despite being outdoors, it was an instant ten degrees cooler than where they'd just been standing – sheltered by lush green trees and copper-red hedges. Mellow music melted into the low buzz of chatter amongst guests and swirled with the rising aroma of freshly baked cheese bourekas. The hostess, a beautiful girl in a thin cotton jumpsuit with flowing honey-brown hair, caught Saira's eye and nodded, leading them to a spacious corner table.

'What did you do, drop a business card?' Faiza grinned.

'I have my ways,' Saira smiled mysteriously.

'Whatever your ways are, I'm just happy we're out of the heat, ugh,' Natasha said, making a beeline for a seat near the mammoth spinning fan.

'What *are* your ways, S? Seriously, I'm intrigued,' Rubani asked.

'Okay, fine,' Saira huffed. 'I *may* have flirted with the hostess a little.' She grinned, wiggling her upturned nose with glee.

Rubani stared at Saira blankly. 'Why would *you* do that?'

'Yeah, I mean, whatever, I just flirted. It's not that big a deal, Bani,' Saira said, a bit offhand. 'Besides, she's probably straight too, for all I know.'

It was typical of Saira, Rubani thought, feeling that familiar surge of anger bubbling up in her chest. The reduction of sexuality to currency; it was what a friend from her Garage84 circle — a queer bar she frequented in South Delhi — had dubbed 'Katy Perry Dykism'. The kind of performative faux lesbianism straight girls put on like a shiny jacket, nothing more than an accessory for the night to appear interesting. She had been turned into the shiny jacket before by several of her straight girlfriends who claimed to be 'too drunk' to recall anything the next day. It was exhausting, and though Saira had never had the gall to try it with Rubani, she reluctantly admitted that Saira fell into that category when she desperately needed a party trick. However, it was a conversation that had all the fixings for a fight. She decided, as she had many times before, during many conversations dangerously in this territory, that she would just let it go.

Saira copped on to Rubani's train of thought only after some delay.

'Oh my god, I'm such an idiot,' she slapped her forehead. 'Bani, sorry I was obtuse. I didn't mean to be offensive or anything.'

'You never do, no?' Rubani muttered under her breath, adjusting her graphic T-shirt dress which kept riding up, to her annoyance.

'Though,' Saira mused, 'she *is* really attractive. Isn't she, Bani?'

'Because she's a nice-looking girl, she must automatically be my type?' Rubani asked rhetorically, her tone snappier than she had intended. It rankled a little that Saira didn't know her type after all these years.

'*Arey*, that's not how she meant it.' Natasha reached across and grabbed Rubani's hand. 'Besides, she looks a little bit like Devika – maybe that's why you thought it?' Natasha looked meaningfully at Saira, hoping she'd catch on.

'Yes! Exactly,' Saira said, taking the cue. 'Except now that I think about it, maybe the cute girl that reminds you of your longest-running ex isn't the best one-night-stand material.'

'Please,' Rubani snorted. 'As if I'm going to have to have a one-night stand.'

'Why not?' Saira prodded, running a hand through her unending auburn curls as she flipped them to one side. 'What could be better after the whole, um …' she quickly looked for a phrase to replace, '… break-up. I mean, after everything. It's perfect!'

'First off, S, it isn't perfect. Sleeping with some stranger isn't going to take away the pain of losing everything Kabir and I had,' Rubani said, holding back tears. 'And secondly, it's not something I'd do anyway. I'm just … not that type of girl.'

Faiza's eyebrows arched as Natasha looked up from perusing her menu. The big decision between shakshuka and chocolate croissant would have to wait.

'Um, what kind of girl, exactly?' Natasha asked, her tone tentative.

'A one-night-stand-kind-of-girl. I just can't do it – there's something so … I don't know … I mean, no judgement, guys; I know you have—'

'Um … is there a one-night-stand kind of girl, Rubani?' Faiza's tone was hard to decipher.

'I mean, no, that's no …' Flustered, Rubani fumbled for words. No matter how she tried to cloak her knee-jerk response to one-night stands, she knew it would come across as critical. 'I don't mean that in a slut-shaming way, Haider; it's just … some people aren't like that.'

There was silence at the table.

'I've had a few, Bani – you know that,' Saira said.

'And me,' Natasha said, quietly. 'But I didn't think I was "that type of girl".'

Rubani opened her mouth to defend herself, but Faiza spoke before she could.

'I've had a couple too, Bani.'

Rubani said nothing. She felt like she'd dug herself into a hole that could possibly swallow the holiday whole. Just as she was trying to think of a suitable apology, Saira said, 'Besides, how the hell have you never had a one-night stand? I mean, given everything.'

'Given that I'm bisexual, you mean?' Rubani asked hotly. The 'up for anything' label was often slapped on by most potential partners, or people who didn't – and didn't care to – know better, but she expected more from her best friends.

'Well, I mean, yeah,' Saira said thoughtfully. 'I would imagine you'd had a few at least in the experimentation stage, when you were figuring things out?'

'Okay, so basically, because I'm bi, you automatically *assume* I'm a slut?' Rubani said in a menacing voice.

'Excuse me?' Faiza shot back angrily. 'Because we've had one-night stands, you automatically assume *we're* sluts?'

'How has this come back on me!' Rubani protested. 'She's the one making generalizations!' She pointed angrily at Saira.

'As are you! How is what you're assuming any better?' Faiza's voice was now dangerously low.

'Okay, *nahi*, we need to stop this *immediately*,' Natasha said, holding up a hand. 'This is our first day in Goa. We will absolutely not fight in the middle of a restaurant.'

'A bloody vegan restaurant,' Rubani muttered under her breath.

'It is *not* vegan; there is fucking fish on the menu,' Faiza said, on the verge of snapping, just loud enough to make the couple at the next table stop mid-bite and turn around warily.

'Zip it,' Natasha said, making a zipper motion across her mouth. 'We are not fighting; *abhi toh* it's too early for the holiday fight. I'll allow it on day six.

'Can it be with Saira because I broke her phone after the fifteenth alarm?' Rubani grinned.

'Hey! It's a nice song; shut up!' Saira said in a near-whine.

The situation sufficiently defused, the girls ordered and chatted about their plans for the evening and the ground they wanted to cover through the holiday. When enough time had passed and their drinks and starters had arrived, Saira thought it safe to go back to the part of the conversation that had stuck with her most.

'Bani, seriously, though,' she said, her tone gentler and more self-effacing this time. 'You've never had a one-night stand? Haven't you ever wanted to?'

Rubani sighed and shrugged. 'I don't know, Saira. I don't think it's for me.' She quickly held up her palms as if to convey, 'No judgement!' 'I mean, there's nothing wrong with it; I just don't think I'm the kind of person that can cut off communication with somebody after a night of meaningless sex, you know?'

The three girls smiled and exchanged looks. Their shared amusement at her statement made Rubani uncomfortable.

'What?' she prodded.

'Nothing, it's funny that—' Natasha started, just as Faiza said, 'I think it's interesting—'

They both stopped to laugh as Natasha gestured to Faiza to carry on.

'I think it's interesting that the general assumption is that it's meaningless,' said Faiza, as Natasha nodded in agreement.

'Yeah, I was going to say the same thing. Like, why does it need to be meaningless just because it's for that one night? It can have meaning without having a future, *na*?'

Saira slurped on her strawberry-chia juice, purposefully squishing the seeds with her front teeth. 'I don't know, Nattu, can't it work both ways? I mean, of course, absolutely, people think it *has* to be meaningless – especially if, like Bani, they've never had one – but they can also be just fun. Proper no-strings-attached, bang-your-brains-out-and-leave fun.'

'Why does fun equal meaningless, though?' Faiza retorted.

'You guys have literally beaten that one word to death, oof.' Rubani joined her hands in a prayer motion. 'I'm sorry I said meaningless, okay?'

'*Arey*, no, Bani, it's a valid assumption,' Natasha said. 'It's also like what you said earlier: "I think I'm not the one-night-stand type of girl." That point of view is more common than you think, but I imagine a lot of women have one-night stands and don't talk about it because they feel like it makes them—'.

'Look like a slut,' Saira completed. Natasha motioned with her hand as if to say, 'Exactly!'

Rubani felt a little cornered. On one hand, it bothered her that Saira had just assumed she'd had a one-night stand because she was bisexual. And on the other, she was irked by the new-found knowledge that they all seemed to have had one, barring her. She'd always known about Saira's liaisons, and had a hunch about Faiza's. But even Natasha? She'd never mentioned anything and she'd met Alex so young … But if all of them had done it, then none of them were going to see her point of view.

She cleared her throat and tried again.

'Okay, let me put it this way: I don't think I'm *personally* cut out for it. I've never done anything except relationships, and I'm a hundred per cent sure that if I try it, I'll get too attached to the person and want to see them again. Which defeats the whole purpose, right?'

'Right,' Natasha nodded.

Faiza speared a piece of feta in her salad with a fork and tacked it onto a chunk of watermelon. Her expression was one of clear disagreement.

'Haider, what? Say it,' Rubani prompted.

'I guess, I don't necessarily think so. I think if you haven't done it, then you actually don't know how you'd react to it, right? For all you know, it might be *exactly* your kind of thing – you just never explored the option.'

'But Bani, for real, it can't be that every time you've hooked up with somebody, it's gone full-scale relationship?' Saira asked. 'That's a *lot* of pressure to put on a hook-up.'

'It doesn't always start with a hook-up for me, S,' Rubani said, rolling her eyes. 'I like to get to know the person first. If I feel like it'll go somewhere, only then do I let it, you know ... go somewhere.' She shrugged.

'Okay, I guess *my* question is: are you curious but nervous about the idea of it, or is it like one of those blanket "yeugh, never" situations?' Natasha asked.

Rubani chewed on her salmon bagel thoughtfully.

She had always felt slightly different from her friends; in some ways, this was one of those differences. They always seemed a little 'cooler' than her; more modern, more self-possessed. It was hard to explain that, for her, emotional attachment seemed a necessary prerequisite for sex; she couldn't be naked with someone without *feeling* it. But it might be because she'd never actually tried ...

'I think maybe the first,' she conceded.

The girls nodded and passed around forks with bites and glasses with sips until Saira suddenly exclaimed, 'I have a genius idea!'

'Ugh,' Faiza groaned. 'Your last genius idea was Goa.'

Saira gave her a look that plainly said, 'Your point being?'

'Fair enough,' Faiza shrugged, waving her fork in assent.

'Have one on this trip, Bani,' Saira said excitedly. 'Your first ever one-night stand, and we'll all be here to dissect it to death after! It is the best, most mind-blowing plan, I have to say.' She clapped with enthusiasm and bowed.

'Yeah, no, thanks,' Rubani said, reaching across the table for a bite of Natasha's pancakes.

'I mean ... it's not a bad idea,' Natasha smiled. 'There are tonnes of travellers here; your Tinder will be *exploding* with options. And maybe there's like an exotic dude from Prague or some hot girl from Brazil you might encounter at one of the parties we'll hit up. I think it sounds very sexy,' she concluded, wiggling her eyebrows for effect.

'I concur,' Faiza said, draining her coconut milk smoothie. 'It's a fucking stand-up idea.'

Saira, elated to have the group's support, announced, 'Okay, then, it's decided.'

'Oy, hello,' Rubani protested. 'Who decided what? Are you going to sleep with a rando on this trip, or am I? I mean, you also can, obviously, but how do you three get off deciding for me?'

'Bani,' Saira sighed, 'you have no idea how great a holiday setting is. My first was on holiday, and if I could go back and redo it, I would do everything exactly the same way.'

'You slept with a stranger? On holiday? You didn't tell me about this one.' Rubani sounded incredulous and a touch insulted. 'You weren't worried about being murdered?'

'Okay, which holiday was this?' Faiza asked, also intrigued.

Natasha mouthed 'Spain?' at her, and Saira nodded. 'Fine, fine, I'll tell you, wait.' She smiled, settling into storytelling mode. 'It happened five years ago …'

SAIRA

IT WAS ALL seeming more and more ridiculous to her as she scuttled down the rain-scented street of Centro, Madrid. Compensating for her late departure had given her an awkward hybrid running walk that had the meagre advantage of a mild increase in speed. *He doesn't even speak the same language!* she thought. It was clear from his Tinder texts – scrambling to find the words to find a place to meet – that he was trying. But it was also an indicator of the disaster the evening to come might be. She had quickly zeroed in on a bar while they had texted, because it seemed low-key and traveller-friendly. It was also close by, so if panic mode kicked in, she was just a short kilometre's sprint from her kitschy underground Airbnb.

She got there first. There was an easy cool about the place, almost exactly like she'd imagined. People were around her age, in their mid-twenties, but there were a few thirtysomethings in the mix as well. Many of them were drinking their cocktails from what looked like repurposed catheter bags, so it was clearly trendy. There were also a lot of gorgeous women, all with hair that seemed far sexier than her long, brown curls (featuring well-hidden early greys) and bodies more effortlessly skinny than her US 12 figure, which impertinent aunts would describe as 'healthy'. She deduced he'd take one look at her, draw the obvious comparison and politely duck out after one drink. That is, if he chose to stay that long; maybe people were rude in Spain?

She sat down and fell back on her usual defence mechanism: her phone. She had refreshed her Instagram feed for the fourth time when the little flame icon popped up, signalling a Tinder message. 'You are here,' it proclaimed, with a follow-up '?' turning it into a question. 'I am,' she typed. She had a small, gnawing feeling in her stomach, the kind she usually got when someone was reading what she'd written and their reaction was en route.

'I come up?' he asked, sending both text and punctuation in one go this time around. 'Yes, I am upstairs,' she typed oversimplistically, because, while she believed language to be the most impressive tool in her arsenal, it didn't work if the man in question didn't speak it. She saw an attractive man in his late twenties walk through the door and look around. He was different from his picture, but who wasn't? He nodded and smiled at a group of gorgeous, gum-baring grins at a nearby table and went over.

Ah. That's why it doesn't look like him. It isn't!

Two other sets of people walked in after, and she felt on the verge of giving up. *Fuck it. I'll have a drink and wander till I find someplace for dinner. Time for an adventure all by myself,* she thought, a little disgruntled. She raised a hand to signal to the waiter, and that's when she saw him walk in. 'Juan,' she rolled his name off her tongue under her breath. That it sounded so intrinsically Spanish only made it sexier to her.

He looked like his picture, but better, she decided – and that instantly made her like him more. He was one of the few men she'd swiped on that hadn't plastered his several slides with his abs or biceps; just old-school crops from photos with his friends, as if it was Facebook, circa 2007. He had the kind of jaw she liked, blue (or were they slightly green?) eyes and a mouth that looked like it could break into the big smile she'd already seen in pixel form any moment. He'd not posted any pictures of his body, so the fact that he was a good head and a half taller than her came as a pleasant surprise. She realized she found him quite attractive.

Saira waved him over. He smiled tentatively. He seemed to visibly embody the awkwardness of someone who wasn't fluent in online dating, and she could only sympathize. She'd assumed it was only unusual for her, so it was comforting to know they might both be equally terrible at this.

She started talking; she felt she should. There were a few silences, but enough broken, part-Spanish, part-English banter to get them both through two pink, punch-filled catheter bags each. They began by talking about themselves and somehow wound up discussing everything, from the differences in medical aid ('Free here, but so much bad!' he'd said, shaking his head fervently) to those in the McDonald's menus of their countries.

She was having to make an effort, to simplify, talk more slowly and clearly than she was used to. But it was nothing compared to how much effort he was putting in, she could tell, because they were almost completely talking in English – she knew about ten Spanish words and didn't think *Donde está la biblioteca* applied in this scenario. But Saira was enjoying herself, despite the struggle. Enjoying herself enough to not want the evening to end after their drinks had been drained dry and their bill slammed callously on the sticky wooden table by a much-too-busy waiter.

'You now go home? I would like, uh, you walk home?' he offered, because that was the precondition she'd set up. Have a drink together, then go home. Nothing else, she had casually reiterated with every third message she'd sent him on Tinder. She supposed he was offering to walk her back because he'd remembered that she had said she was staying right there, in Centro. The walk would take under ten minutes. Much too little time.

'Um ... no,' she decided. 'Where else can we go now? What is still open?'

He cracked a smile and told her that everything was open. It was 11 p.m. in Madrid and the city was only just coming to life. The capital's myriad cantinas and tapas bars would brim with colour, music and infectious sensuality – until the first streaks of twilight and the fiesta had to give way to real life.

It's not like she didn't travel often, but moments like these, every time she left Delhi, reminded her of how constrained she felt by her city. The idea of meandering with an attractive stranger around a she had no map for (quite literally, for she was data-less, and hence, Google Maps-less) was so liberating. And it saddened Saira that her beautiful exception was the norm her date probably took for granted.

They chose a club on his phone, its local chest puffed proudly with data. There seemed only one bar that was a cross between cheap walking distance and not reviewed abysmally by scorned patrons. *Besides*, she thought, *I'm on holiday. I can drink cheap booze and sleep in to deal with it.* They paid for their catheters and walked out together ('I insist,' she'd said, tossing her share of Euros over his, pleased that he threw up his hands in resistance in lieu of arguing her down).

They got into the elevator and Saira was suddenly very aware of him. He was close to her without it being uncomfortable, but it was his fingers, just millimetres away from hers and twitching gently, that kept inviting her. To touch them might be a bit much. She had repeatedly asserted that this was only a 'friendly drink', but she *really* wanted to break that rule. And, before she could fully process her thoughts, she did.

He pulled her fingers into his own easily and she leaned into the moment, letting the intimacy engulf her like warm water in a swimming pool. Without taking things further, they stayed, fingers looped, till the old elevator grumbled to a halt on the ground floor. As the door opened, she was abruptly flung into the brisk night air and an impatient crowd. The moment quickly dissolved.

Saira walked alongside him towards the club, close, yet apart. In an attempt to meet him halfway, she touted the few Spanish phrases she knew, mangled by her wildly inaccurate accent. Juan smiled patiently, and corrected her. There was a warmth she felt she couldn't describe. *How could it be this easy to talk to a man who barely spoke the same language as her?* She'd known her share of men, but she couldn't articulate the intimacy she felt with this utter stranger. She couldn't describe the delicious sense of familiarity there was between them, despite everything about tonight being as unfamiliar as it could be. It was new and yet it felt safe.

The moment picked Saira up in a giddy swirl for just an instant, making her do something out of character. The juxtaposition of that feeling against the way he looked under the looming lights of the street – tall, imposing, beautiful – nudged her on. It felt so right to ask, 'Could I take your picture?'

He grinned, raising an eyebrow in amusement. 'Oh, *si*, sure.' Every expression, every piece of off-track language was becoming more and more suffused with a wonderful glow. She didn't know if it was the alcohol, and she certainly didn't care. She took one single photograph – his frame marred a little by the haze of the light and an old smudge on the lens – but it was enough. The moment now existed on her reel of memories.

They finally got to the club, but they still seemed to have arrived early. Save for some stragglers and a group of disconcertingly cool teens that had clearly fake ID'd their way in, the club was empty. The dance floor was sparse, and it made more sense to start drinking the three shots and two drinks they had each been handed tickets for with their cover charge than to attempt to dance.

When she recalled the conversation later, his words weren't as broken as they probably had been. 'It's rare to meet someone you can talk, eh, so easily; you can feel close to so *gfhgfh*,' he had said, breaking into, from what she could decipher, Spanish and then quickly replacing it with 'so fast' when he remembered. She recollected being glad it was dark because she was blushing; it made her feel so silly and childish. *What grown woman blushes?* she chided herself, grateful he was unlikely to notice under the dim lighting.

She had moved closer now; she could tell by the loop of rings her drink had made on the chalky pinewood table as she edged her drink towards Juan's. It was sweet, but now also a little frustrating, how physically careful he was being with her. She wanted an accidental brush of hands, or, even better, his arm around her waist. He seemed inclined to do neither and she wondered if it was her. For an instant, she had a visual of him with a graceful Spanish girl from the last bar. It seemed natural because they were both so beautiful. It is *me*, she thought and felt something cold clutch at her insides.

Right then, he locked eyes with her as he reached for his drink. His eyes stayed firmly transfixed on her, and in them was – she hoped – desire. Ugh, desire. She'd always hated that word because it had a tacky romance-novel connotation she couldn't dismiss and yet there was no other word that could fill its shoes. His eyes had an unspoken directness about them and, in that moment, she could stake her life on the fact that he wanted her.

He was talking about the horrors of absinthe when she leaned forward and kissed him, mid-sentence. For a fraction of a second, she felt his mouth moving, still forming words against hers, until it understood her kiss and moved into it. The kiss was intense, but there was still something sweet about it. Sweeter than you'd expect a kiss with a stranger in a bar to be. She pulled away and he smiled at her. They leaned closer, talking as they kissed, kissing as they talked. She barely noticed that the blue strobe lights of the darkened club were now sweeping across many more dancing bodies than when they'd come in.

She was down to her last shot now and the haze of tequila

had caught up with her. Everything seemed a beautiful, blurry blue until Juan's face came before her. She was used to the warmth of the alcohol burning through her, but not so much to it's emboldening effect. In a move that surprised her, she took his hand and led him through the club, moving quickly past the thickening crowd. They found a corner just out of the reach of the interrogatory flashes of neon that skimmed the club in time to the music. She pressed into him and kissed him with an urgency that she'd never thought herself capable of.

Old adages and social warnings from her growing years started ringing faintly at the back of her mind: 'This is so dangerous', 'You're a slut', 'What if he does something to you?', 'You don't even know his last name – have some shame.' The voices soon grew to a loud, mosquito-like buzzing and she shook her head to get rid of them, in turn breaking the kiss.

He instantly cupped her face, his eyes full of concern. 'You are okay?' he asked and seemed so sincere, she couldn't stop herself from kissing him again. The kisses turned harder, more pressing – his body was melding with hers now and she could feel the effect she had on him. The sweetness of those kisses at their table had disappeared, replaced with a hungry heat that had taken hold of her. She would go wherever that heat took her.

And it took her to the bathroom of the club. She pulled him into the ladies' room and pushed him against the dilapidated wooden walls of a stall with her body, kissing him almost violently, as if she wanted him so much that reality wasn't enough. They both fumbled desperately with the lock until he told her in struggling words and succinct gestures that it simply wouldn't lock. It was the ultimate deterrent, the snap-back to reality.

That is when she heard high, animated women's voices talking in right outside, but Saira realized she didn't care. Maybe it was being here, in this land where no one knew her, where she felt protected by her anonymity and the city's liberalism. There was something so hot about – both at the time it was happening and when she replayed it years later – leading this man to a public restroom with a door that wouldn't lock, and fuck him anyway. The risk seemed insignificant compared to the moment, *that* moment – full and passionate – and she knew it was worth it. She slid her hand down his abs and onto him. He was hard – but he pulled back gently, uttering a soft, massacred version of 'Are you sure?'

She was. She didn't know *why*, exactly, but she felt sure.

His manner shifted from aroused but tentative, to truly-take-charge for the first time since Saira had kissed him, and she was fuelled by it. They played off each other's almost biting hunger, each kissing harder, touching more urgently. The blazer she'd worn to protect herself from the soft nip in the air had been cast on the filthy, footprinted floor. The corset top she'd felt so brazen putting on – but had hidden all evening out of Delhi-girl instinct – was now in disarray, riding up unpoetically against the midriff she'd been nervous about exposing. It seemed so strange that, not two hours ago, she'd been hugging her blazer tighter for fear of peekaboo skin, and now, she was one degree of separation from being buck naked in a grimy bathroom stall.

There was no space to move, and her landslide of desire

(there was the word again) had not accounted for that. Cinema had been her only real barometer of what sex in a restroom looked like, and the aesthetic angles never entertained its limits. But as she was trying to figure out her next move, he decided for them, hoisting her up onto him and propping her against the wall. She could feel him against her, the tension and longing suddenly commingling into impatience. She pulled him inside her and, all at once, it was real. It was *her* – not this out-of-body experience it had felt like up until that second. It was she, Saira Baruah, who was against this wall, being fucked by a Spanish man she knew nothing about, as she tried to suppress the moans that came unbidden, for fear of the girl-gaggle outside overhearing. This wasn't in a book, or a bad porno. It was happening to her. In the here and now. And she waited for the cold crash of consciousness to ruin the moment.

But it didn't. Not when he moved her from the wall and sat down on the seat, pulling her onto him as he grew harder inside her. Not when he gently moaned the name she'd given him on Tinder in her ear, as she moved against him. Not when he finally undid the laces on her corset, enough to reach her breasts and grasp at them in an uncoordinated frenzy. She kept waiting, but it never tipped over into insanity for even a second.

'You go first,' she directed, hastily buttoning her jeans when they were done. When he'd left, she sat in the stall and tried hard to extract the strands of memory from the blur of alcohol, eager to save the images for later. It was like trying to quickly put out a burning photograph to salvage whatever she could for her album; it would fade anyway, but this moment was crucial. More than his skin under her fingers or his lips on her breasts, she tried to hold on to the way she'd felt in this last electric hour of her life. Unbelievably free.

He was waiting for her outside with a drink and she smiled as he told her it was a whisky sour. She hated whisky, but he didn't know that – and he'd never need to. They finished their cocktails in silence, exchanging grins with colour in their cheeks, until he offered to walk her back to her Airbnb. She was still drunk, and the idea of having a hand to hold as she walked through unfamiliar streets of Madrid at this late hour was too appealing for her usual panic instinct to kick in. 'Yes, please.' She smiled coyly, riding the wave of that feeling.

It was nearly 2 a.m. by the time they left the club and stepped out into the city's sublime streets, cobbled with waterworn stones and glistening under the corner lights. The streets were by no means deserted, but that didn't impede her sudden need to swing around the lampposts and repeat the three Spanish phrases she knew with loud, gay abandon. There were several witnesses to her bout of light-hearted madness, but it didn't seem to bother Juan who, Saira realized, was smiling at her. Watching her.

She swung right around a lamppost and into his arms, and they kissed. In that moment she knew she'd never forget that kiss because, in the wildness of the night, it was a moment that was truly cinematic in its romance. They walked hand in hand, her randomly spouting 'por favor' and 'Donde esta la biblioteca' interspersed with a zillion soft kisses on the street. Every so often, a little burst of chatter from an opening restaurant door or incomplete wisps of conversation from passers-by would remind them that they weren't the only two people the city had left.

They finally reached the gothic, brick-lined archway of her Airbnb in the narrow lane of La Encomienda that she already felt like she knew so well. He stood there for a moment, staring at her in that way someone does right before they tell you what they're thinking. She felt a certain wistfulness clutch at her, like when summer vacation ends and it's time to go back to school. He leaned down to kiss her and pulled her smaller frame up into his, the kiss deepening, intensifying, dizzying.

When he released her gently, her head was spinning, but she'd made up her mind. She raised a finger to her lips and let out a furtive 'shhhh' as she noisily turned the clunky key to the house. As she snuck him past the common area and into her room, terrified she would wake her strict-seeming host, Saira felt a frisson of excitement. It was as if every time she surprised herself by pushing her limits, she'd push them some more – and the rush was fantastic.

They made love for the next three hours straight. Saira wasn't sappy – she didn't bandy the term about as a replacement for the cruder 'fucked' when it was more accurate. But with Juan – in the warmth of her Airbnb bed, skin on skin against the cool sheets – it felt too intimate to qualify as anything but that. The melting depth of their kisses that sometimes went on forever and only ended for oxygen. The way their hands clasped as she came. The way he kissed her eyes after he did ...

As she stood on the street, with twilight doing its morning stretches, it all seemed like a phantasm. She couldn't believe it hadn't even been twenty-four hours since she had landed in this country and already she felt a connection with it that was too deep for her to ever forget. With this man, who stood in her doorway, with his kind amber eyes and his lightly tanned skin, that had been nearly enmeshed with hers not an hour ago. He was looking at her like only lovers do, with a familiarity that's so tangible you could almost taste it in the air between them. She looked at him the same way, knowing how beautiful this experience was in its ephemerality; or rather, because of it.

She knew this was the last time she would ever see him, and the exquisite allure and sadness of that thought filled her up to her fingertips. They had an unspoken understanding – neither would try to reconnect. It seemed cruel to drag to death through distance a moment that could instead be immortalized in memory, becoming a delicious blanket of reminiscence they wrapped around themselves when they needed it most.

She leaned up to kiss him goodbye, taking in the taste of his lips, the traces of tequila and cigarettes lacing their softness. She memorized the scent, the faint remnants of his cedarwood cologne mingled with notes of her dark cocoa perfume. The feeling of his hands on her waist, making their way up to her face as he kissed her. He pulled away slowly, the kisses getting shorter as they forced themselves to part.

As he walked away, doused in streetlight, his towering frame fading into the nighttime shadows of Madrid, Saira felt a pang, an urge to run to him for another 'last kiss', like a craving for a second (or third) helping of dessert. He took a turn, looking at her from afar and smiling before he was swept clean from her sight. The streets were empty now and he was just a dream.

FOUR

'WOW,' RUBANI BREATHED. 'I mean … wow.'

A hush had fallen over the group as Saira's impassioned recounting soaked in. The whole experience read too quixotic for Rubani's taste. It was alright for Saira, who was adventurous enough to put a crocodile hunter to shame, but a handsome stranger with a language barrier had always seemed more Dahmer than dalliance-worthy in Rubani's eyes.

'I have too many questions,' Faiza said, bursting through Rubani's thoughts.

'Yes!' Natasha squealed excitedly. 'Like, first of all, are you still in touch? I've always wondered. And was it *really* your first one-night stand? Because I'm pretty sure in college there were—'

'Okay, sorry, no. You all will just kill it with too much probing. I'm instituting a two-question rule, okay? I really don't want to ruin the memory of it.'

'How the fuck is *that* fair?' Faiza grumbled. 'Unless you mean two questions each. I should be able to ask you whatever I want.'

'Two questions total – sorry, Haider.' Saira shrugged. 'It

was honestly one of the most beautiful nights of my life and I don't want it pulped at this public forum, thanks.'

'Okay, fine, Bani? You want to go first, since this is all for your benefit?'

'I'm good.' Rubani smiled, pushing down the inquest bubbling in her stomach. *Didn't you worry he'd hurt you? How were you okay getting drunk with a stranger? Did you get an STD check after? Do you ever regret it?*

There was a recklessness to it that Rubani envied, a pull she knew she'd never be able to give in to. As a young girl in a foreign city, letting yourself fuck a total stranger – in a goddamn public bathroom, for crying out loud! It seemed to leap wildly from the pages of something *Fifty Shades*-esque, pragmatism and real-world consequences be damned. She would have been far too governed by trepidation to do it herself – not that an opportunity would ever present itself. She was nothing like her free and flighty friend and, hence, her life would never come to junctures that called for free and flighty impulses.

'Okay, fine, then. Faiza, you go first,' Natasha offered generously.

'Why did you give him a fake name?' Faiza asked, without missing a beat.

A slow smile spread across Saira's face. 'Ahhh, caught that, didn't you, you little minx,' she replied, grinning. 'I didn't want to be traceable. Like, in case he turned out to be nuts, I didn't want to give him any access to my life.'

'But isn't that kind of unfair?' Faiza mused. 'I mean, would *you* be okay if he had lied to you about his name?'

Saira thought about sweet Juan, with his kind eyes and

stirring touch. It was the name she cried out sometimes when she was on her own. It was the name that made her ears prick up if a character was called that on a Netflix España series. It was the name that brought back every warm kiss, every rousing graze with a visceral intensity. And then there was the possibility that it had never been his name at all.

'Nope,' Saira declared. 'That was his name to me. And that's good enough for me. Now, just a reminder that you have one question left.'

'I'll take the last one, then?' Natasha looked over at Rubani for confirmation.

'By all means,' she complied.

'Babu, weren't you *scared*?' Natasha asked. 'I mean, a total stranger. In a strange country. *Spain*, for God's sake – what if something had happened to you?'

'Yeah, okay, I'm going to piggyback on that,' Rubani chimed in. 'Saira, he could have *literally* been a rapist. He could've been a serial killer. How the hell did you put that aside?' Realizing her voice had risen a few octaves, she pulled back. 'I'm not trying to yell at you – but thank god you're okay. And you're an *idiot*.'

'I know, I know.' Saira sighed. 'I told you – I thought about that myself.'

'Yeah, fleetingly. Not enough to stop you,' Rubani pointed out.

'To be honest, as ridiculous as I know it's going to sound, it was instinct. There was something about the vibe, from the first minute, that didn't make me feel like anything was off. I'm generally not reckless—'

A soft 'pffft' from Natasha's direction made Saira shoot her a withering glare.

'I'm ballsy, you assholes, not *suicidal*,' she scoffed, loud enough for two Goan men, struggling past with a heavy water bottle they intended to change, look up in surprise.

'You *do* do some pretty crazy shit, S,' Faiza said. 'Remember that time you literally jumped a turnstile when we were coming back from Gurgaon and you couldn't find your metro card?'

'I lost it on the train!' Saira objected. 'How the hell was I supposed to get out of the station?'

'By paying the fine, like regular humans?'

'Whatever! I got away with it. And, like, worst-case scenario, I would've feigned ignorance and paid the fine. Anyway, this wasn't like that. It wasn't so much a "calculated risk" as it was just ... trusting my gut.'

'Well, he could've physically wrenched your trusting guts out,' Rubani mumbled, disapproving.

'Okay, fine. You know what, *this* is why I didn't want so many questions. You both have had one-nighters too, right?' Saira gestured at Faiza and Natasha with a forkful of tuna. 'Why am I getting all the heat? You guys aren't even talking about yours!'

'Wow, what is this rush?' Natasha asked. 'We're on *chhutti*. We'll all talk about it when we feel like it, *na*?'

'I mean, it's not a fucking seminar.' Faiza grinned, looking over at Natasha. 'We're not sex evangelists, here to convert the non-believer.'

The shared look of kinship between the two irritated Saira enough for her to be completely done with this conversation. 'You know what?' She raised her hand, beckoning for the bill. 'Let's just go. I'm sure Faiza needs to get a workout in.'

Natasha opened her mouth to retort on her behalf but decided against it. It was a fight for another day.

As Rubani parted the toran door hangings of the indie store Saira had dragged her to, she was glad she'd decided to come. The alternative had been wakeboarding with an overzealous Faiza, who was convinced the trip, though only in its second day, would wane without her working in some water sports. She had suggested an activity none of the others endorsed. Natasha had gone with her as an act of solidarity, even though Rubani knew her friend would much rather have been here, perusing pretty silver earrings instead.

The cool climes of the eggshell-hued store offered much-needed relief from the unforgiving coastal sun that glowered outside. The woman behind the counter smiled distractedly, too consumed with a colourful European woman exclaiming about a pair of block-printed babouches. The walls were lined with the handiworks of homegrown designers and organic merchandise, making the fast-fashion-rejection ethos of the store acutely clear. It held little interest for Rubani, who thrifted most of her wardrobe from Instagram stores and Sarojini Nagar; nothing here warranted the extra zeroes slapped on for its spurious 'sustainability'. To her, it was performative-bougie, a masterclass in vaingloriousness. There were local women a little ways down the road selling similar jewellery and patchwork handbags, but because they sold them under the harsh southwestern sun as opposed to the attar-scented AC climes, they didn't quite have the same cachet. But she knew Saira loved this kind of thing – and there was a bar next door where they could knock back a few daiquiris afterwards, so it wasn't a total loss.

True to form, Saira was delighted to have discovered the store. The sun streamed in through the shamrock-green shutters, dousing the space in molten gold light. The open white shelves creaked under the weight of the wares, from necklaces spun with brass and yarn to block-printed coffee mugs, depending on where your gaze landed. Homey corners with earthy-hued cushions cuddled up next to myriad wooden racks, lined with kaleidoscopic clothes in organic fabrics. Burgeoning designers' works were on display with the pride of a mother holding an A+-rife report card. Saira could have spent hours drifting through the store by herself, scoring indie finds, but it seemed unfair to let Rubani tap her feet with the boredom of an unamused adolescent while she pored over paper jewellery. Besides, it was their chance to catch up one on one.

'Thanks for coming with me, Bani. I mean, I know you mostly came to escape adventure-sports time, but still,' Saira smiled.

'Aye, no, I like this place,' Rubani said, feeling forgiving. 'Besides, we're drinking after, no?'

'Oh, friend, we are *always* drinking after,' Saira said. The big sell of being on holiday was being able to have the stem of a cocktail glass between her fingers at any hour without being labelled an alcoholic. 'The bar next door is supposed to have nice live music. And, who knows, maybe we'll find your one-night boy,' she wiggled her eyebrows. 'Or girl,' she added hastily.

Rubani sighed and wondered if she should let it go. But it was just the two of them and, in a way, that made it easier without the unit of Faiza and Natasha to contend with.

'S, can I say something? And you won't take this the wrong way?' Rubani ventured.

'Uh-oh.' Saira, thumbing through a rack of funky button-downs, turned around. 'Am I in trouble?'

Rubani rolled her eyes.

'Okay, so, I don't want to fight about it, but it kind of bothered me that you assumed I'd had, like, multiple casual hook-ups because I'm bi—'

'Oh my god, Bani, that's not what—' Saira cut in.

Rubani held her hand up. 'Let me just please finish what I'm trying to say?'

Saira stopped, leaning on a shelf full of open-toed flats. She nodded in quiet assent.

'The thing is, I get that bullshit from people. I get a lot of it. More than you can imagine. I've had my boyfriends ask me if I'm up for a threesome. I've had my girlfriend tell me that she always felt worried I'd end up with a man instead of her, because I've been with more men than women. I've even had queer friends assume it's a stopgap to being gay, like it's not who I am, it's just, like, orientation indigestion. There's this assumption that you're more likely to be a cheater because you have 'more options'. I've dealt with a lot of this crap and I don't fight back most of the time because it's exhausting. But I just – I kind of don't expect it from you, you know? You're my best friend, you and Nattu and me – it's been thirteen years, and *you* shouldn't be stereotyping me. You should be shutting down the people who are stereotyping me, you know? And I'm not saying you're an asshole – I know you're not. I know you mean well. But just … don't do shit like that, okay?'

Rubani looked at Saira to gauge her reaction to her tirade. Saira was quiet, thumbing the beads of a glass matinee necklace.

'Okay, please say something?' Rubani said.

'Honestly?' Saira began. 'I'm sorry, Bani. I didn't think I was stereotyping you. But I mean … for me, that assumption was just based on this idea that 'we've all done it, so I'm sure you have too; it wasn't okay to think that you would have simply because you're bi. I didn't mean for it to come out that way, at least. Maybe that's part of the problem. Like, I don't think I got it until now,' Saira said in all earnestness.

Rubani smiled. '*Abey*, I don't think you'll get it for a while, but that's okay.'

They were interrupted briefly by a saleswoman with an open smile, both to ask if she could help and to inform them there was a sale on the fabric jewellery. They nodded politely until she finally sauntered away.

Saira grinned. 'Can I tell you something, though? I think you might kill me for it.'

'*Haan*, say?'

'In the beginning, when you first told me in third year, my first reaction was: *does she find me attractive?*'

'Ugh, no. No, no, you know my rule about friends! And this is *exactly* what I meant about the stereotyping,' Rubani said, her tone lighter because she knew Saira was just trying to be honest.

'No, I mean, yeah, obviously, man, I know your rule now.

And I know it's a dick thing to have thought. But back then, when it was all fairly fresh, I did kinda, sorta, maybe … wonder if you had a crush on me. Like, I know that was arrogant as fuck and that's why I never said anything, but I thought it for a bit.' Saira shrugged sheepishly.

'Wow, you *are* arrogant as fuck.' Rubani raised her eyebrows, reining in her irritation. *Saira knew better now and would do better*, she assured herself. 'Just an FYI: I've never had "a crush" on any of you. Friends are not something I do, after the whole Asha fiasco. That disaster completely put me off.'

Asha Desai had started out as Rubani's friend from her college theatre club. Over many shared mid-practice glances, and some post-practice evenings at the shady bar near their college over tetra packs of bad port, the friendship had grown. Certain that these moments were nothing more than simple, friendly encounters in Asha's mind, Rubani had pushed back her sprouting feelings for fear of being embarrassed. The slow swirl of exquisite torture began: falling in love with her straight friend, watching her bounce from boy to boy, coming back to regale her with stories of her animalistic bedroom exploits, realizing with each passing Jack-and-Coke they split and every movie night they cuddled together and fell asleep that her love would go unrequited.

One day, with the patina of alcohol clouding her judgement, she had given in. She had seized a moment when the two girls lay side by side on Asha's bed, drinking beer and rewatching *Legally Blonde* for the tenth time. She had reached up to Asha's face and kissed the lips she'd memorized the contours of over the course of the last several months. And Asha's reaction had broken Rubani's heart. The lives of the two friends quickly unbraided over the next few weeks, with Rubani's apologies finding no soft landing. It was the most heartsick she'd ever felt, and she couldn't even pin it on a failed relationship. It was then that she had closed herself off and made a rule: if someone was a friend, she simply never let herself go there. And she'd managed well, for twelve years.

'Yeah,' Saira recalled with a shudder. 'We were just becoming friends then, but I still remember how much that fucked you up. I'm sorry, Bani. Like, in general. There's so much you must deal with that I'll never have to, and I know I don't get a lot of it, but I'll try to do better.'

Rubani, awash with fondness for Saira, reached in and gave her a hug. 'I love you,' she said, her voice muffled, her face buried in Saira's shoulder.

'Oh my god, I *knew* you had a crush on me,' Saira teased, and hugged her tightly.

'Jackass.' Rubani punched her friend and grinned.

Across town, Natasha struggled against the saltwater to walk back to shore, a few paces behind a faster Faiza. Their afternoon of wakeboarding had actually been a lot more fun than a grumbling Natasha from that morning had imagined it would be, and despite being covered in sea spray and sneaky granules of sand, she felt fantastic. She was still coasting off the rush and owed her bestie for pushing her to partake of it.

Natasha's automatic reaction was to think of Faiza as her best friend, even though she knew that if Rubani and Saira were to ever find out, the result would be a head-slicing of

Antoinette proportions. She felt a little guilty as she watched the lissome, bronze figure of Faiza swish easily through the glimmering blue waters towards the shore. With her beautiful skin, ridiculously ripped, I-work-out-every-day abs and arms and a dishevelled, lopsided bob that glinted with natural, sunbleached copper, Faiza looked exactly like Natasha wanted to.

She'd always found her own looks too pandering to the Indian archetype of beauty – the pale skin and Delhi-girl straight hair may be coveted by the mothers of the arranged marriage market, but Natasha found it uninspired. While she believed her face and frame to be the epitome of the Fair & Lovely commercial, Faiza's beautiful skin and athletic body were an easy mark for her envy. She looked coolly, nonchalantly sexy in a way Natasha knew she could never pull off.

The two trudged back to the shack at Candolim where they'd dumped all their belongings, their initial burst of full faith in the friendly, gap-toothed owner to stand guard having paid off. They waved to let him know that they were back, and he held up a beer and wiggled it as a question. With wordless ease, two crisp IPAs were soon slammed down on a table beside the two women as they threw their kaftans over their soaked swimwear. The thin cotton clung to both Faiza's sparse black bikini and Natasha's blush pink maillot, drawing sunglass-lowering stares from many a male passer-by. None of which went unnoticed behind the girls' mirrored aviators.

'These boys are fucking shameless, no?' Faiza said, amused.

'This is why I wanted to carry a thicker shirt,' Natasha said, tugging uncomfortably at her kaftan.

'Um, excuse me? Why should you have to? You're on the

beach, for fuck's sake. In an ideal world, you should be able to wear this on a Delhi street, but that you're feeling weird about it here is really stupid, Nattu.'

'Well, I don't want to be stared at, Faizoo! It's not fair. I'm literally just having a beer and being ogled – it's irritating.'

'Listen, if they stare, just stare back. I promise you, most of these little dipshits freak out when you make eye contact and glare. They're so used to women averting their eyes that they can't stomach the sass.'

'And what if they do something?' Natasha asked. She hated herself for the thought (and wouldn't dare say it in front of Saira, for instance, who was the human equivalent of bra-burning), but it did cross her mind often. It was the aftermath of her upbringing, of being a former lieutenant general's only daughter. 'Army conservative' took years to shake off, and she had never managed to completely forsake the 'proper' ways her authoritarian father had instilled in her, much to the dismay of her well-meaning but ineffectual mother. It still took a lot to be able to wear an audacious neckline or a daring pair of shorts without the niggling feeling that it was both indecorous and dangerous.

'Babe, what will they do? We're in broad daylight. And I'm here.' She patted Natasha's hand supportively. 'And I lift. I'll kick their ass.'

'Hahaha. I love you, Faizoo,' Natasha said, squeezing Faiza's hand in response. 'Besides, some of these boys are cute, so I actually don't mind,' she said, shaking her head with a smile at a local woman who had stopped to ask if she'd like to get her hair braided.

'Oooh, remember that sexy white boy we saw when we were coming in?' Faiza asked, making a mock-lascivious face. They'd seen a slightly sunburnt but still very attractive man on his cellphone as they'd padded on the Candolim sand, and caught a fragment of a Scottish accent as they'd passed him.

'Ugh, yes. He was very cute. It's a good thing we're both married, *na*? Or we'd have been fighting for all the same boys.'

'Excuse me, who are you calling married?' Faiza retorted. 'Not all of us had the urge to be a child bride like you.'

'I mean, living with someone for more than three years legally counts as being married in this country, so your fifteen years definitely qualify.'

'Ugh, it's barely been six – and that's if you count like Zaden does, from our first "date", which was just me eating at his bloody restaurant.'

'How do *you* do the math?'

'Duh. First time we fucked, obviously,' Faiza shrugged. 'That's what matters, no?'

'Not for all of us, but yeah, I can see that with you,' Natasha grinned. 'Besides, in my head I always think of you as married. Like, for all intents and purposes, you are. You're as … tethered as I am.'

'Tethered,' Faiza mused. 'That's an interesting choice of word.'

'I mean, it's apt, I guess. We're not stuck – we're in good relationships. With good men.'

'Well, as good as men can be,' Faiza scoffed.

'*Haan*. See, the point is, they're our partners because we chose them and love them – but it *does* change things. It does make us different from Saira, and now Bani, because they're free in a way we aren't, you know?'

'I mean, in a way *I'm* not, but whatever.' Faiza grinned and Natasha whacked her arm. 'No, but I get it,' she conceded. 'They don't have to factor somebody else into every decision.'

'Exactly! Like, they can decide to up and move to Italy tomorrow for a project. Or go on a three-day bender without checking with someone.'

'Honestly, babe, I think we're all too old for a three-day bender.'

'Ugh, but you know what I'm saying, *na*?'

'I do, I do. I think about that a lot, in fact. It's an interesting duality, because I also ask myself if I would trade in what I have with Zaden for that "untethered-ness". And I don't think I would.'

'Nor would I. Alex and I work – and that means something to me. To have that kind of support system in the person I'm with. It's taken nearly a decade to build this level of comfort and trust, and it makes much of my life possible to have that … emotional cushioning.'

'I feel like it's quieter with Z, because our lives are less intertwined than yours and Alex's. But at the base of it all, yeah, it's that feeling of someone who's there and gets it. Like, he gets my family and my dynamic with them and with you guys, and he's accommodated for it. I don't get pushback about things that matter, which makes it easier to do my shit. Thing is, I love that. And sure, I wouldn't give it up for that single-person freedom. But that doesn't mean I don't miss it.'

Natasha felt a warm glow, the kind she often felt after talking to Faiza about something like this, because she felt her friend understood her in a way even Alex didn't sometimes. He always rolled his eyes whenever she declared it to him amidst fights, or during her random fond reminiscences of Faiza.

'Sometimes I think *we* should've got married.' Natasha sighed.

'If only we didn't love dick so much.' Faiza sighed back.

'Ugh,' Natasha said, raising her clammy-bottomed beer in a toast. 'Touché.'

FIVE

'AREN'T WE TOO old for Silent Noise?' Rubani asked as they trudged across the cool evening beach sand towards the mini-field that served as an open-air club in Palolem. 'Is it even a thing anymore?'

The road trip all the way to South Goa for just one night of nostalgia seemed a misfire to her. They had gone twelve years ago to this very party on their first trip to Goa, and returning after all this time felt like a desperate attempt to relive a night that had gone down in their hall of fame. For everyone barring Faiza, who had agreed to come good-naturedly, the 'headphone party' held the fading memory of spending 500 bucks on a whim, despite it being a trip where they'd been pretty broke. It had seemed a cool concept back then, sold to them by an amiable Italian who'd been holidaying in Goa for three months, and it had turned out to be the most memorable night of the trip – save for some karaoke-gone-wild on their last. Both Saira and Natasha were too consumed by the idea of doing it 'for old time's sake', to account for the possibility that it would fall short of the warm remembrance.

'Listen, I know it might actually be really tacky now, but

who gives a shit?' Saira argued. 'There's likely still going to be some cuties to buy us drinks,' she said, grinning at Rubani. 'You two,' she pointed at Faiza and Natasha, 'can stand in the corner like old wives and get lots of FOMO.'

'Will you fuckers stop with the wives bullshit!' Faiza grumbled. 'Besides, what if it's just full of creepy uncles? Like 'hey-bebby' types from ladies' nights in Hauz Khas. That'll serve you right.'

'Ugh, really?' Natasha made a face. 'It better not be. I'm so excited about this. Remember that weird guy who was obsessed with you, Bani? The one in that gross Ed Hardy hoodie that kept blowing you kisses from the DJ booth?'

'Oh my god, *yes*! I remember him!' Saira clapped excitedly. 'He's the one that got away, Bani.'

'I mean, just think.' Natasha chuckled. 'By now, you could have had lots of little baby Guns N' Roses.'

'Ew.' Rubani laughed. 'Not if he was the last fauxhawked douchebag on the planet.'

'The fauxhawk!' Natasha and Saira said in unison, laughing. 'Who doesn't love a good fauxhawk,' Natasha said, smiling.

The idea started to grow on Rubani a little. Sure, it might not be particularly fun, or wild. But it definitely would be nostalgic and that wasn't an idea she was averse to right now. There was a comfort about college that she missed. Saira and Natasha often said they hated their college selves because they had no idea who they were back then. Rubani, on the other hand, sometimes wondered if her sense of self was still more or less the same as it was at nineteen.

As they clomped through the last bits of leaden sand and onto the smoother surface of the Silent Disco space, it felt as if they were entering a time capsule. They entered, and it almost seemed like a poster moment from a movie about a fun girls' holiday. With Natasha's powder-blue sundress, Saira's red shorts and giant cotton blazer, Faiza's black bralette and boyfriend jeans and her own white-and-teal printed kaftan, they looked like a freeze-frame from *Sex and the City* – minus the head-to-toe pink. The open field was peppered with palms and boulders, strategically placed for breathers from frenetic dancing and breathless make-out sessions alike. The neon lights pounded in a trio of colours, each indicative of the different stations playing retro (lime green), pop (aquamarine) and hard trance (vivid red) music.

The name 'Silent Noise' explained itself better than it intended visually, with a sea of inebriated dancers moving to myriad rhythms in surround-sound stillness. The crowd had changed, from being filled with European travellers and locals in the know over a decade ago, to a smattering of foreign faces amidst the exact sort of overdressed partygoers Rubani had left Delhi to avoid. The odds that she'd meet someone interesting here grew slimmer with every Axe body spray-drenched popped collar that swaggered past her.

Natasha, however, was filled with fond nostalgia. Twelve years ago, she ended up having one of the happiest nights of her life with Saira and Rubani. And sure, the place had lost some of its original underground cachet, but anything that caught the popular eye was bound to over time. What it *had* held on to was its big, breezy space, its still somewhat authentic concept and that film of ridiculousness that came with watching people dance to no music shed just as quickly when she put her headphones back on. Natasha threw on a pair – pop, always – and Lil Nas X filled her ears with a song she'd heard on Instagram reels. She closed her eyes and began swaying to the music, parting from her friends, and into the disparate herd of fellow roisterers.

Faiza and Saira made a beeline for the bar – instinct for Saira, the lure of a special occasion for Faiza. 'What'll you drink?' Faiza called out, disappearing into the throng away from Rubani, whose shout of 'vodka soda' cut through the shuffling silence audibly. Faiza found the whole thing amusing: the strobe-lit field, the surreal view of people seemingly dancing to silence, the fascinating mixture of the crowd itself. She suddenly felt an overwhelming surge of relief that she wasn't single, that sifting through this motley wave of tourists and try-hards for a spark of something hadn't even crossed her mind. It seemed like forever since she had 'dated', or had a battery of casual encounters with men whose appeal expired after twenty-four hours.

She'd always fancied herself a master of sexual encounters of the shallow kind and Zaden had factored heavily into changing her stance. While most men were left shell-shocked at her not wanting a relationship – and countered the rejection by coming on stronger – Zaden had accommodated her disdain for commitment by letting the relationship go at her pace. A year in, she had wanted nothing more than to be with him, full-time and for good, and he had welcomed the call because, as he'd then told her with a twinkle in his eye, 'It's what I've wanted all along.' She'd moved into his beautiful Defence Colony flat and hadn't had the urge to revive her youthful days of bedhopping since.

'I'm going to take this to Rubani,' she said to Saira, as

a friendly bartender slammed their drinks down on the counter and sheepishly apologized for the reckless spillage. 'You're okay here?'

'I'm good.' Saira smiled and waved her off encouragingly. She liked the idea of having a little time alone to scour the party for a cute face – or two – so she could take one back for Rubani. The party wasn't exactly as Saira remembered, but she'd expected that. The warm glow of nostalgia had a tendency to paint every memory in technicolour, an experience routinely ruined by revisiting it. This was why she usually never rewatched a show or movie she loved; it was destined not to live up to expectations the next time around. But when Natasha had come up to her, all bright-eyed with the idea of going back to Palolem for this, Saira couldn't help but say yes. Reliving their own wild capers was reason enough – the party wouldn't need to do it for them.

She sat at the bar and looked around. It seemed that time had amended the unspoken 'no locals' code, and a few stood around looking a bit bored – a stark contrast to the tourists who had completely submitted to the party's unique energy. She swirled her LIIT, taking measured sips of the potent drink. Her friends wouldn't dare have one, but for Saira, who sipped champagne at fashion events as often as most people eat eggs, drinking was second nature – and an LIIT simply got the job done faster.

'That's a terrifying drink,' a smooth male voice said from behind her, as if reading her thoughts.

She turned around to see a handsome man, a clean foot taller than her, standing a pace behind her at the bar. His accent was indubitably Indian, almost recognizably Bombay, but he didn't look it. He had the cool undertones of a well-to-do Caucasian, his eyes on the border of brown and cobalt blue. Dishevelled hair curled around his ears, a russet hue that she wasn't used to seeing on Indian men. *Is he or isn't he white?* she wondered.

'Why, have you roofied it?' she asked with a half-smile, raising an eyebrow.

'Wow.' He let out a breath. 'Not the response I was expecting.'

'Okay.' Saira laughed. 'I'll try again in a baby voice and flutter my eyelashes this time.'

He laughed warmly and held out his hand. 'Maxime,' he said, shaking his head.

So he is white!

'Saira.' She smiled. 'Maxime – what is that, French?'

'*Oui*,' he said jokingly. His pale pink mouth arced up when he smiled, creating little crinkles at his eyes that Saira fell in love with instantly. She made a mental note to make him smile more.

'Then why do you have a Bandra accent?' she asked point-blank.

Maxime held up a hand to his chest, as if he'd been stabbed.

'It's a Colaba accent, thanks very much. And it's because I grew up there.'

Saira shook her head. 'I'm confused: why were you growing up in Colaba if you're French and could have grown up in Le Marais. What is your origin story?'

'Ah, so you've been.' He grinned. 'I'm actually not from Paris at all. My mother is from Rouen.'

She loved how his accent changed during the French sections of his sentence. It was that familiar Bombay inflection until he broke into 'pah-ree' or 'roo-awn'.

'Indian father, I'm guessing?'

'You guessed right. My father is born-and-bred Bombay,' Maxime offered. 'And now, if you've finished giving me the third degree, can I maybe buy you a drink?'

'Sure, you filthy little mudblood.' She smirked.

'That is so racist!' Maxime laughed. 'But I applaud the reference. I don't meet many Harry Potter fans anymore.'

'Um, sorry, Maxime, but white people can't call other people racist.' It was Saira's turn to laugh. 'And thank you.'

'*Half*-white!' Maxime protested, leaning over the bar to procure her a second LIIT. 'And call me Max, please. Only my grandmother calls me Maxime.'

The conversation glided as smoothly over the next forty-five minutes as warm caramel on a sundae. It had been a long time since Saira had found such ease in parleying with a total stranger and, if her friends hadn't been lost to the bacchanal, she'd have stayed there until the darkness of the sky cracked with morning light. But alas, she was here with them and had stressed too heavily on how important a bonding experience this was to decamp with the first attractive man she met.

'I should go find my friends,' she said wistfully, just as he was wrapping up an anecdote about his dog hating children.

'I take it you don't like dogs?' Max enquired.

'They're fine; I just don't see what all the fuss is about.' She shrugged. 'My friend Faiza is obsessed, though – she's properly one of those aunties that sends out a dog meme a day.'

'You've brought up your friends twice now,' he pointed out. 'That really *is* my cue to leave, isn't it?'

'Well, I really do need to get back to them,' Saira sighed. 'But maybe come say hi? Faiza will care more about your dog stories.'

'You're very cruel, Saira … um, I meant to say your last name with gravitas, but I don't know it.'

'Baruah. You're going to find me on Instagram, aren't you?' Saira said, her eyes twinkling this time, as she picked up her clutch and slid off the bar stool.

'You know, just for *that*, I won't,' Max said, mock-huffily, following her through the crowd.

'Don't bother.' Saira shot him a smile. 'Take my number instead.'

They shared a look – a quick, charged moment. Just as Natasha spotted them and weaved her way over.

'Listen, this place is still so nice, ya!' Natasha said, clearly enjoying herself. She noticed Maxime and smiled politely, unable to discern whether he was with Saira or simply standing next to her.

'Nattu, this is Max,' Saira said by way of introduction. 'Max, Natasha.'

'Hi Natasha, nice to meet you,' Maxime said, his expression friendly, Saira noticed, and not at all the gaping one she was used to seeing on men's faces when they first laid eyes on Natasha. With her shampoo-commercial hair, petite frame and translucent skin that had never known a pimple – despite her obsession with liquid foundation and her penchant for cheese – Natasha was a show-stealer in Saira's eyes. Side by side, they were both beautiful and almost similarly pale, Saira observed: Maxime's tallness was a fitting contrast to Natasha's smallness. A flash of feeling like a lumbering giant overtook her, but subsided quickly. She hated herself for the little nip of insecurity she felt when a man she was interested in met Natasha for the first time – the contrast, she always told herself, was knockout versus knockoff. It helped immensely that Natasha was happily married.

That Max, however, hadn't gone goo-goo-eyed was definitely a point in his favour.

'Heyyy Max,' Natasha said, shooting Saira a look that said 'wow'. 'So you're what's been keeping our friend away, huh? She seems to have completely forgotten that we exist.'

Saira opened her mouth to object, but Maxime replied instead.

'In her defence, she mentioned you existed. Several times. Too many times actually,' he said, flashing his pearly whites at Saira. 'It was almost insulting. I'm the one who asked her to stay.'

Natasha shot her another look. *I like him*, this one clearly said.

Faiza and Rubani jogged up, each bearing a cocktail that looked almost too iridescently bright to drink.

'I don't know what's in this,' Rubani said, with the slightest of slurs. 'But it's working.'

'She should know.' Faiza rolled her eyes. 'She's fucking had twelve.'

'I have had four!' Rubani held up four fingers, mentally reconfirming and then nodding in assertion. 'And fuck off, Haider; you wanted me in a good mood, I'm in a good mood. Who is this white boy?'

'Bani!' Natasha said, alarmed. 'Okay, just come with me.'

While Natasha carted Rubani off to the side, Saira introduced Faiza and Maxime. A conversation about dogs ensued quickly and went on far too long for her liking. Talk flowed from pets to parties to a fondness for Goa and how Max always found a way to return every few months. Nearly a half hour later, with a promise to meet again before their trips ended, Maxime parted from them, leaving Faiza and Saira sipping on the chromatic cocktails together.

'Should we go find those two? I think Bani might throw up,' Saira said, just as Natasha returned, her hand locked with Rubani's.

'Okay, so she threw up a bit, but she's had some water and is feeling much better now,' Natasha said.

'I'm much better now,' Rubani confirmed, sounding far more sober than she had a short while ago.

And she really was. She was actually feeling pretty damn great. A beautiful, long-haired girl had held her bag in the bathroom and told her that she loved her cropped hair. Rubani had shouted thank yous to her through the stall door when Natasha had come looking for her. The girl left after giving Rubani a long hug, and she had felt a fuzzy glow of happiness. It wasn't sexual, just warm and wonderful, the kind only girls who lift each other's spirits in public restrooms would truly ever be able to understand.

'Yes, but you *do* need a breath mint.' Saira pulled one out of her straw crossbody handbag. 'Just suck on this before you say anything else in my face, please?'

'Can you two handle her for a bit?' Natasha asked. 'I'll be back in a few.'

Saira caught Faiza smiling into her drink and her latent frustration at the passing thought that Faiza knew something she didn't bubbled to the surface. 'Yeah, yeah, go – I'm here,' she said, her tone snappy.

She turned to Faiza. 'So, what'd you think?'

'Of?'

'Max, obviously!'

'Ah, yes, sorry. He's really nice! *And* his dog is adorable.'

'I knew you'd love his stupid dog.' Saira pulled a face. 'He's cute, isn't he? Like, *really* cute? Or is it just me?'

'He *is* pretty cute. But now I'm wondering if maybe you have a white-boy fetish,' Faiza teased.

'Hey!' Saira smacked her hand. 'Actually, *wait*. Oh my god, do I have a white-boy fetish? There haven't been any others, except Juan.'

'Are you suuure? No secret flings with white boys in college?'

'Shut up!' Saira grinned. 'I think I'd remember, no?'

They talked for a while and Saira, who spent very little time with Faiza one on one, found herself surprisingly comfortable in her company. She'd always been padded by the others around her and often wondered if they would simply drown in a sea of awkward silence if left to fend for themselves any longer than ten minutes. It was, on the contrary, so comfortable that they lost track of time – and Rubani.

Spurred by her newly emptied tank and newfound ability to walk, Rubani had wandered off in search of Natasha. The breath mint had hit refresh on her confidence, and she smiled sloppily at strangers as she meandered through the field, her eyes peeled for her friend's flowing powder-blue dress.

She spotted a quick flash of the colour a few yards away and quickened her pace. After pushing past a head-bobbing wannabe Rastafarian and a couple practically dry-humping on the dance floor, she found the wearer of the blue. Her back was turned to Rubani, but she could clearly tell from that impossibly tiny waist and the sheet of shimmering hair that it was Natasha.

Just as she decided that she was in good enough spirits to run the distance between them and jump on her shoulders to surprise her, she saw a strong arm wind itself around that svelte waist. A man, an easy six-foot-something with broad shoulders and a dimpled smile, was whispering into her ear. There was something so intimate about the act, about the way the two people were dancing and smiling at each other, that Rubani instantly deduced it wasn't just a friend. Then the man leaned down and kissed her.

Rubani felt a sinking feeling in the pit of her stomach. The last time she'd felt that gripping unease was when she'd heard the zipper of Kabir's duffel bag. There was a finality in the sound that had sickened her. It had changed everything. She felt it again now and she knew that she didn't need a full-frontal view to confirm things. It *was* Natasha. And she was kissing another man.

Rubani felt the hot sting of vomit at the base of her throat and swallowed hard. She suddenly pictured Alex. Sweet, quiet Alex who had always been her favourite of her friends' partners. She had a visual of their last group dinner at an Italian restaurant Natasha loved. Alex had tucked her hair behind her ear several times as Natasha had talked animatedly, as strands kept snaking their way into her carbonara. He'd eventually just moved her plate further away, as she continued to chat, oblivious to his thoughtful little manoeuvres. Rubani remembered thinking, *That's what I want. The intimacy that comes with a decade of pure partnership.* And wondering if she'd ever have that with Kabir. The prick of nausea returned.

Her instinct was to run. Not physically – the faint ghosts of cocktails past wouldn't let her. But to move away, quickly, before Natasha was spun in a twirl by the man and saw her there. She couldn't face her friend. And she couldn't bear to be gaslighted – told she was seeing things because she was drunk. It would be too much right now.

Rubani stumbled just far enough, to a boulder on the open field, out of Natasha's sight and, much to an unsuspecting couple's chagrin, threw up. As she sat on the ground, now dry-heaving, she felt a hand on her back and an instant stab of alarm.

'Bani, baby, are you okay?' Saira's voice wafted from behind her. *It's not her*, Rubani thought with relief.

'I think we should head back now,' came Faiza's tempered tone from a little farther. 'Let me just find Nattu and we'll go?'

'I'll stay here. You go find her?' Saira said, stroking Rubani's hair fondly.

As Faiza disappeared into the crowd, Rubani stood up and brushed the dust from the ground off her kaftan, miraculously still a Tide white despite all the spewing. They moved to the bar close by, where Saira settled Rubani on a stool and signalled for a glass of water.

'Sai?' Rubani said. 'Does Nattu seem happy to you?'

'What do you mean? Here, first drink this, then tell me.'

Rubani glugged down the water gladly. The aftertaste of vomit had lessened, but lingered still.

'Can I have another breath mint?'

'Of course you can,' Saira said with fondness. Rubani popped three in her mouth and crunched thoughtfully.

'Does she?' Rubani repeated. She'd seen her favourite aunt devastated by her uncle's cheating for many years, and this recent incident with Kabir ... That Natasha was willing to be that person could only mean she was miserable ... right?

'Does who what?'

'Nattu. Does she seem happy to you or no?'

'Like, on this trip? Yeah, I think so. Bani, we're all happy to be here. I hate that it took all this shit with Kabir to make it happen, but this trip is a good thing.'

'Not this trip,' Rubani shook her head as if to clear it. 'Like, in life. Does she have a happy life?'

'Okay. Weird question. Um, yeah, I think so. She should def quit that sexist piece-of-shit agency of hers, but other than that, yeah. What are you getting at?'

Rubani debated telling Saira. It would be easier to split the burden, to have someone to freak out about it with. But Saira wasn't exactly known for her discretion. The idea that she could confront Natasha and cause a holiday-imploding scene was more than her currently-too-delicate stomach could handle.

'Nothing.' She smiled. 'I just worry about you guys sometimes.'

'Awley, baby.' Saira hugged her and held Rubani's head to her chest, kissing the top. 'It's our turn to worry about you.

You just focus on having fun – and a one-night stand, like you've been instructed.' She smiled mischievously.

'Ugh, enough with that,' Rubani said, but her tone was soft. 'By the way, did I tell you? I started texting this girl on Tinder.'

'Oh my god, what? Is she in Goa?'

'No, Delhi. But she's cute. Like, really cute. Like, if Summer from *The O.C.* was Indian?'

'SHOW ME IMMEDIATELY!' Saira bellowed.

'Not now!' Rubani laughed, feeling lighter. 'I'll show you at home or something; *abhi* I don't want to move much.'

'Okay, fine, but I'm so glad! It still shouldn't stop you from having a one-nighter, though. Like, what happens on holiday stays on holiday. And then your thangs can happen in Delhi also,' she teased, winking.

'Yuck,' Rubani groaned. 'I'm mostly only used to saying this to men, but you really have a one-track mind.'

Faiza and Natasha appeared beside them, laughing, and Rubani felt a pang as she made eye contact with Natasha. Seeing her up close in good light confirmed to her what she was still hoping was a drunken delusion. Natasha's lipstick, usually perfect, was mostly gone – and what remained was just smudged enough to prove that damage had been done. Her hair was tousled enough to testify that someone's hand had run through it. And it was, in fact, the exact same dress.

'Shall we head?' Faiza motioned toward the exit.

'Yep,' Rubani said, her momentary good mood evaporating. 'I'm done.'

SIX

SOFT SUNLIGHT DAPPLED the waters of Candolim, playing off the Colgate-white of the freshly painted dolphin boat Natasha had dragged them to in the wee hours of the morning. Faiza didn't mind – it was her favourite time of day – but by the look on Rubani's and Saira's faces, that train of thought was carrying a party of one. Natasha was struggling between her natural instinct to sleep in and her holiday desire to watch jumping fish. And leaning towards the latter, she had fallen into a cycle of nodding off and jolting awake with a big 'I'm up, I'm up!' smile.

'Tell me why we're here,' Saira grumbled into a near-empty cup of coffee. 'Please explain why we are anywhere but in our beds at this ungodly hour. While on holiday!'

'Nattu, this is a testament to how much they love you.' Faiza grinned. 'No, Bani?'

Bani turned to Faiza and smiled tightly. *Weird*, thought Faiza.

'Guys, I'm sorry, okay? I actually wanted to do this. And I *told* you I'll go with Faiza if you don't want to come so it's really your fault only,' Natasha huffed.

Saira let out a scathing noise, as if she wanted to give the two of them more opportunities to run off together. She could imagine a holiday retelling where she was constantly left out of the most fun anecdotes and the idea was unappealing, to say the least. No, thank you, she would be part of this story.

Faiza caught the scoff and instantly realized why Saira and Rubani had agreed to come. She supposed it should bother her that the two were insecure about her friendship with Natasha, but it didn't anymore. She couldn't help who she was close to, and she considered both of them close as well. It was Saira's nature to be a little immature about these things, she'd concluded. While Rubani didn't seem it in other respects, she'd always found Saira coming off a little anxious.

She couldn't fathom why. Saira was far more successful in her field than Faiza had been at her age. And she seemed to live a great life, wrapped in an almost vagrant sense of independence except for the aeonian series of perks from her job. To help matters further, Saira was also attractive and funny. Faiza couldn't understand what there was to be bothered by.

'I'm glad we just chilled yesterday,' Rubani said. 'I'm getting too old for this party-every-night thing, even on holiday.'

The girls had slept in and then spent the day by the beach. They'd done a low-key dinner and catch-up – an early night for the early morning that would follow suit. It had been nice and mellow, but Rubani seemed off again, which niggled Faiza. It had just seemed as if their friend had been getting back into the swing of things – she'd been her adorable old self at the Silent Noise party – but all of yesterday she'd appeared a touch uncomfortable.

'I mean, we're on *chhutti* so I'm definitely down for the party-every-night thing this week,' Natasha said, smiling at Rubani, who broke eye contact and stared out to sea.

She knew she was being weird, and the group would eventually cop on, but Rubani couldn't reconcile what she'd seen the night before with the friend she knew. What she'd witnessed effectively made Natasha a cheater. And to have to file her in the same category as so many of the men who had broken her heart in the past was too much to bear. Even Kabir, though she couldn't quite confirm it. She knew in her heart that his school friend had been on the periphery far longer than he had even let on. And Murphy's law of relationships held especially fast for cheating; if they *could* go astray, they usually did.

But still, cheating was the MO of her scumbag exes, not her incredibly kind best friend. She couldn't imagine confronting Natasha, of course. A face-off would be the absolute worst outcome; she'd be presented with some flimsy excuse, goaded into a reaction, called 'judgemental' with a flippant snort once more. But if believing in fidelity, in not breaking the vows of marriage, made her judgemental, well, then maybe it was her friends who needed a sharper moral compass.

'Unngnngg,' Saira grumbled loudly from her corner of the boat, startling the four other passengers who were sitting a little ways away. 'Where are your dolphins, Nattu? Have you seen any yet?'

'I did!' Natasha protested. 'And I shook you also, but you had no interest in seeing them.'

'I have *no* interest in seeing them,' Saira retorted. 'They are the rapists of the sea.'

'Excuse me?' Natasha exclaimed.

'You know this.' Faiza laughed. 'Remember I sent you that *Slate* piece about violent dolphin sex?'

'You send me so much stuff, how am I supposed to read everything?' Natasha squealed. 'What does that even mean, that they're … rapists?' Her voice involuntarily lowered on the last word.

'It means they are rapists, Nattu; they are actually gang rapists, and they do it to humans too, so don't pet any of the cute ones,' Saira said, gleefully watching her friend's expression change to one of misery.

'Gangs of two or three male bottlenose dolphins isolate a single female from the pod and forcibly mate with her, sometimes for weeks at a time,' Faiza read out from her phone, clearly having retrieved the *Slate* article. 'To keep her in line, they make aggressive noises, threatening movements and even smack her around with their tails. And if she tries to swim away, they chase her down. Horny dolphins have also been known to target human swimmers.'

'Oh my god,' Natasha said, moving away from the low, striped edges of the boat to the seats under the aqua-blue canopy. 'I can't … This is deeply disturbing.'

'Miriam Goldstein,' Faiza said cheerfully. 'Really good writer. You should read more of her stuff.'

'Okay, I'm officially over this.' Natasha sighed. 'You,' she pointed at Saira, 'have ruined it for me.'

Getting her vengeance for being woken up early, Saira grinned and drained the last lingering drops of her macchiato.

'So, S, are you seeing that French guy again?' Faiza asked.

'Mmmm, he was dreamy, wasn't he?' Saira smiled, batting her eyelashes comically.

'He was gorgeous,' Natasha chimed in. 'His eyes are so sexy – what colour were they? Were they blue or not?'

'Kind of, but like an intensely dark, deep blue,' Saira sighed. 'Like Titanic diamond blue, but if someone had spilt some coffee on it.'

'How romantic,' Faiza laughed with mock sarcasm. 'You should write for a living.'

Saira stuck her tongue out at Faiza and they grinned.

'Do you remember him at all, Bani?' Natasha asked, turning to her. 'Or were you too hammered by then?'

Faiza couldn't be sure, but she thought she saw Rubani flinch, just the slightest bit.

'I don't remember him that well,' she said quietly. 'The whole night is a bit of a blur.'

'A fun blur,' Saira added. 'I think you were right, Nattu. It *was* a nice idea. I mean, I definitely had a good time.' She blushed.

'Ooh, someone's in loooove,' Faiza teased, elbowing her.

'Love is for plebs like *you*.' Saira laughed, rubbing her back. 'But I'm in lust, hundred per cent. Man, I was hoping Rubani would also find lust, but this girl, I say.' She shook her head.

'I've been texting that Tinder girl, though,' Rubani smiled gently. She had contemplated keeping it to herself until she was surer but Rubani always found a certain joy in sharing things with the girls that nothing else would ever replicate. And so, she caved. 'She's really hot. Like Jackie from *That '70s Show* hot.'

A passenger's ears pricked up and he turned around to listen. His family, oblivious, was busy taking posey photos

against the cerulean sky. Faiza noticed and shot the man a
withering look. He quickly averted his eyes, making a show
of focusing extra hard on his innocently posing wife.

'I thought she was Summer from *The O.C.* hot?' Saira
asked. 'But yeah, I guess they look kind of the same. You
were supposed to show me pictures.'

Rubani laughed and pulled out her phone. The three girls
clustered around it, swiping through her Tinder and making
appreciative noises.

'Well, she's a fucking stunner,' Faiza said, handing Rubani
her phone back. 'But then, so are you.'

'Hardly,' Rubani said, but felt a pang of warmth for Faiza.
'She's a ten. I'm a six at best.'

Faiza frowned and shook her head. She was pretty sure it
was Rubani's beautiful, open smile and Bambi-big eyes that
got her videos on the content platform Goddess the millions
of views it boasted. Between her tiny frame, shaggy pixie
cut, pert little pierced nose and a butt that could be easily
mistaken for a Kardashian's, she couldn't believe Rubani
thought of herself as anything less than gorgeous. Maybe this
was one of the things that had bound these three together
in college – tens who thought they were sixes because self-
esteem was a near-unconquerable beast.

'I disagree completely.' Natasha shook her head with
force. '*You're* the ten. She's cute, but maybe an eight, eight
and a half.'

'Are we really ranking women, friends?' Saira snorted.
'What's next, a best-butt list that we circulate through the
school?'

'Bani would win best butt too,' Natasha pointed out,
winking at Rubani.

There it was again, Faiza observed, as Rubani responded by tensing up and smiling with restraint. *Maybe she and Natasha had had a fight?*

'Okay, this is true,' Saira said, reaching out and smacking Rubani's upper thigh. 'She's got the ass. She's just not *getting* any ass.'

'Hey!' Rubani protested, but with a smile. 'I will do something about the local Mila Kunis when I go home, okay? Now can we get off the subject?'

'I think something should happen on this trip too,' Natasha said. 'Like, holiday romance. Your Laila from *Zindagi Na Milegi Dobara*?'

'Which one was Laila?' Faiza asked.

Natasha stared at her, aghast.

'Katrina Kaif.' She shook her head.

'Not all of us memorize this shit like you do, okay?' Saira smirked at Faiza.

'Um, excuse me, I know you pretend to not like Hindi movies as much as me, but what other reason is there for you to have seen *Kuch Kuch Hota Hai* seven times?'

'I've seen it three times, because childhood,' Saira mumbled. 'And I watch it ironically.'

'Yeah, yeah. Saira is a cheater,' Natasha sang, teasing 'CHEATER!'.

Rubani stiffened up again.

'But okay, point is, you should definitely hook up with someone here – and do it fast. We only have five days left,' Saira pointed out.

'I don't think that's what this trip is about for me,' Rubani shot back, staring back out at the ocean.

The ride came to an end soon after, with far less leaping 'rapists of the sea' than Natasha had hoped to spot. Moving towards the shore, they passed a group of smirking surfers, and Rubani felt sure they were mocking the tourists who had chosen the dolphin excursion. She averted her eyes as they docked. The girls stepped off carefully the moment the boat seemed steady, and headed straight to a shack for beer, and coconut water for Faiza. After about an hour of talking about everything, from how much Goa had changed to whether they should check out a salsa club they'd heard of on Friday night, Faiza picked up her stuff.

'I'm heading back, guys. I have a video I need to shoot,' she said, dusting herself off and gathering her clear beach tote.

'You are NO fun,' Saira said. 'Stay, Haider!'

'Stay, *na*?' Natasha agreed. 'It's a *chhutti*.'

'I told you bitches I'd have to work,' Faiza said, pursing her lips. 'It's why I could swing going away on such short notice.'

'Okay, fine, go. But you'll meet us at that place for lunch? We'll leave in a bit from here.'

Having finalized plans to reunite at their next stop, Faiza headed off. They were to meet at the villa of a chef friend of Saira's, who ran one of her most beloved restaurants and was opening his home only to them for an authentic Goan lunch – Faiza headed off. The rest of the girls ordered another round. The thatched cane of her chair was sticking to Rubani's bottom and she cursed herself for wearing denim shorts on the excursion. If she'd gone with her first instinct – a pair of white pajamas scoured from a bin in a makeshift

Lajpat Nagar market stall – the backs of her thighs wouldn't have been tattooed with rattan impressions.

'I like this place; it reminds me a little of when Britto's used to be good,' Saira said, cracking open her local craft. 'Same vibe, before the noisy Indian family contingent discovered it, I mean.'

Cane chairs and sea-facing tables were pretty much 101 for any beach shack in Goa. But there was something about the sloped chocolate-brown roofs, wicker lanterns, stained-glass windows and gargantuan specials boards that were terribly reminiscent of the iconic Goan restaurant Saira had grown up with.

'I was just thinking, it reminds me of something too!' Rubani exclaimed. 'Remember that night when we ran into that weird actor and he thought we were dying of excitement because we couldn't believe we'd met him?' She laughed her most genuine laugh of the whole trip so far, Saira noticed fondly.

'Aftab Shivdasani!' Natasha squealed. 'And speak for yourself, okay, I was legit super-excited to meet him. You two were just so drunk that you physically scared him off.'

'Why on earth would you be excited to meet that dude?' Saira asked, rolling her eyes.

'You guys don't remember *Mast*? He was *so* cute!' Natasha sighed. 'Y'all just think you're too cool for this. And it's a lie, because, we all grew up with these movies.'

'Um, yes, we also grew up with Barbies and irritating *masis* and shit but you don't see us still pining for them?' Saira pointed out.

'Okay, whatever, I'm not having this conversation with

you again,' Natasha held up her hand and turned to Rubani. 'Bani, did you meet anyone fun at the party?'

'Nope, sorry,' Rubani responded in a rather cool tone her previously chipper air having evaporated.

'Oh, okay,' Natasha said, feeling a bit confused by her reaction. 'S, are you seeing Maxime again?'

'I want to, for sure,' Saira said. 'I just haven't decided when yet. I figured maybe in a couple of days – I literally saw him the day before.'

'*Haan*, but I mean—' Natasha was interrupted by the ringing of her own phone.

'Ooh, it's Rohan!' she squealed, watching the phone flash with the name of her best friend from school. 'Guys, can I take this? I haven't spoken to him in two weeks.'

She started FaceTime, first putting Saira and Rubani on so they could say hi, and then parting to talk to him on her own.

When they were alone, Rubani turned to Saira and opened her mouth as if to say something but closed it again. Saira quickly cottoned on to her hesitance.

'What, Bani?'

Rubani shook her head and smiled. 'Nothing.'

Saira stared at her with a look of impatience. 'Tell me,' she said, tapping her foot restlessly.

'It's just …' Rubani trailed. 'Um, have you spoken to Nattu lately?'

'You mean, apart from ten seconds ago?' Saira frowned, lowering her wooden-framed sunglasses.

'No, I mean, like, since the party. Since Silent Noise.'

Saira furrowed her brow. 'You're being weird.'

'How am I being weird?' Rubani asked. Saira had a habit of making her always come off uptight. It was an all-pervasive fear she experienced anyway; that 'uptight' was how people perceived her inability to express herself freely. She'd grown used to it in a grudging way – it was easier than bringing the matter up with her. But today, it made her especially irritable. 'It's a simple question.'

'Okay, um, we've all practically been together every minute except for whenever Faiza does her workout fuss and you go off to talk to *Jia*.' Saira's inflection changed on the name Jia, Rubani's closest friend outside the group. Though Saira had invited her to come as a courtesy, Jia had politely turned her down, saying she didn't want to interrupt a 'group thing', and Saira had been silently grateful.

'Yeah, she worries.' Rubani smiled at the thought of her responsible, ever-concerned best friend. It was a phrase she couldn't use in front of the girls, because to them college ties beat out a friendship that came from being closer to a colleague's friend than the colleague themselves. She and Jia had met through her video editor four years ago and been thick as thieves since. 'Anyway, I didn't mean it like that. Has she said anythi—'

Rubani stopped as she saw Natasha making her way back to them, skirting an overzealous local offering a range of shell necklaces. 'I'll tell you later.'

Saira stared curiously at Rubani and then turned to Natasha and smiled.

'All good with Ro?' she asked.

'Yes, yes, all good,' Natasha said, sitting down and adjusting her pale-yellow sundress. 'He was just telling me he bumped into a friend of ours from school that we hated. Funnily enough, it reminded me of the last time we bumped into her. It was *insane*.' She laughed.

'Why, what happened?' Saira prodded.

'Don't we have to be at your friend's by 1:00?' She held up her smartphone that showed 12:30 p.m.

'We have time, ya.' Saira waved her away.

'*Achha*, chug your beer – I'll tell you in the car,' Natasha said. 'Becaaause ... it's also kind of my own one-night-stand story,' she sheepishly revealed.

'Oh my god, what?' Saira said. 'Did you sleep with Rohan?'

'Didn't you say you and Rohan had never hooked up?' Rubani asked, looking at her with suspicion.

'*Arey*, no, we haven't. Sai knows this story. Both of you do too; just not the details. Remember that night at the Temaki launch party? We were talking about the wildest place we'd ever had sex in and I told you mine was in somebody else's garden?' Natasha prompted.

'I remember! But I just assumed it was Alex,' Saira admitted sheepishly.

'Wait, it wasn't? So who was it?' Rubani pressed.

'Oof, *chalo*!' She signalled for the bill, pulling out a wad of notes. 'I said I'll tell you in the car!'

NATASHA

'WHAT DO YOU even wear to something like this?' Natasha asked her cat, who had been staring at her from a corner as she stared at herself in the mirror. She had held up six dresses over the last forty minutes in a mixed rotation, finding problems with each one and throwing it back down on the bed. She studied her most faithful white skater dress and turned to OJ, her ginger stray, raising her eyebrows in question. He had now begun to stretch and yawn; it was clear even he was bored by the exercise.

Normally Alex was here to help her decide and undo all the irritating zippers, but a business trip had conveniently catapulted him to Japan and away from Longchamp Hall at the Taj on Man Singh Road that would hold all the ghosts of high school past, no doubt hotter and richer than ever before.

She dialled the one person she knew would have an opinion, simply because he always did.

'Rohan, can you help?' she said, her voice a little whinier than she would have liked.

'Yes, yes … what, you still haven't picked out a dress?' her oldest friend asked, with no intention of masking his disdain. Her girlfriends were great seconds, but Rohan's instinctual understanding of aesthetics and brutal honesty usually made him the perfect person from whom to solicit this kind of advice. Besides, he'd actually be at this thing, so he would, in all likelihood, understand the assignment better.

Something about his tropical printed shirts, healthy appreciation of couture and healthier appreciation of attractive men at the gym they shared often made people assume Rohan was gay, but his indignation at the inference was always terribly righteous. Natasha, who had seen him through passionate relationships with both men and women since school – and because of Rubani – knew it was the oversimplification that bothered him. It wasn't that people thought he liked men – he'd explained to her on a drunken night at the start of their friendship – it was that they assumed he couldn't *also* like women. 'All this progress and everyone still thinks bi is a gateway,' he'd sighed, sipping on a brazenly blue Breezer. 'People are so pedestrian.'

She'd completely missed Rohan's attraction to both sexes – much to her chagrin at the start. But to her relief, as they grew older, she was grateful for the friendship they'd developed in its stead. She may have missed out on him in boyfriend mode, but long-term-friend mode was a pretty great trade-off.

Besides, ex-boyfriends wouldn't tear apart dress after dress over video call and help her settle on the only one she didn't have the confidence to wear.

'But this one!' she pled, holding up her fail-safe meekly, knowing he would shut it down because she wore it too much.

'I think you need to burn that now – it's time,' he scoffed.

'Don't clothes have rules? Like, spontaneously combust after the thousandth wear?'

'Ugh, your exaggerations are exhausting.' She rolled her eyes and grudgingly held up the slinky wine-coloured number he was pushing for. 'This is so cleavage-y. I'll look like I'm trying *so* hard.'

'Excuse me, everyone at this shindig will be "trying so hard",' he quipped. 'That's the point of high-school reunions. You need to look sexy and successful even if you're unemployed and single.'

'I am neither and you are both,' she shot back.

'Ah, you're single-ish. Or, like, just single enough. That's my point. You always look so expensive and pish-posh, it's damn irritating. Even when you're wearing Sarojini it looks like Saint Laurent. Try *harder*, look *sluttier*.'

Natasha caught a glimpse of herself in the mirror, positively aghast.

'I am not single! You can't *call* it that! And anyway, I can't *look* like I'm trying, no? That defeats the purpose.'

'Please, when men see a hot girl in a slutty dress, you think they care?'

'So you *do* think it's slutty!' she exclaimed, before looking in the mirror wistfully. 'And I'm hardly a girl now. We're practically thirty.'

'Speak for yourself. I'm twenty-eight and that horrid number is still two years away, so don't you *dare*,' he hissed.

She was more nervous about this than the average party. Everyone would be dressed in their best, *being* their best, trying to come off far more successful and attractive than they usually were – it was a total impressions game. The last thing she wanted was to be the one woman in the room who turned up in a clingy dress while everyone else was in power suits or delicate saris.

'Everyone will be wearing something sexy, okay?' Rohan said, reading her mind. 'You think if these idiots have aged decently, they'll hide it under layers? Please. You have it, so kindly flaunt it.'

'Fine,' she sighed. She would let his taste win over her reserved instinct. That way, if she looked out of place, she'd have someone else to blame.

'You know, Thin Megha used to wear this kind of shit all the time back then.' He'd now pulled a Mars bar out of the fridge and begun chewing loudly. 'You think shdwearmmg thakingd now?' Trying to decipher his words over the munching was exasperating.

'Finish chewing, you beast,' she scolded.

A loud swallow was followed by, 'You think she'd wear that kind of thing now?'

'God knows.' Natasha sighed. 'Is it horrible to hope she fatted out?'

'Oh god, NO,' Rohan gasped. 'I used to pray for it in school, okay? I would keep trying to give her Mumma's cakes and condensed-milk sandwiches, but madam never ate anything. Bitch.'

'You really go from zero to savage in one minute, don't you?' Natasha laughed. 'Okay, whatever she wears, I will look like an idiot unless I have time to do my make-up properly, so *bye*.'

'Bye,' Rohan said, distracted by the ping of a notification. 'Wear concealer.'

'Asshole,' she shot back and hung up.

She slipped into the dress and undid her hair, letting it tumble down her back. It was, thank god, still fairly thick – with mostly the same nonchalant volume it had ten years ago. Though, now, it took products aplenty and regular salon care to give it the beautiful sheen it had. Back then, she sometimes even swapped out shampoo for a bar of soap and the results were still surprisingly lustrous. Luckily, it was still raven-hued like no Garnier product could create – she was terrified of greys and hoped they were waiting only on the far side of her thirties, as they had for her mother.

She also had her mother's bright eyes that always looked a little like they were smiling, and her lithe physique, which in Natasha's case, she often felt, was undeserved because of her monstrous appetite. Losing her mother at twenty-one had been tougher to get past because she could see parts of her mom in herself, sometimes to an all-too-terrifying degree, if the mirror caught the light a certain way.

She shook her head, snapping out of her reverie and focusing once again on the mirror. Thankfully, she looked enough like herself today to push back the sting of tears – and assess the cling of her dress. It set off her lissome lines in a graceful manner; a daring dress, by her standards, but one that didn't at all veer into the off-puttingly risqué territory. The softness of the dark hue made her eyes even brighter, played off of her skin – 'Marie-biscuit-coloured,' her mother had called it when she was a child. It was a *good* dress.

The 'good' dress, however, began to feel like a bad idea from the minute she walked in. The event room at the hotel was filling slowly with men in tuxes, women who looked far more expensive than her, decked out in their best DVFs or Schiaparellis. Her non-couture slip dress seemed out of place, like a scholarship kid at a private school. She wished she'd gone for designer over daring – not that she had a vast selection of the stuff – but it was too late now.

She wished Rohan would turn up fast.

Can you please hurry the fuck up? her fingers texted furiously. *If you're trying to be late to make an entrance I will lose my shit, Rohan.*

'Tasha? Is that you?' She heard a slightly shrill voice call out from behind her.

Ugh. Tasha. The nickname instantly brought back memories of Orkut scrapbook posts and cringeworthy teenage email IDs. The effort to be cool always intermingled with an effort to align themselves to Americanized nicknames, interests and habits. Years later, when they had begun to come into their own, the memory of it always stirred up a flood of deep awkwardness.

'Oh my god, Ria!' She faced her ex-classmate, plastering a superficial smile on her face. Natasha remembered Ria Bajaj most for the snide comments she'd make about how it was 'so gross that some girls are so hairy', whenever Natasha would walk by. Oblivious until then about her body hair, as any thirteen-year-old should be, Natasha had been stung and begged her mother to let her have at it with Anne French, the pungent hair removal cream of yore, but her father had intervened and left her with a firm 'no'. She'd been fodder for Ria's jokes for another three years.

Ria hadn't been conventionally pretty as a child, unlike Natasha – but she had the kind of thin 'mean girl' vibe that people had responded to. Of her childhood appearance, only the perfect, glossy hair remained, now a salon-bought honey hue that matched the colour of her skin. Everything else she'd been displeased with had been fixed by the fine doctors of South Bombay, of course.

'You look *so good*, babe!' She sounded as fake as her lips looked, Natasha thought, surprising herself with the bitchiness of her own simile. But then again, not really.

'Thank you!' Natasha tried to match her pitch, adding a touch of nasal excitement. 'So do you! *Love* the dress.' It was Amit Meherwal; she'd always buy more designer bags than clothes (when she could), but that didn't mean she didn't know her stuff.

'Oh, thanks, babe. Amit's a friend, so I was like, "Sweetie, can you quickkkkly do this in my size?"' she said, swivelling to show off a body on which a sample size would've worked with ease.

'Lucky he's a friend,' Natasha said, trying not to sound too frosty.

'I swear, right?' She pulled back and surveyed Natasha's dress. 'Love what you're wearing too. Who's it by?'

It was 'by' Zara, from five years ago, but that was akin to the local vegetable market to the people at her moneyed former school. 'It's this indie designer from Vietnam, a really cool guy I met last time I was there,' Natasha talked out of her arse like a pro. 'I'm more into newer, homegrown labels. I feel like their stuff is so fresh, *na*?' she said evenly.

'Oh, yeah, absolutely, same.' Watching Ria flummoxed at being outcooled was enjoyable and Natasha had to work hard not to instinctively smile. 'Does he ship to India? You must give me his number,' Ria added.

'He does it for me, but then, he's a friend,' Natasha said, unable to resist. 'But I'll check and let you know. Sorry, just a sec, I think I see Priyanka from 9C. I'll see you around?'

Natasha cut out, figuring it was good to leave on a strong wicket. She went up to a few girls from one of the other sections of her batch and, in sharp contrast to Ria, actually had a warm conversation. They had ended up in myriad jobs, some routine (lawyer, CA), others more glamorous (news anchor, fashion photographer), and most of them were easy to talk to. They hadn't been popular in school and, because Natasha had wanted to be, she had paid them less mind than Ria and her gaggle of lip-glossed cronies. Now, several years in, she felt that same all-encompassing sense of stupidity that anybody feels looking back on their adolescent errors in judgement. They were wonderful people and probably had been all along – she'd just been too caught up attempting 'cool' to notice.

As the conversation moved from the sweet canteen guy they had all loved (who would always let them have a samosa even if they came up short on change) to the final-year camping trip, Natasha saw a flash of someone eerily familiar. He slipped behind a small crowd towards the other end of the room, but the fleeting glimpse had been enough to fill her with an escalating mixture of excitement and dread. It was that very specific and curious unease at sighting someone you thought you'd never see again.

It's probably not him, she thought to herself dismissively. Dismissing her own thoughts had been her coping mechanism through the years; it was easier to tell herself she was worried for no reason than to acknowledge she had a reason to worry.

There seemed no sign of him now, though, so she pushed herself to bring her focus back to the group. But their reminiscences of sports days and fights over which house was best no longer held her attention. She was acutely aware of the fact that, somewhere behind her turned back, was the man she'd slept with – and run out on – nine years ago.

It was definitely his frame – that imposing, athletic six-foot-plus frame with the solid shoulders that had drawn her instantly. For some reason, she'd always fetishized tall, 'big' men in contrast to her five-foot-three slightness – and he had fit the bill perfectly enough for her to be able to recall it in the span of that flash-in-the-pan glimpse.

It can't have been him, she tried to convince herself. *He's Bombay-based, he's not an alum, so there's no reason for him to even be here …*

Her phone lit up with a soft buzz, and she was glad for the distraction. Her tendency to overthink had kicked into overdrive and it was smart to stop it.

'Where the fuck are you?' she nearly growled. 'I've been on my own for an hour; you always do this shit.'

'Calm down, bitch.' Rohan was, as always, infuriatingly blasé. 'I'm, like, basically here.'

'Which basically means twenty minutes on GPS?' She knew him better.

'Which means, like, eleven minutes but fine, okay, I'm sorry. The shirt was all wrong and it was making my paunch stick out.'

Okay, eleven minutes wasn't the worst. She could handle eleven minutes. She cracked a smile and allowed herself to be wicked.

'No shirt can help that paunch, babu. Maybe try lipo?'

'You're such a bitch!' he said with a gasp, but his tone was friendly. 'See you in ten now!'

She slowly walked over to the bar, trying to fill the seconds. People-watching presented itself as an option, but it was an activity best carried out in the company of her savage friend. She made a mental note of the former long-jump champion's zebra-print dress to ridicule later as she sashayed past and ordered herself a shot of Patrón. Because why the fuck not?

Two shots later, her courage significantly bolstered, Natasha decided she needed to find him. It *was* him; who did she think she was kidding? Her gut wasn't just *telling* her, it was shouting obnoxiously through a megaphone, and she had the time to indulge it.

She had just done a casual sweep of the ex-basketball team's side of the ballroom, trying to look behind their impossibly high heads and distractedly smiling through a conversation about who still had the best jump shot. She was just about to walk over to the dance-club girls when her phone buzzed again.

'And now where the fuck are *you*?' Rohan asked, his voice somewhat drowned by the same background voices and clatter as on her end. He had reached! Thank *god*!

'I'm near Sandhu,' she said, referring to the tallest ex-player in the group, who was an easy-to-spot six-foot-four.

'Oh, nice, I've spotted him – obvs.' He cut across the room quickly and Natasha was engulfed with relief on seeing him. Never had his lanky, too-tall frame and toothy smile been such a welcome sight.

'Please don't ever leave me alone like that, okay?' she said, ruffling his floppy hair. She was happy enough that he was here for her anger to dissipate.

'Okay, legit, I'm sorry. But I'm here now. And we need to talk about the zebra fiasco on Mihika – what the *fuck*!'

'Yes, yes, we do.' She laughed. 'Anyway, forget about that. I'm about to have a serious fiasco of my own.'

'What happened – was Ria nasty?' He rolled his eyes. 'Shouldn't you expect that from the bulimic bitch at this point?'

'Oof, you are *horrible*!' She gasped and then grinned. 'No, she was actually pretty fake-nice. It's something else. There's a guy here. Ugh, okay, how to explain?'

'Just say, *na*? Like a creepy guy? Or ex-type situation?'

'Um, kind of. Not an actual ex. Unless a one-night counts as an ex?'

'Nata-SHA! Did you have a one-night stand in school? I thought you were a late bloomer. Very impressive!'

'It was in college, okay?' she answered in a huff.

'I mean, I thought you were kind of a Charlotte till your twenties, though.' He shrugged, referring to Natasha's least favourite character from *Sex and the City*.

'Makes sense – you're definitely an Antony,' she retorted with a withering glare.

'Ooh, burn. Okay, don't distract me; start telling me everything. Like begin at the beginning, and what year was this even?'

'First year, *duh*,' she said with a slight smile. 'There was Nathan after that, for most of it, *na*?'

Her ex, Nathan, had been a second-year crush that had grown into a far-too-intense two-year-long relationship that was an on-again, off-again mix of shouting matches and rough make-up sex. It had ended with her giving up half of her books, her two favourite hoodies (that were technically his) and a solid chunk of her self-esteem.

'Ew, I always block out Nathan. Okay, so like eighteen–nineteen types?'

'Ya, about that-ish. I met him a few months before Nathan, at Juicy's.' A fruit juice shop that also sold cigarettes, Juicy's had inexplicably become the hub for all the kids at her college who wouldn't fancy being seen at the campus canteen.

'Yuck, I remember you telling me about that place. Your college was so gross, ya.'

Natasha ignored his Bangalore-bashing – something he was wont to do, as was making comparisons with his buzzier Bombay college life – and went on with her narration.

'So, he was really cute. Like that kind of tall, lean-ish guy you find incredibly cute in college with the slightly overgrown hair and, *oof*, those kissable lips. I'd stare at him from afar every time I went there between classes with my classmate Nam. I started going with her during every smoke break and drinking weird things like butterfruit milkshakes just to see if he'd be there, smoking his Gold Flakes.'

'What the fuck is a butterfuit milkshake?' Rohan's face was abject horror itself.

'Um, I think it's avocado? But also something else with it? I mean, it looks grosser than it is, but the Juicy's guy used to make it pretty decentl—'

'I'm sorry I asked, please go back to the story,' Rohan cut her off.

'Ugh, fine. So, for a few weeks, it was basically just, like, looking at each other. And then the looking got really intense, like … sexually charged-ish.'

'It's called eye-banging,' Rohan offered helpfully.

'Sure.' She grinned. 'But I didn't know what to do after that. Like, picking up men was *not* my thing for a long time, you know that.'

Rohan nodded in agreement, with an eye roll for effect.

'So, I kind of just thought that would be it, and I'd basically given up. But one day, I'd gone for this party at Pandey's,' she said, referring to a friend who lived nearby, whom Rohan had met as well. 'She was the only one with a house that could have a party because we all lived in such gross little boxes in SG,' Natasha reminisced, smiling as she remembered SG Palya, a truly godawful neighbourhood behind her college. It was what many out-of-towners gravitated to when they couldn't handle the austerity of hostel life. The rent was far too expensive for an area that terrible, but hey, it took five minutes to walk to class.

'I don't know how the hell y'all lived there.' The horror returned to Rohan's face as he remembered his first (and only) long-weekend visit. 'That place made Bombay chawls look like the Marriott by comparison.'

'*Anyway*, this isn't where the party was – *keep up*,' Natasha said, with a touch of annoyance. 'She lived in Koramangala. It wasn't a BYOB thing, which was very rare for us, and there were a bunch of her random friends from other departments. Like, she was friends with strange people from BBM also, for some reason.'

'What's BBM?' Rohan asked. 'I can only think of Blackberry Messenger.'

'Funnily enough, most of them had Blackberries also,' she mused. 'But it was Bachelor's in Business Management. Those were the weirdly rich, nerdy boys that none of us arts people would even acknowledge on campus. There were about ten of them at this party. And *still* wearing suits, like they had to on campus, yeuch!'

'Oh, yuck, was he a Blackberry?' Rohan's tone was dripping with judgement. 'Baby, those are the ones you marry and cheat on, not the ones you sleep with for recreational purposes. They should only give you Dior, not dick,' he said, looking very proud of himself for coming up with a campaign slogan for BBM boys.

'Hi, I'm not a Real Housewife, okay, these are not my goals in life,' Natasha scoffed. 'Anyway, I'm at this party and this was during my denim shorts phase, so I was wearing the most risqué ones I had—'

'UghughSLUTTYuhuh,' Rohan fake-coughed.

Natasha rolled her eyes. 'Fine, slutty. I will lose my train of thought, I'm telling you,' she warned.

'Okay, sorry, sorry. Party. Koramangala. "Risqué" shorts.' He made air quotes with his fingers. 'Then what happened?'

'So, mostly, I was just there for the free booze, which never happened back then. She had Tanqueray – and back then we only drank shit like DSP and Old Monk, so it was a really big deal to have a non-petrol type of booze.'

Rohan motioned to his watch and gestured for her to hurry up with her retelling.

'No, this is context!' she whined. 'You have to understand, there was a reason I was getting drunk off my face.'

'Okay, fine, so you had a lot of the fanciest gin in the whole wide world – then what?'

'So I was on my fourth drink and then some guy was like, "Shots! Shots! Shots!" And then, obviously, I did shots,' Natasha shrugged.

'Obviously,' Rohan agreed.

'I did *four* shots, which was the really fucking stupid part,' Natasha winced. 'I ran out of the party to the garden in front of her house, because for a second I felt like I was going to throw up directly in everyone's faces.'

'*That* would have been a fun story.' Rohan sighed.

Natasha shot him a sharp look. Rohan raised his hands to indicate he was backing off.

'So, I'm in the garden, and it's pretty cold, and I'm in my stupid tiny shorts and this stupid thin muslin-y T-shirt so I'm feeling even *more* cold. And then, suddenly he walks out to the garden, holding a beer, looking casual as fuck.'

'Gold Flake?' Rohan asked.

'Gold Flake,' Natasha affirmed.

'Oh my god, please don't tell me you threw up on him …?'

'Right?!' Natasha nodded enthusiastically. 'I was so afraid of doing exactly that, because I swear I felt really sick. So I just kept swallowing awkwardly and smiling at him. And obviously trying really hard to think of anything except throwing up.'

'Natasha! Rohan! How are you guys?' a girl they vaguely recognized from a different section of their batch cut in, ambushing them with overenthusiastic hugs. 'It has been sooooo long!'

A five-minute conversation ensued about how time had flown, with ambiguous memories being recalled and crisp smiles from Natasha and Rohan eager to be rid of her quickly.

The minute she spotted her old EVS teacher, the two quickly excused themselves, encouraging her to go say hi.

'Okay, yes, you're in the garden, about to projectile-vomit and he's there looking sexy as fuck,' Rohan hastily recapped.

'I think I said casual as fuck, but whatever, yes,' Natasha grinned. 'So he's there kind of just … watching me. I'm also sort of standing there, trying really hard not to look at him.'

'You want to seem cool,' Rohan pointed out.

'Exactly. I'm freezing, but I'm *super* aware of him. And suddenly, he starts walking towards me. Then he's standing right next to me – and I swear, Rohan, I felt this chill, like this sexy chill run down my whole body just because he was so close he was practically touching me, but he wasn't touching me, you know what I mean?'

'Frisson!' Rohan exclaimed. 'That chill, it's called frisson. I got that from a Sidney Sheldon I read when I was a kid.'

'Oh god, yes, I remember your weird obsession with that MPD book. What was it called? Something really strange …' Natasha wondered.

'*Tell Me Your Dreams*,' Rohan muttered. 'Great fucking book. And it's called DID now.'

'Anyway,' Natasha continued. 'It was driving me insane. Like, I *really* wanted to touch him, maybe put my elbow next to his … I just wanted our bodies to touch in some way. I was consumed by that thought; I was just thinking of ways to do it and, suddenly, he looks at me and says, "Butterfruit milkshake, right?"'

'Oh my GOD, hahaha.' Rohan chuckled. 'That is hilarious.'

'Ugh, ya, *now* it is, I guess. But at that moment, it was mortifying. So I just tried to be all casual and said, 'Uh, ya, it's better for you than Gold Flakes.'

'Ooh, decent recovery,' Rohan said in an approving tone. 'But also, hi, way to say I'm watching you closely enough to creepily remember what you smoke.'

'*Hai na*? I had the same thought as soon as I said it. But I think it worked on him, because he looked at me and said, "Rishaad," and held out his hand.'

'No "Nice to meet you?"'

'Nope, just "Rishaad", cool as hell. So I shook his hand, and said, "Natasha. But everyone calls me Tasha." I know it was lame,' she quickly added, as she saw Rohan stifle a giggle. 'I was a kid, okay?'

'Okay, okay, so then?'

'So, he grins and goes, "Hey *Tasha*," with, like, this bemused inflection. And I swear, Rohan, when he shook my hand, that frisson was like full-on zinging around my body. I had no idea something that stupid could have such a physical effect, you know?'

'Oh, I know.' Rohan nodded sagely. 'It's called intense fucking sexual tension.'

'God, yes, it was. At least it was to me; I had no clue what he was thinking at the time. I just knew I really wanted to be out there with him. So I looked at him and just started talking about Pandey. I figured he was at her party so obviously he knew her.'

She stopped to laugh, remembering the moment with relish.

'But he didn't know her,' she continued. 'He just looked at me and said, "Who's Pandey?"'

'Ah, college,' Rohan said, feeling fondly reminiscent.

'So I was like, "Um, the girl throwing this party? You're just at some random party without even knowing where you are?"'

'That is the point of college, no, Nattu?' Rohan shook his head disapprovingly. 'You're such a nerd sometimes, I swear.'

'So he was like, "My roommate dragged me to this place; he's got a thing for this girl who asked him to come," and shrugged, all chill and nonchalant. "I was just doing him a favour," he said. Then he smiled at me and added, "But now I'm kind of glad I came …"'

'Such a line.' Rohan grinned.

'*Such* a line,' Natasha agreed. 'But it worked. I was young, he was hot. So we started talking, and we kind of stayed out there for a couple of hours. He kept going in every once in a while to bring us drinks, like these really *sick* Old Monk and Cokes, which were way too strong, but I kept drinking them—'

'Can you *get to the fun part*!' Rohan had clearly had enough context.

'Okay, so, we were arguing about some douchey college thing, like, what Rashomon really says about the idea of truth, and *was* there even a real truth or only versions, etc., etc. And suddenly he just kissed me.'

'Mmmm, finally.' Rohan smirked. 'Good kiss?'

'Goooood kiss,' Natasha said, remembering. 'Or, at least, it felt like a good kiss after 86,000 drinks. And it was … this really … intense kiss. In a couple of seconds we were kind of grabbing and pressing into each other. Like it was so …'

'Urgent?' Rohan asked, with a wistful sigh.

'Yeah … At one point it was somewhere between a kiss and an attack – we just couldn't get enough. It was *amazing*. But the thing is, we were getting super turned on in a garden, so we thought, what the hell do we do? Do we go inside and risk dealing with people? Do we just kiss and end it there?

Because we did *not* want to end it there,' she said, with a bit of a snort.

'You're such a prissy thing sometimes.' Rohan shook his head in disdain. 'Why can't you ever be spontaneous? I am so sure you could've fucked him in the garden if you wanted.'

A slow smile spread across Natasha's face.

'Oh. My. God. Natasha, *no*. You actually fucked him in the garden!' Rohan's voice rose just enough octaves for the former poetry jam champion of his school and his wife standing nearby and to hear.

'Can you shut UP!' Natasha said in a strangled voice, slapping Rohan's hand.

'But *did you*, though?' he asked, more discreetly this time.

'It was pretty dark and the inside of the house was really full, you know,' Natasha powered on, ignoring him. 'I knew that if we tried to go in, we would just end up, like, getting distracted and not doing anything. And Rohan, I swear, I cannot tell how much I wanted to do something …'

'*You fucked him in the garden*!' Rohan said in the loudest whisper she'd ever heard.

Natasha nodded proudly.

'Like those old Hindi movie innuendos, Ro. We found this one super dark part of the garden and *literally* went behind the bushes.'

'This is so exciting,' Rohan marvelled. '*You* of all people. Who won't put a Fendi bag down on a table without wiping it first.'

'I only own *one* Fendi bag; excuse me for trying to look after it,' she hissed.

'Okay, whatever, please go back to the garden sex.'

Natasha made a face. 'You make it sound so cheap.'

'Well, it isn't *tasteful*.' Rohan rolled his eyes again. 'But,' he added quickly, 'it's incredibly hot, so please continue.'

'Okay, so we basically kept kissing until we sort of, like, sank into the lawn. He had a surprisingly good body for a stoner, which I'm guessing he was – I remember seeing him with rolling papers once,' she mused. 'Anyway, it was intense. I was incredibly turned on, and all I wanted to do was just, like, tear his clothes off. And he was very turned on as well,' she added, with a bit of redness creeping into her cheeks.

'You're blushing?' Rohan laughed and shook his head. 'Are you fucking eleven years old?'

'Listen, it's awkward to talk about it, okay? Gory details aren't my specialty.'

'Ugh, okay, so give me the basics. Did you legit manage to have sex in the garden?'

'I most certainly did.' The pride was back.

'Condoms? Pregnancy scares?'

'Rohan! *No!* I always use one – and that's the part you care about?'

'I mean, who knows where this story is going! You're taking so long to tell it.'

'No scares, all safe, all clear,' Natasha confirmed, gesturing with her hand that he move on.

'Okay, so now more fun stuff. Was he big?'

'To be honest, I was too drunk to really give a shit, but yes.' She grinned.

'Mmmm, excellent. And technique?'

'Surprising technique for college – remember how everyone mostly just fumbled around back then? But he had a way with his hands. And his mouth …' she trailed off coyly.

'*No! He went down on you in a garden?*'

'Is there something about gardens that is just mind-blowing to you? Because you keep saying it like it was in a spacecraft.'

'I mean, it's gross and muddy, no?'

'It was a dry lawn, okay? Not some jungle sex scene from *Lost*. Anyway,' she cleared her throat. 'He did go down on me. And it was insane. Like, it wasn't the best sex I've ever had – top five, though – but I still think about that orgasm. No one else has ever made me come with their tongue like that …' Natasha gazed into the distance, visibly distracted by the recollection.

Rohan snapped his fingers in front of her face. 'Focus,' he barked. 'Also, *wow*.'

'Yup. I'm not kidding, I literally blacked out for a second when I came.'

Rohan sighed at the thought of that full-strength orgasm.

'And the best part was, he seemed to really enjoy it. There's a lot of men who don't, or they kind of just do it so that they can use it as leverage to make sure you blow them.'

'Oh, yes, indeed, men are terrible,' Rohan agreed.

'But with him, it was like he just … loved it. It was the wildest turn-on. He made me come twice with his mouth before he was actually inside me.'

'Oh my god,' Rohan looked around, scouring the room. 'I need to see this guy – where is he!'

'No, WAIT. I haven't even got to the best part!'

'Great-at-head stranger who gives you multiple orgasms in a garden *isn't* the best part?'

Natasha had a Cheshire-cat grin on her face. 'He was *really* into the fact that I was coming so hard. Even after the second time. I was legitimately telling him I'll pass out if he makes me come again, but he just kept going; I think that spurred him on. And then, when I was on the verge of coming the *third* time and I told him – I always announce it,' she smiled sheepishly, 'he stopped and asked if it was okay if he, you know, "stuck it in".'

'He did *not* say "stick it in"!' Rohan practically gasped.

'No, obviously not. But he was hard and we'd kind of put on the condom earlier – before he started going down on me. Oof, sorry, I forgot to tell you that part …'

'Not important; continue.' Rohan waved it off.

'He just kind of stood up and gave me this look as he leaned over me, as if to say, "Can I?" And I was actually delirious, so I was like, "Yes, yes, oh my god,"' Natasha yelped and then suddenly realized how loud her voice sounded. 'And then,' she continued, more hushed, 'he was inside me. And he kept going till I finished that orgasm—'

'With his dick!' Rohan was awed. 'Genius. Love it. Very creative, especially for a college boy. Okay, so why was this guy a one-night stand again? I would have kept that D on lock.'

'I mean, I guess I was just kind of embarrassed? I was *way* too drunk that night to care about what he thought, or how good it was for him, or if he thought I was some major slut for sleeping with him, like, five minutes after we met.'

'Oof! Seriously?' Rohan scolded. 'I mean, I get it. It sucks that you'd have to think that last bit, but I get it, I know how it is for you.'

'I think that's pretty much most of us after random sex, to be honest,' Natasha said. 'But anyway, especially in college, I was mortified by what he was thinking or what he might say to people. So I kind of just … left the party after I went inside on the pretext of "cleaning up". And then I avoided Juicy's for a long, long time.'

'I'm sorry, sweetie,' Rohan said, surprising Natasha with his sudden empathy. 'That doesn't sound like much fun.'

'Ah, well.' Natasha shrugged. 'It's a great memory. And I think in retrospect I'm kinda glad, because, like, at least I have that. It was the first time I had ever just slept with someone I did not mean to start a relationship with, so the whole one-night thing was kind of a rush, you know?'

'I get it now,' Rohan said. 'Like, why you're freaking out that he might be here. Seeing a one-night stand out of the blue after a decade is awkward as hell.'

'You know, I haven't seen him since that one time I thought I did. Now I'm just feeling stupid. Like, it probably wasn't him but I just sort of imagined it because some guy looked a little like him.'

'Ugh, that happens.' Rohan nodded in agreement. 'I'm always seeing exes everywhere. And I have enough also that half the time it's them only,' he chuckled.

'Okay,' Natasha let out a long breath in a whoosh of air. 'I ate up so much of your time *bewajah*. You should go say hi to people, *na*?'

They did the rounds, lingering with their favourite groups (the 9B girls, the Deb Soc) a little more, putting in just enough time to be polite with the rest. Finally, they were left with the popular girls, and even though Natasha was dreading seeing Ria again, she knew that Rohan would be a fast hit with her because of her tokenistic fetish for the 'gay best friend'. It was what Rohan had accurately predicted in the run-up to the reunion.

'Rohan daaaarling, you look fabulous!' Ria drawled, as Rohan shot Natasha a quick I-told-you-so glance. 'I love what you're wearing!' Ria exclaimed, predictably, even though Natasha felt that there was nothing remarkable about Rohan's dark grey silk shirt and black trousers. But it felt like an appropriately Ria thing to say.

'Right back at you, babe!' Rohan said, leaning into the role. 'Is this Amit?'

'Of course! Would he let me wear anyone else?' Ria laughed and Rohan joined in. Natasha resisted the urge to throw her drink in Rohan's face and shot him a chilling look instead.

'I was just telling Natasha it's so sad Alex isn't here. I know he would've loved this!' Ria, who'd met Natasha's husband all of once, wouldn't let that stop her from acting overfamiliar.

Which, naturally, Rohan cottoned on to and volleyed back at her.

'Really? Alex pretty much hates anything social, so I'm not convinced he didn't skip this on purpose,' Rohan said with a jolly laugh. Ria looked a little thrown so he quickly added, 'I jest, I jest,' in a light-hearted tone.

'*Achha*, but wait! You've never met my husband, *na*? I have no idea where he's disappeared; let me just call him.' Ria's fingers had flown to her phone before the two could have stopped her. She held on to Natasha's hand, as if she'd seen through her formulating plan to French-exit.

'Baby? I want you to meet some friends. Can you come in, please?' There was a demanding impatience in her tone that catapulted Natasha right back to school, and she felt a slight shudder.

'He'd just gone to get a smoke; he's on his way in,' she explained, even though no one had asked.

'So, um, how long have you been married, Ria?' Natasha asked politely, under the awkward pressure to fill the time.

'Oh god! I mean, it's been, like, four years now? I mean, we dated for a year before that, but I think I pretty much just knew from day one,' Ria said, an inescapable redness spreading across her perfectly contoured face.

'That's amazing!' Rohan offered, in a tone faker than Ria's eyelashes. 'You know what they say: When you know, you know!'

'Ya, and with Rishi, I just knew, from, like, the first time we had dinner at Hakkasan. As if on cue, Rishi appeared in a sitcom-perfect entry.

As it turned out, Rishi was short for Rishaad.

'Baby!' Ria squealed, kissing the lips Natasha had last seen disappear into her groin ten years ago. 'This is Rohan! From school! And Natasha!'

It was a short pause, but nothing had ever seemed so long. Natasha could feel her blood run cold and, judging by the expression on Rishaad's face, he was experiencing similar symptoms.

'Um, hi, I'm Rishaad. It's nice to meet you.' The years had not damaged the laidback drawl. He was still stunning, but the hair was cropped neat and his leanness had filled out nicely, perhaps courtesy of some overpriced Bandra gym Ria made him go to. The lips, somehow, had become even more kissable.

'Natasha,' she managed, her voice part-squeak.

'Rishaad,' Rohan mused. 'Unusual name.' He raised an eyebrow at Natasha, obviously having figured it out. 'But lovely, of course. It's so nice to meet you.'

'Likewise,' Rishaad replied, not having taken his eyes off Natasha.

'Oh my god!' Ria smacked her forehead with emphasis. 'I totally spaced! I just realized you both went to Christ! Different courses I think; you were BBM, right, babe? And Tasha, you were arts?'

'Oh god, wait, so he *was* a Blackberry?' Rohan asked Natasha in a low, strangled voice.

'I was actually Commerce, but close enough.' Rishaad smiled at Ria. 'Yeah, I was at Christ too. Which batch?'

'University batch,' Natasha said without thinking, since it was the only year Christ had been given university status, only to later find it revoked. 'I mean—'

'I was university batch too,' he grinned. 'Funny we never met,' he said, his eyes twinkling.

'Yeah,' Natasha said. That twinkle in his eye suddenly made lightning flashes of that drunken night rush back. His face looking up at her while he was buried between her legs and that intimate moment when they locked eyes as she came. His rum-soaked lips warming up her cold, gin-laced ones, their kisses a swirl of second-hand liquor and slow-burning heat. That borderline feeling between pleasure and pain as he traced his fingers up her torso and into her shirt. His body moving against hers as she stared up at the night sky, not knowing her body was capable of making her feel this good. His eyes when he saw her come … again. And again. And again.

'Yeah,' Natasha smiled, her eyes twinkling as well. 'Funny.'

SEVEN

'LISTEN, THIS NEEDS to be turned into a movie,' was Saira's first response, her eyes glittering.

'It's insane, *na*?' Natasha laughed. 'Every time I feel a sense of injustice about someone horrible doing better than me at life, I remind myself that I slept with Ria Bajaj's husband.'

Natasha pulled up outside the beautiful Portuguese villa Saira's friend called home and slid the bulky Kia into a spot meant for a smaller hatchback with the ease of a parallel-parking pro. The lane was clearly a residential one, calm and green in a way that even the most curated, bourgeois sections of a tourist's Goa could never dream of being.

'Were you not tempted to, like, tell her?' Saira asked.

'Is that one of your two questions?' Natasha quipped.

'Heh?' Saira furrowed her brow.

'It was your rule,' Natasha pointed out. 'Two questions, no? Otherwise you kill the story?'

'That was for me, man,' Saira complained. 'And technically, this wasn't the story. It was you telling Rohan the story. I bet Faiza also knows.'

'Yeah.' Natasha shrugged sheepishly. 'Faiza knows.'

'Faiza *always* knows.' Saira scowled.

'Whatever,' Natasha shook her head, as the car beep-beeped to indicate it had been locked and they opened the gate of the garden-encircled villa. 'The two-question rule applies. But let's get settled in first?'

They stood on the cobblestone pathway as Saira rang her friend. A short, broad-chested man ran up, wearing a pleasant smile and a slogan-emblazoned apron that said 'Bringing Home the Bacon'.

'Wags!' Saira squealed in excitement. 'Look at *you*, stud!'

'Sairaaaaa,' he responded affectionately, ruffling her hair and then picking her up. 'How many years has it been?'

'Too many fucking years, man,' Saira smiled, now firmly back on the ground.

'Hi, I'm Warren,' he said, extending his hand to Rubani, then Saira. 'It's so good to see you guys. Saira talks about you every time we meet.' They smiled and introduced themselves.

Rubani liked him instantly. She wasn't usually drawn to men with muscle, but his warm, brown eyes and dimpled smile balanced it out well. His warmth was genuine, something she never associated with restaurateurs. She'd dealt with them a lot in her early years at Boys Club, the men's video platform where she'd started her career. There had been restaurant reviews and chef interviews aplenty, and the aura that seemed common to anyone who donned the hat was smugness. A deep, oblivious smugness that was often a challenge to be around for a young, opinionated Rubani, who gave herself a virtual medal every time she didn't shout 'You're not ending world hunger!' in response to their self-important answers.

'The last time was ages ago, no?' Saira mused. 'When I'd come to review that awful Mehervaan's Asian place. Is it still open or did he bore enough customers to death for the tourism board to shut him down?'

'She's awful, isn't she?' Warren said, looking at Natasha with a glint in his eye. 'But come, come! Let's not stand at the entrance. I have a big meal planned for you guys, so I hope you're hungry!'

'Can't wait!' Natasha said, earnestly, as they walked up the path to a table draped in red-chequered cloth under the shade of a colossal tree, laden with baskets of freshly fried prawn crackers. 'Saira told me that no place in the city does a better poi or balchão than you.'

'She's being generous – or setting me up to fail when my food is just average,' Warren smiled modestly.

'Not a chance,' Saira shook her head with conviction. 'These con artist places in Assagao could learn a thing or two from our man here.'

'Oof.' He smiled. 'Excuse me, ladies, I'm just going to make sure everything is in place. Can I start you off with a cocktail?'

'Daiquiris?' Rubani and Saira said in unison and exchanged a smile. 'If you have them,' Rubani added shyly.

'We can absolutely whip up some daiquiris. Shall I make them guava? I just got a fresh crop.'

'Sounds perfect,' Saira said, waving at him as he left and focusing her attention back on Natasha.

'Back to business,' she said, popping a whole prawn cracker into her mouth.

'Two questions,' Natasha reminded her. 'So, one each. You clearly want to go first, S – *bolo*?'

'Hmm ... so many to choose from.' Saira stroked her chin

thoughtfully. 'Wait, I've got it. You ended very mysteriously. Did you ever get in touch with him again?'

Natasha smiled. 'Well, he found me on Instagram. And followed me.'

'Oh my god, I love it!' Saira grinned. 'And then?'

'Then nothing,' Natasha flipped her hair innocently, breaking a cracker in half. 'We DM sometimes, that's all.' She saw Saira's mouth open to say something, so she quickly added, 'That is all. Like, "How is Ria?" or "Your cat is so cute." Nothing more exciting than that. *Bas*, now it's Bani's turn.'

'Okay, fine,' Saira said, sulking, just as a tray of chilled martini glasses brimful of coral-pink daiquiris with wedges of fresh guava was set on the table.

'Everyone eats seafood, yes?' Warren asked, looking around the table.

'Yes!' said Saira, who preferred it to everything else.

'I know you eat it; you practically ate a family of fish the last time you were here,' he teased. 'Everyone else?'

'Yes, most definitely.' Natasha smiled.

'Not a fish fan, but squid, prawns, mussels, crab, all a go,' Rubani said.

'How about lobster?' Warren asked.

'Wags, you're making us *lobster*? You are not!' Saira exclaimed.

'Lobster's great,' Rubani smiled, locking eyes with Warren. He held her gaze a fraction of a second longer than the others', then nodded with a smile and excused himself.

'Can I please take a boomerang before we drink? Thanks!' Natasha said and took about seventeen till she had herself the perfect clinking on loop.

'Done? Can I drink my drink now, please?' Saira sighed.

'Yeah, yeah, okay,' Natasha nodded.

'Bani, your turn,' Saira said.

Rubani chewed thoughtfully on her guava wedge. She was quiet long enough for the sounds of the villa to seep in – the soft tweeting of the birds, the gentle rustling of the wind through the cashew trees, the faint hum of nearby motorcars.

'Bani?' Natasha prompted.

'What did Rohan mean,' Rubani asked, avoiding Natasha's eyes, 'by single-ish?'

'Oh my god, YEAH! I also remember thinking that, but I forgot in the middle of all the telenovela drama that happened afterwards,' Saira chimed in.

Natasha stared awkwardly at her glass, stirring the pink drink with her slice of fruit.

'Um … Okay, yeah,' Natasha said, tentatively. 'I'll explain. But first, you both have to promise me something.'

Rubani's heart quickened. Had Natasha and Alex split up? She wouldn't hide something so major from them. *No, it can't be*, Rubani reminded herself. *Her story is from three years ago. There's no chance.*

'What?' Rubani said, her tone drier than she'd thought it would be.

'Alex and I, we're … um … we're open,' Natasha said, with some difficulty.

Saira's eyes, already saucer-esque, looked like they would pop right out of her head.

'Oh. My. God. *What?*' Saira said, grabbing Natasha's hand and almost spilling her drink in the bargain.

'Ladies, your first course – rissóis de camarão,' Warren said, putting down a platter of fried turnovers from which wafted the tantalizing scent of seafood and melted cheese.

Saira smiled at Warren impatiently. She loved the man, but he had terrible timing today.

'Oh wow! Fried carbs and cheese! Everything I love in one place,' Natasha exclaimed, happy both for the distraction and the delicious dish in front of her. She knew an ugly conversation may be forthcoming, and it would help to not have it on an empty stomach.

'Thank you, Wags!' Saira said, sounding a little too bright. 'We can't wait to dig in!'

He excused himself, and both girls zeroed back in on Natasha, who was already onto her second rissole.

'Please put that down and continue NOW,' Saira demanded.

Natasha finished her bite and wiped her mouth delicately with a cloth napkin.

'I mean, I don't know what else to say, really.' She shrugged.

'What else to say? You spring something like this on us and you don't know what to say?' Saira said, visibly upset.

'I don't know, Saira; what do you want me to say? I didn't think it would be something you, um, that you …' Natasha trailed off.

'That you what?' Rubani narrowed her eyes.

Natasha was quiet. She picked up the half-eaten rissole and started tearing it apart, crumb by crumb, with her fingers.

'What did you think, Nattu?' Saira asked.

'I thought you'd judge me. I didn't think you'd understand – and it's not your fault. Most people wouldn't! Most people are quite sceptical about the idea itself, and that's why I don't really tell anyone, ever. It's not like you guys are the only people I haven't told. It's not as if Alex's friends know. I mean, I don't think they do. They'd better not. No one really knows at all. We don't want the judgement it comes with. Everyone is always like, "Oh, open relationships are so great, but you know, I'd never be able to do that." There's always this thin veneer of "We're better than you because we're monogamous", and I guess I just – I didn't want that,' Natasha babbled, her words tumbling out in an unshackled rush.

'Nattu,' Saira said, her tone kind. 'I would never judge you. I can't believe you'd think that. I mean, sure, it's a shock. And I have a *lot* of follow-up questions.' She grinned. 'But I hate that you didn't think we could know. We would absolutely never – come *on*. I'd bury bodies with you, baby.' She smiled, reaching over and giving Natasha a tight hug.

The two held each other for a second longer than necessary, soaking in the warmth of the moment. Saira let go first and squeezed Natasha's hand affectionately as they parted.

Natasha looked hesitantly at Rubani. Her expression was very different from Saira's.

'Bani, I'm …' Natasha started, but stopped when she saw Rubani shaking her head.

'I want to know one thing,' Rubani said.

'Anything,' Natasha pleaded.

'Did Faiza know?' Rubani asked, sounding eerily calm.

Natasha shifted uncomfortably, smoothing the wrinkles in the soft lemon-yellow fabric of her dress with extreme focus.

'I can't believe it.' Rubani breathed. 'I should've fucking

known. Faiza *always* fucking knows,' She couldn't explain why, but there was something about not knowing the truth about Natasha's marriage – and Faiza knowing – that stung as badly as the thought of Kabir having cheated on her.

'Wait,' Saira said, her expression hurt. 'You told Faiza, but not us? So this whole time, Faiza's known this huge, like, *huge* fucking thing about your life – this thing you said you didn't tell anyone, but clearly that was a lie. Because Faiza knew.'

'And clearly, so did Rohan,' Rubani added, her voice dripping with disdain. 'So when you said "everyone", you basically just meant us. Your two longest-lasting friends, your college … your "closest" friends, who were fucking stupid enough to think they knew you better than anyone, didn't know that your eight-year-long relationship … marriage, now it's been a marriage for the last five or six years, right? That relationship has been open all along? You've been fucking other people while you were bloody married to the nicest guy in the world, and you didn't tell your best friends about it. It makes me sick,' Rubani fumed.

'See,' Natasha snapped. 'That's it. Right there. That's why I didn't tell you. You, especially, Bani. And what you just said made me realize I made the right call. I shouldn't have told you, even now.'

'Excuse me,' Rubani said hotly, setting down her drink and leaning towards Natasha. 'What the hell does that mean?'

'It means that you go off on Saira about how she's judgemental about you being bi, but Saira wasn't. She was literally shooting off her mouth, and she does that – we know she does that.'

'Hey!' Saira said, holding up her hands, but Natasha was not to be stopped.

'You gave her *so* much grief about being judgemental but you were equally judgemental about us in the *same* conversation. You implied over and over that girls who have one-night stands are "sluts" – she held up a finger to stop Rubani, who had opened her mouth to offer a rebuttal. 'And you basically kowtowed and laid off only because it was three against one. Right now, just now, you made me feel so *cheap* for sleeping with other men. Like I was hurting Alex, who is "the best man in the world" but I'm too promiscuous to care about his feelings. You equated me with a cheater. And I'm not surprised because it is so typical of you to judge people – and if they *dare* call you out on it, you turn it around on them and play the victim.'

Natasha stopped, breathless from her rant, and the two stared at her in separate silences – Saira's uncomfortable, Rubani's fuming.

'Crab xacuti and rice!' Warren announced, enthusiastic and oblivious, arriving only a moment after Natasha's tirade. A little oohing, aahing and fake smiles later, he left each of them with a generous mound of rice and delicious, steaming coconut gravy-soaked shellfish on their plates.

The girls ate in silence for a few moments. Then, Natasha breathed deep and long and looked at Saira. 'I'm sorry, Sairoo,' she said, employing a lost college nickname. 'I should've told you. There was no reason not to, and it's not okay. I should've known you'd be okay with it, and I lumped you in with – I'm just … I'm sorry.'

'It's okay, Nattu,' Saira said, with visible discomfort at being given an apology when Rubani wasn't. 'I guess the Faiza thing hurt me more. It always feels like you two are a little … you know.'

'No, I don't know,' said Natasha, feigning innocence in the hope that Saira would drop it.

'Well, closer. You have these little looks and inside references and it sounds stupid to say it aloud, but it bothers me. Maybe it shouldn't, but—'

'Oh, it should,' Rubani said, with a spark of anger in her eyes. 'It should because she treats her like a priority. We let Faiza in – and she was your friend, Nattu. You don't see Jia being part of the group, or Andrea,' she said, naming the art director from Saira's magazine, who was also one of her closest friends. 'They're not on this trip. They've not hung out with the three of us practically every day since you decided to make her a part of the group. But we gave her a chance, became friends with her. But she's always been more important to you. And it's not fucking fair.'

'You're a child, Rubani,' Natasha said, her expression disgusted. 'Faiza doesn't think of herself as "my friend". She thinks of herself as "our friend"; just that she met you through me. It's messed up that you'd even say that.'

'She doesn't mean it,' Saira said, trying to defuse the situation. 'It's just something she's saying in anger, that's all.'

'I absolutely mean it,' Rubani spat back. 'And I absolutely stand by it. It's so irritating to watch you two smirk and laugh, like there's always some inside joke to which S and I are not privy. And you,' she said, turning to Saira, 'can stop speaking for me! Stop trying to decide what I think, what I mean. I don't need you to explain my reactions. I don't need a fucking one-night stand. I don't need your opinion at *all*.'

'Get your shit together, Bani,' Saira's tone changed to one of cold calmness. 'I don't give a shit if you want to fight later, but we're not doing this now, when we are guests in my friend's home. Capiche?'

Rubani stared at her plate, fuming. The remainder of the coconut curry that had spilled off the rice to the edges of the plate had started to congeal. Of course her feelings had to be tabled for the sake of appearances. She was used to them getting lost in the fray; she rarely fought to revive them with the group, especially where Saira was concerned. It felt so much worse that Natasha had apologized to Saira. They would come out of this stronger and leave her, once again, on the sidelines.

It had happened in college, on occasion. Moments when there was a tacit understanding between the two girls about things that made her feel left out. It had always seemed petty to her to address, because she knew they went out of their way to make her feel included, especially after she'd come out to them. They had wanted to seem nothing short of completely supportive, so much so that she wasn't always able to tell when they were being honest, and when they were – what Jia called – yasss kween-ing her – her phrase for unquestioned encouragement in a bid to seem like a real ally.

Saira turned to Natasha and held her hand.

'I'm sorry, too. I guess the Faiza thing shouldn't bother me as much as it does. And I'm sorry if I ever made you feel like I would judge you. About anything. I meant that part.'

Natasha's eyes were glossy with unfallen tears. She tilted

her head back as if to keep them in, but they rolled clean off her face and onto her and Saira's entwined fingers.

'I'm sorry,' she said, in a hushed voice. 'I really am.'

'Okay, whoops, I've come at a bad time clearly,' Warren's voice cut through their moment.

'No, no, just silly, sentimental feelings, don't worry,' Saira brushed it off, handing Natasha a napkin.

'You sure? Alright if I bring the next course?'

'Yes, please.' Natasha smiled, dabbing her eyes carefully. 'We've loved everything so far.'

'Phew, I thought the food was so bad, you'd started sobbing,' he teased.

'Your progression to "uncleji" has officially begun, Wags,' Saira said with a wry smile.

'Please.' Warren laughed. 'I've had my uncle jokes on since I was fifteen!'

A giant platter proudly bearing three grilled pomfrets smeared with fragrant tamarind-ginger paste emerged from behind Saira, who was already rubbing her hands in gleeful anticipation.

'Are you crazy?' She whacked his shoulder playfully.

'This is so much food!' Natasha chimed in. 'This is the last course, no? I'm absolutely stuffed.'

'Just that one lobster I made a big show of promising,' he grinned. 'And some homemade bebinca for dessert, if you have room?

'Oh, I promise we will have room,' Saira said, feeling truly excited.

Warren slid whole fish onto fresh plates for the girls and bowed out. For a moment, there was silence, broken only by the chirruping of bulbuls nearby.

'So this is how you're going to play it,' Rubani said – the first thing she'd said in a while. 'I'm the bad guy. Saira gets an apology, an explanation, but I just get told I'm judgemental and vicious because *you* lied to *me*.'

'No,' Natasha said. 'You don't get an apology because you still don't get it, at all. You still don't see why I was afraid of telling you. And you still don't see how you reacted exactly how I was hoping you wouldn't react. This trip has been about *you*, Bani, from day one, but don't you dare think that's an excuse to dismiss how I feel.'

'Oh, bullshit,' Rubani said, her voice close to yelling. 'This trip has been about me? Did y'all even bother to ask?'

'Oh, so now we forced this on you?' Natasha was visibly upset. 'You're a hostage? Oh, poor me. My godawful boyfriend left me and instead of saying "I told you so" like they should have – and Saira did, but yeah, Faiza and I weren't brave enough – they cleared their schedules to spend ten days with me. Isn't my life just *so* hard.'

'Oh fuck *off*, Natasha!' Rubani bellowed. Saira immediately turned to look for Warren in a panic. Luckily there was no sign of him.

'I don't need you to clear your fucking schedule.' She stood up and angrily began to stuff her sunglasses and wallet back into her bag. 'I don't need your fake bullshit and I-told-you-sos. And I *definitely* don't need judgement on my relationship from someone who clearly can't deal with her own.' Rubani leaned on the tree for support and put her mules back on. She then skirted around the table and walked away.

'Are you fucking serious?' Saira shouted after her. 'You can't just leave! There's no Uber even – come *back*, Bani!'

'You can go after her if you want,' Natasha said, terrifyingly calm as she cut into a piece of fish. 'Oh my god, this is delicious!'

Saira looked at Natasha, worried, and just then spotted a pair of neon sneakers stepping past the gate. Faiza was here. Saira ran towards her, and then past her, trying to catch up with a now-out-of-sight Rubani.

Faiza barely had time to acknowledge the whorl of speed and movement that was Saira as she sped past her. She walked up to Natasha and sat down, swinging her nylon duffel across the arm of her chair.

'Wow, what'd I miss?'

EIGHT

WHEN THE TWENTY-FOUR-HOUR clock on the fight ran out, Faiza decided she'd had enough. Natasha and Rubani had not said a word to each other and the other two had been coerced into dividing their time between the two across meals. That they didn't share a room had made it easier for the bitterness to simmer separately, with neither making any attempt to reach out to the other.

The result for Faiza had been a dinner with Natasha that involved a lot of livid ranting. And, as the un-aggrieved two had decided to avoid accusations of favouritism, an uncomfortable lunch at a popular thali place that had been too crowded and noisy for any real conversation; which Rubani had refrained from anyway because Faiza had been part of why the fight had begun in the first place. In real time, she'd have given them a couple of weeks to work through their feelings, but being on holiday called for expedited action. Already having lost a day, Faiza was in no mood to spend the remaining four wading through deepening tensions.

Bring Bani to the pool bar? she texted Saira. *Let's make them sort this shit out?*

Oh thank Jesus, came Saira's prompt response. *See you there in ten!*

Faiza sent a hug emoji in reply and tossed her phone aside. She started rummaging through her cupboard and settled on a black lycra monokini, with a cut-out at the navel, to change into.

'Get up,' she said to Natasha firmly, almost like an order.

'Why? You just got back. Let's laze for a bit, *na*? It's only three,' Natasha responded, reclining on the bed and flipping through an old issue of *Vogue* she'd stolen from the lobby.

Faiza stripped down to her underwear and rolled on some deodorant. 'We're meeting S and Bani at the pool bar,' she said. 'Why don't you wear that pretty bikini you keep chickening out of wearing? The pale pink one with the white on the sides?'

'Um, I think I'll pass. You have fun, though,' Natasha said.

'Oh, no, nuh-uh,' Faiza said. 'Get the fuck up and wear a fucking suit – we are *both* going.'

'Faiza, no, okay, I just do not want to deal with her *abhi*,' Natasha protested. 'You have no idea the kind of things she said.'

'Don't I? Because I recall you telling me in vivid detail last night,' Faiza said.

'No,' Natasha shook her head. 'You can't just come back from things like that. Not so quickly, like it didn't matter.'

Faiza, now naked and brushing out her hair, sighed.

'Nattu, I get it, okay. And I know the shit she said was really fucking cruel – I'm sure she thinks it, too. But, babe, we don't have time for you two to deal with it now. At least, not like this. We have four days left, and this is not what Saira and I signed up for – having to split our time with you both, like children of divorce. So either fight like motherfuckers and make up, or put a pin in it till you get home and then make up. Either way, figure it out so we can go back to our holiday, please?'

Natasha sighed. Faiza had a point – this wasn't their fight, and they shouldn't have to suffer the consequences. She and Rubani needed to deal with it. And so they would. She looked up at Faiza, sliding into her swimsuit and half-falling as she nearly put both legs in the same opening by mistake. She felt the pang of envy that she always did when Faiza stripped down to nothing in front of her. Her body and her confidence about it were amazing, and Natasha wished she had both.

'Okay,' she said, setting down the magazine and walking to her side of the closet. 'But I'm borrowing that white lace cover-up of yours – you never wear it anyway.'

Twenty-five minutes later, the two girls walked, an unplanned yin-and-yang in their black-and-white cover-ups and swimsuits. Saira and Rubani were already floating in the pool, the former with a cocktail in hand and the latter talking animatedly until she saw the two approach. Faiza tossed off her cover-up and jumped into the pool, splashing Saira who laughed and splashed her back. Natasha began climbing the stepladder to the pool, tentatively unfurling her robe-style cover-up till it was shed and placed exactly by the pool's edge for a quick retrieval on exit.

'Hey,' Natasha said gently, making her way to the other three.

'Hi friends! Long time no see,' joked Saira, who'd just had lunch with her.

'Hey,' Rubani said quietly. She'd missed Natasha, and had contemplated apologizing, but hadn't been able to bring herself to doing it.

'So, are you two going to get over yourselves or what?' Saira said. 'Please do it stat, because Haider and I love you both, but we're not doing this fifty-fifty dance anymore.'

Rubani and Natasha were silent. Faiza and Saira looked at each other, a little worried.

'Okay, so, er, we're going to get a drink,' Faiza announced. 'We'll be back in five. Just … start, okay? One of you, just start?'

They bobbed away from the other two and towards the bar.

Being in a pool meant abject awkwardness – no phone to stare at or hide behind, water impeding your ability to simply (or at least elegantly) walk away. It was after a few moments of contemplating exit strategies that Rubani finally spoke.

'I said some shit,' she sighed. 'And I'm sorry. But you also said some shit, Nattu. And you lied to me. That still fucking hurts; it hasn't gone away.'

'Yeah, no, I know,' Natasha said, her tone soft. 'And I know it must hurt you, but I also want to be able to tell you stuff like that. In a way where we're talking, not *screaming*,' Natasha said.

'I'm not screaming,' Rubani said, even-toned. 'Tell me now.'

'The truth is, it's not an easy thing to explain to people. To even the closest people – or, I don't know, maybe especially to them. People just assume a lot of things, and I guess it's easier to let them assume we're monogamous than to, like, risk their judgement.'

'But you told Faiza,' Rubani pointed out, just as Faiza and Saira swam back up to them clumsily, balancing a piña colada in each hand.

'*Do you like piña coladas,*' Saira sang, '*and getting caught in a catfight!*'

Rubani shot her a glare. Was there anything Saira would ever take seriously?

'Whoops, okay, sorry, clearly we walked into something,' she shrugged, handing Natasha a cocktail.

'Actually,' Rubani said, her voice calm, 'I just asked Nattu why she told Faiza but not me. Sorry, I mean us.'

Faiza looked down at her drink uncomfortably. Saira, sensing discomfort, grabbed Faiza by the hand and floated off with her to one side.

'You do that,' Saira called out as they drifted away. 'We'll be here taking selfies so Haider can make me Insta-famous.' They stood at a safe distance, pouting into the camera, just within earshot but without being part of the conversation.

Natasha sighed. 'Fine, you know what? I told her one night because we were drinking, and it felt … right. I just felt like I could tell her and she'd understand. And she *did*. She's known for a while – and, in fact, kept telling me to tell you guys, that you would get it, too. But it was I who couldn't, so stop hating on her, Bani.'

'I'm not hating on her!' Rubani's voice rose an octave, before she quickly reined it in. 'I said your …' she waved her hands to indicate a connection, '… whatever bothered me, but not Faiza. I've never had a problem with Faiza.'

Natasha was tempted to suggest that Rubani had waxed lyrical just yesterday about how Faiza was 'Natasha's friend' but chose not to.

'So what if I'm close to her, huh, Bani?' Natasha shrugged. 'It doesn't change the fact that I'm close to you both, too. Why can't I love you the same but just have different relationships with you? Why is it a contest?' Natasha knew she was lying a little, but the situation called for it.

The last point struck a chord with Rubani. It was something she could relate to; it never really came up because her myriad circles and spaces rarely intersected, but there was a closeness she felt particularly towards her queer friends that she could never replicate with this group. Well-intentioned though they might be, they would never quite understand the nuances of what she went through – the journey, the self-doubt, that niggling feeling of unbelonging in most spaces that were often slightly reductive of her worldview. It was something that, say, Jia got, without any work to get her there. And it was easier. But it wasn't necessarily that one set was closer than the other. The equations were just ... different.

'I guess I get what you're saying,' Rubani sighed. 'But I still feel like it's unfair that you thought I would judge you.'

'Your reaction was to imply that I was cheating on the best man in the world and it made you sick!' Natasha exclaimed.

Rubani stared at her for a second and burst out laughing.

'Oh my god, I fucking did do that,' she said in a fit of giggles. 'I'm a dick.'

'I'm a dick too,' Natasha said, laughing with relief at Rubani's reaction.

'Oh, you definitely are,' Rubani said, smiling.

Faiza and Saira, who had huddled together a little ways apart, also smiled. If their friends were laughing, that meant it was working. They continued to drain their drinks and eavesdrop with caution.

'Which is why we've been friends for a hundred years.' Natasha said gently. 'I love you, Bani. I should've told you, and

I should've known you'd be a dick about it, but I should've told you anyway and dealt with it.'

'You should've,' Rubani smiled. 'But I'm sorry I made you feel like you couldn't. I'll be less … judgemental.' She turned to Saira and Faiza, gesturing for them to come closer. 'But, like, I'm not *that* judgemental, am I?'

Saira raised an eyebrow sarcastically. 'Remember when I got drunk and kissed that lawyer boy while I was still dating Sarab? And you made me feel like a Marvel supervillain?'

'Ooh, and remember when that video co-host you had for like five minutes had just joined Goddess, and you went to his house?' Faiza added.

'His house was fucking filthy!' Rubani protested. 'And he had a huge cross on the wall, ew! You know those ones are psychos.'

'Oh, oh, and remember when you called your best friends hoes because they'd had one-night stands?' Saira teased.

'Okay, yeah, yeah, fuck off,' Rubani smiled, embarrassed. 'I get it, okay? But, Nattu, I still have a question.'

'Say?'

'You haven't told me how or why you guys decided to be open. Like, where did it come from, and how does it even work? Don't you guys get jealous?'

'To be honest, I'm also curious,' Saira added.

'Yeah, I figured you would be. So, okay, just ask me stuff, and I'll answer because that way is easiest.'

'First, tell us *why* you decided to be open in the first place?' Rubani asked. 'Not, like, in a judgy way,' she added hastily. 'But, like, whose idea was it?'

It hadn't been as much an idea as a solution. One night,

about two years into the marriage, Alex had been away on business – and Natasha had had a lapse. She'd got drunk and slept with an old friend, someone she'd had almost animalistic tension with for years. Alex had been away a lot, and a formidable cocktail of loneliness, arousal and, of course, actual cocktails had made one thing lead to another … then another and another, till they'd had sex five times through the night. It had been meaningless to her, but it wouldn't be to Alex if he were to find out. After three whole months of the most soul-crushing guilt, she finally told Alex, despite Rohan's advice not to. His stance was that it didn't matter; she'd sacrifice a great relationship for a moment's weakness, just to relieve her own guilt. She, however, couldn't bear the thought of living with the lie any longer.

When she did finally succumb and tell Alex, his reaction surprised her. He wasn't upset about the sex – it was the *lying* that unnerved him. 'I thought we were always honest with each other,' he'd said, distressed. She explained in a fluster, that her fear of losing him superseded her desire to be honest – couldn't he understand that? And, after a few hours of raw, unfettered conversation, he did.

'But the sex didn't bother him?' Saira asked.

'Not really – he has the same view on sex as I do. It can be very meaningful, as it is with the two of us. But it can also be just sex: physical, hot and not laced with a thousand emotions.'

'I could never do that,' Rubani said instinctively. 'But I'm probably the anomaly.'

'No, you're not – you're probably more "normal" about it than we are,' Natasha said. 'On that day, though, we talked about it for a long time and realized that, because we had married so young, we never really got a chance to have the sexual experiences many people have had by the time they're our age. I mean, I had that one time with Rishaad and that was really it.'

'Fair point,' Faiza said.

'So that's when we decided that we would be open. Not, like, actively Tinder-swiping, on-the-prowl open – but just that we would give ourselves the freedom to go with something if we really wanted to. If the only thing that would've stopped us from letting ourselves be with someone we were attracted to was the fact that we weren't single.'

'Wow,' Saira said. 'That actually sounds pretty evolved.'

'Yeah, I mean, of course it took a while to get there. It was pretty imperfect for the first year – I slept with a couple more people than he did, so there was jealousy, etceter—'

'I was literally just about to ask,' Rubani interrupted, stirring her cocktail, which had now separated into murky pineapple and thick coconut sections.

'And it was definitely tricky. It took time,' she added.

Natasha thought to herself about the one time it could have torn her marriage apart. She'd met a guy at a warehouse party in Delhi whom she'd grown a little fond of and told Alex about. She hadn't been able to stop thinking about what he'd be like in bed. He had these beautiful, gold-flecked eyes, strong shoulders and the kind of slightly crooked smile that really did it for her. She'd fantasized more than once about him fucking her that night itself, at the warehouse party, hidden in a dark corner, safe from the neon-red glow of the rooms throbbing deliriously with music. Alex had chanced upon a string of texts once and the frequency of their communication – not to mention the intensity of it – had really bothered him. One time, she'd seen him up at 4 a.m., scrolling through the texts, unable to sleep, and known she had to cut the other guy off. She'd never actually slept with him, but it felt more like cheating than anything else. She decided not to mention it to the girls.

'There were some dodgy moments – he'd be a little bothered by something, or I'd get a bit upset that he had met some really smart, sexy girl, and it would throw things off.'

'I can't imagine Alex with anyone but you, for some reason,' Rubani said.

'I know,' Natasha smiled, watching a stray child bob past in his SpongeBob SquarePants swimming wings. 'I think that was part of why I was never sure if I could talk about it with anyone. It was just as much his private life, his secret to tell.'

'Yeah, I get that …' Rubani said slowly. She wasn't sure if she would ever be capable of it herself, but …

'Do you sometimes get jealous?' Faiza asked. 'Like, I've never thought about it, because you don't seem like a jealous person, but you ever feel like, "Fuck, I want to kill that bitch?"'

The stray child's mother, who had swum up near them to take her son back to the shallow end, looked a bit aghast. Natasha apologetically mouthed 'sorry' as she collected her child and waded off in a huff.

Natasha laughed and shook her head. 'I mean, sure, I've had my moments, but, mostly, no. I think, I know somewhere deep down, that what we have is unshakeable. Our bond is too strong – we've weathered too much together to let a casual thing burn everything to the ground.'

'Do you have, like, ground rules and stuff, or is it a sexual Wild Wild West?' Saira grinned proudly at her own quip.

'Not like a whole list, and sometimes we add things as we go,' Natasha answered. 'But we try never to sleep with the same person twice. And we're honest with each other. About everything. No secrets, nothing that can spring up later and hurt our feelings.'

'Close friends,' Faiza prompted, softly.

'Oh yeah, we'll never sleep with anyone we know well, or a friend,' Natasha added. 'Way too messy.'

Rubani was thrown by the honesty prerequisite; it seemed like a hurtful prospect. She thought about sitting in bed with Kabir, having to hear him describe his encounters with another woman. How they kissed, how they touched … the thought made her shudder.

'Doesn't the hundred-per cent honesty thing mean telling each other, like, what you did with somebody else? And isn't it painful to hear about it?'

Natasha looked thoughtful for a moment. 'Sometimes, it can dredge up a lot of insecurities: Was she prettier? Was she better in bed? Does he want to see her again? But, just as often, it's actually … kind of hot. Does that sound weird?'

'It doesn't; I can totally get the appeal,' Saira chimed in, just as Rubani said, 'A little, but maybe that's me.'

'Like, we'll tell each other about what we did with the other person and it really turns us on. It has led to some of the best sex Alex and I have ever had. It's kinky, I know, but it just works for us.'

'So,' Rubani cleared her throat, 'something you'd recommend?'

'Not necessarily. Like for you, probably not, Bani. But

someone like you, S, maybe. Faizoo, I don't think would want it with Zaden.' Faiza nodded in agreement. 'It works on a case-by-case basis. I think the one thing that matters most is you and your partner being on the same page. Because if one of you is doing it to make the other happy, there will be *so* much resentment, oof.'

'How can you know for sure that Alex is on the same page, though?' Rubani mused. She wondered a little if Alex did it only to make Natasha happy. He would do pretty much anything for her, and Rubani loved that about him.

'I guess I can't ever know a hundred per cent,' Natasha said. 'But if he's not, he's a very good actor. Has been all these years.'

'Okay, I think enough interrogation. More alcohol, *si*?' Faiza said, sensing that her friend was done being questioned.

'I just want to say one last thing,' Saira said. 'I have thought about it a lot since yesterday and I can see what you have is pretty great. I feel like it's so much more fucked when people cheat – and, let's face it, most people cheat. Like, just the idea of Kabir cheating and lying messed with your head so much, Bani, and I hate him for it. But you guys, Nattu, you're solid. You're honest in a real way, and almost nobody has that kind of trust and understanding. It's so much more than monogamous sex. I see you two together, and it fits – it always has – and knowing this doesn't change the way I feel about the two of you. I think I'd be lucky to find what you guys have.'

Natasha felt a little swell of emotion. '*Rulaayegi kya, pagli?*' She laughed and gave Saira a hug.

'Please,' Faiza scoffed, 'as if you need an excuse.'

NINE

THE RUSH OF uptempo Latin music and voices screaming over it broke the silence of the quiet Anjuna street as the girls opened the door to the club. Dançando, one of Goa's coolest underground salsa clubs, was another Saira find. It had once been two dilapidated bars that shared a wall, each barely breaking even. Until, of course, the neighborhood was labelled 'upcoming' in the early 2010s; its inevitable gentrification followed suit. Apart from a few nostalgic favourites, the other three had left it to her to lead the way; she was the one with the inroads to the cooler counterculture of the city, due in part to her job, other than her long-standing connection to the club itself.

The first time Saira had come to Dançando was seven years ago, when it was still ripe with the scent of a new launch. Kept under wraps for the purposes of exclusivity, the club was only in the cultural repertoire of certain locals and some especially well-versed tourists – of which Saira was one. Fifteen years of coming to Goa, mixed and shaken with her charismatic, extrovert personality, had led to her creating a network in the city, one that kept her abreast of the most exciting new things. While she was often happy to share the wealth with friends and fellow travellers who DM'd her on Instagram, she'd always kept this place a secret. Its dark granite walls, seductive yellow light and tucked-away location on an innocuous, run-of-the-mill street in Anjuna only added to its in-the-know-only reputation. Saira had never been compelled to share it with anyone else – until now.

'I love this place,' Natasha said, leaning into Saira's ear, her voice straining against the pounding clave of the music.

'I know, right?' Saira grinned back. 'I never bring anyone here. Only you guys.'

'Aww,' Rubani said, giving her a hug. Since making up with Natasha, her general mood had lightened considerably. It was nice to feel close to her friends again; she'd had a long chat with Faiza as well this morning before the others had woken up. They had talked about Natasha, about her friendship with Faiza and Rubani's resentment of it. And about Kabir. She'd found it funny that, of the three, she'd had the most real post-break-up conversation with Faiza, delving deep into how much it had shaken her. She knew Saira would have had a smug face throughout, and Natasha would've been almost too sympathetic – but Faiza gave it to her straight, which was something Rubani realized she really needed. 'If you're sitting here later questioning everything about what you had, that means he never really made you feel safe,' she had said wisely and it dawned on Rubani how true that was. She'd had moments of happiness, intimacy, great sex – but nearly never safety. 'And you need that in a relationship. More than anything,' Faiza had said, squeezing her hand.

In the years they had been a group, Rubani had never

disliked Faiza; she'd just always unconsciously competed with her for Natasha's affections, in the quest to be her confidante. It soon became a conscious effort (just to her, she hoped) and any kinship she felt with Faiza was always coloured by Natasha's presence. But this morning, Rubani had left feeling aglow out of a fondness for Faiza. One that, for the first time in their group dynamic, seemed to be on par with what she felt for her two other friends. Natasha was right – Faiza wasn't just *her* friend and Rubani felt it more than ever now.

'What are you thinking about?' Faiza asked, shaking Rubani out of her thoughts. 'All okay?'

'Ya, ya,' Rubani smiled. 'Thinking about our talk in the morning.'

'I'm sorry if I overstepped,' Faiza said. 'I simply felt like we were being honest with each other.'

'Aye, no,' Rubani shook her head dismissively. 'It's the opposite. I was just thinking about how it was such a good talk. Getting your opinion separate from everyone's; it helped me.'

'Really?' Faiza asked, a mix of hopeful and sceptical.

'Really,' Rubani reassured her, reaching out for her hand. 'And now I'm going to buy you a drink to prove it.'

She held up her hand to signal that they were leaving, and Natasha and Saira smiled and nodded in acknowledgment.

'You don't want a drink?' Saira asked.

'Maybe in a few,' Natasha said. 'Let's just walk a little, *na*? I want to see the rest of the place.'

They made their way deeper into the club, bobbing and weaving through sweaty, spinning dancers as they turned and spun to the rhythmic beats. Some were in serious dance mode, the girls in swingy, halter-neck dresses and towering heels, and the men in half-unbuttoned shirts, executing a practised progression of *enchufla dobles* and *dos taros* that could put professional dancers to shame. The others, comfortingly, were in beachy shirts, shorts and dresses that indicated this was more a fun Thursday-night stopover than a display of technical mastery. They fumbled, misstepped, laughed and made it easier for everyone else to lighten up and do it wrong.

'So, is tonight an "open Natasha" night?' Saira asked, raising an eyebrow. 'And by that, I mean, is your vag open for business?'

'Ew!' Natasha laughed, swinging today's designer bag at her – Marc by Marc Jacobs Snapshot, a new but fast favourite of hers.

'Seriously, tell me?' Saira prodded.

'This night is about you, babies,' Natasha said, cupping Saira's chin in her hand. '*Vaise*, why are you so keen to see me get laid on this trip?'

'I just want someone to get some action, man,' Saira whined.

'Why can't it be you?' Natasha raised her eyebrow this time, grinning. '*Tere Maximillian ko kya hua?*'

'Yuck, he's not a textbook company, ya. His name is "Maxime",' Saira said, pronouncing his name with an exaggerated French inflection.

'That's *Macmillan*, you imbecile, the publishing house.' Natasha laughed, almost snorting. 'Yes, okay, where is "Maxime"?' she asked, imitating Saira's pronunciation.

'He texted a couple of times.' Saira smiled slyly. 'I'm trying not to come off as desperate. Maybe I'll call him when we go to the night market. What do you think?'

'Good idea,' Natasha agreed, as they passed a pirouetting woman with a skyscraping ponytail and a broad smile. 'Lots of people, casual, I get it.'

'Right? I think less pressure that way, and if I feel like it later, then I can leave with him.' Saira winked.

'You clearly have a thing for white boys, no?' Natasha laughed.

'Why does everyone keep saying that!' Saira protested. 'This is just the third ...' she stopped short, and did a quick mental count, touching the tips of her fingers '... um, okay, maybe fourth. Are Turkish boys white? Okay, whatever; is that a lot?'

'Well, it's four more than me.' Natasha shrugged.

'Seriously?' Saira looked at her in disbelief. 'Not even one? Never even close?'

'What can I say, babu?' Natasha shook her head. 'I like my desi boys.'

Saira laughed. They stood together and watched the couples dance for a bit, enjoying the mix of personalities and vibes. Just as they were obsessing over this one woman's beautiful moves, a tall, striking woman in a red organza dress came and cut into their chat, tapping Natasha on the shoulder.

'Oh my god, *Tasha*?' the woman said breathily. 'I can't believe it's *you*!'

'Mohini! Oh my ...' Natasha leaned in and hugged her. 'Saira, this is Mohini. Mo, Saira.'

'Nice to meet you,' Saira said with a polite smile.

'Mo and I went to school together,' Natasha explained.

'Ah, that explains the nickname, *Tasha*,' Saira teased.

'Wait, what do people call you now?' Mohini looked confused.

'*Arey*, forget it,' Natasha laughed. 'Tell me, how've you been? Is Sagar here?' she asked, referring to her husband.

'Guys, I'm so sorry, I have to take this,' Saira interrupted, motioning to her phone. The fake phone call was her oldest go-to for stepping out of a conversation. Natasha gave her a placating nod and made a motion to suggest she'd catch up. 'It was nice to meet you, Mohini,' Saira said and ducked out.

After a few minutes of expertly navigating the spinning arms and legs of the fervent dancers, she managed to push her way through to the sticky, wine-stained bar where Faiza and Rubani were standing, heads together, laughing about something.

'Ugh, I thought you ditched us,' Saira said, pulling herself up onto a stool and beckoning for the bartender.

'*Sai*, babe, how the fuck are you?' The sexy bartender with the pierced ear leaned over the counter and squeezed her shoulders. 'I haven't seen you in a long time, man. You don't come anymore!'

'*Tony*! There's so much work, bubs. You know I'd live here if I could,' Saira said, and she meant it. Despite the influx of metropolitan millennials who had recently relocated their lives here, Saira still felt a greater claim over it, and a fondness that hadn't ebbed with the rise in the upscale eateries and dime-a-dozen distilleries that made it the new nexus of cool.

'You met my friends? This is Faiza and Rubani.' Tony smiled, introducing himself, and proceeded to slam down three tequila shots on the table. 'For Saira's friends.'

'Saira's friends!' the three said in unison, glugging the tequila – Saira and Rubani with ease, Faiza with an expression of some disgust.

'Shots? Are we fucking twelve?' Faiza grumbled under her breath.

'Such an old, married lady you've become,' Rubani teased.

'Guys, don't joke about it, okay?' Faiza shook her head. 'My mother has been on me for the last three years, *and* she's been nudge-nudging Zaden. I'm getting pretty stressed about it.'

It was rare for Faiza to bring up her parents with the group. She did it with Natasha often, but it was a subject she didn't enjoy in general. Her faux-progressive parents still held a lot of conservative values at heart, which had led to a don't-ask-don't-tell relationship that Faiza had fostered carefully over the years. They knew enough to not be completely in the dark, but never enough to warrant a real discussion. She was sure they knew she used to drink regularly as a teenager, yet the idea of having a drink in front of them – let alone *with* them – was unfathomable. It was a method her older brother Amaan and she had perfected over the years, covering for each other when they had parties or dates. They knew she was with Zaden, but not that she lived with him, and the only reason she'd finally even told them about him was because he was Muslim too – one less thing to disapprove of.

It was a strange affection she'd felt for them. She loved them, in a they-are-my-family-so-I-have-to way, but she'd never felt the need to lean on them. She'd always leaned on Mira in school, and now Natasha, more so than she ever had on her parents. She and Amaan had a good enough dynamic, but not one that qualified as a friendship. As a paediatrician who'd moved to New Jersey when she was twenty-one, their long-distance chats were piecemeal and surface-level, circling the subjects of their partners, his daughter and work. Her father wasn't much for conversation, saying a few token sentences about the weather in Bombay and how she should visit soon whenever her mother handed him the phone. Her mother taxed her most of all, her quiet disapproval never voiced but omnipresent. That, and her regular reminders that thirty-four was no age to be unmarried, made the chats unpleasant weekly necessities, like paying taxes, where the only good feeling it produced was that now it was done.

'Ugh, I know this, man. I haven't even been able to tell my mom about Kabir; she'll be so disappointed. She loved him.'

'But your mom loves everyone!' Saira said. 'She's just like that.'

She was, Rubani conceded to herself. She'd been lucky that way – it was something her Garage84 friends constantly reminded her of. She'd had the privilege of acceptance; something most of them hadn't, and she was never allowed to forget it. Most of them had to struggle far more. Her trans friend Abida always came to mind; she had been shipped off home to Jaisalmer while her family tossed all the things from her 'debauched' city life out of her studio apartment and onto the street. Rubani had received a call late one evening from a PO booth in Jaisalmer while in college in Bangalore, with a sobbing Abida begging her to go pick up whatever she could of her belongings from the street outside her home. Rubani had run and tried to salvage what she could from the haphazard pile, but her friend's carefully curated things – stilettos, poetry books with pressed flowers, Madonna CDs – had all been pillaged, trampled upon or kicked down the street. It was a sight she drew back from memory every time her parents were difficult.

'That's definitely true,' Rubani smiled. 'She's good like that. But, sorry, no, we were talking about Haider; I got distracted.'

'No, nothing, really. Just that. I don't know how to break it to her that I don't want to get married yet; I don't even know if at all. If someone, then, yeah, Zaden, but something about actually being legally married still fucks me in the head. And kids are just a whole other ball game.'

'You don't want them at all?' Rubani asked, a little surprised.

'I'm honestly not sure. There are times I think it would be nice to have one – something Zaden and I created. Our own little person.' She laughed. 'But most of the time, I don't. I like my life the way it is. And I have no burning desire to raise a child.'

'Amen,' said Saira, 'to the second part. Not creating a little person. I think I've just always known that kids are just not my scene, bro. I knew when I was ten and these dumb bitches in my school were obsessed with playing *ghar ghar*, pretending to cook dinner for our "husbands" and getting our "kids" ready for school.'

'Pretty fucked up that we were playing *ghar ghar* when the dudes were getting Hot Wheels and doctor sets, no?' Faiza smiled.

'Yeah. It would always piss me off. At least you had a brother. You could steal his shit and play with it. Being an only child meant being carted off to neighbour gal pals for Barbie dates; it was extremely *not* fun.'

Rubani smiled at the idea of Saira, who would've been

pegged as a 'tomboy' by the colony mothers for certain, having to suffer through playing with Barbies and 'girlie' toys. Her being in fashion often made people mistake her for someone who grew up obsessed with clothes, but her introduction to the world had only come via a chance internship at a women's lifestyle magazine post college that had blossomed into a full-fledged career. Saira knew fashion, understood it and enjoyed it in an almost academic way – but she had never been consumed by it. As a friend of hers from her pre-work college era, Rubani, who'd known her to wear ragged Metallica tees and grey cotton pajamas, stood testament to that.

'Anyway,' Saira continued, 'every time I said to Mum's friends or any of the various aunties that kept coming over that I didn't want them, they would laugh and say, "Just you wait. You'll change your mind one day."'

'At what age did they finally stop?' Rubani asked with a laugh.

'I'll let you know when they do,' Saira smiled wryly.

'Your folks are fine about it, though?' Faiza asked. 'No pressure from them?'

'Well, I mean, with Pa, when *isn't* there pressure?' Saira rolled her eyes. 'I've just learned to drown him out now. Ma, I think, will be happy if I just date someone seriously to begin with. She thinks I'm incapable of commitment.'

'Well, you are, though,' Rubani teased. She'd never admit it aloud, but Rubani envied Saira's ability to stay detached. Her own method of relationshipping – hardcore monogamy with often ill-advised partners – had only always led to heartbreak; a feeling Saira had expertly avoided for three decades.

'Capable, or do you mean incapable?' Faiza asked.

'She means incapable only,' Saira clarified on Rubani's behalf. 'And ya, maybe. I like the idea of having someone sometimes. But then I think about having to share my space and my house and having to check in with someone constantly. Then it quickly loses its appeal.' She sighed dramatically. 'Maybe I'm just too old now; I'm set in my ways.'

'On the other hand, I'm going to have to figure out how to go back to life on my own again,' said Rubani. 'I'd gotten so used to Kabir that I'd let myself get spoiled about the little things. Like reaching the high shelves, or chasing out lizards in summer.' Her tone was just a bit dismal. 'On the plus side, I can eat in bed again! It used to drive him mad – he'd find crumbs in the bed and do this whole *naatak* of yanking off the sheets and dusting them with so much drama. I'm going to eat fucking Oreos in bed to celebrate when we're home.'

'Does Zaden *allow* you to eat in bed, Haider?' Saira shook her head in disbelief at Rubani and looked over at Faiza so they could mock her together.

Faiza's eyes, however, had completely glossed over. It was almost as though she were in a trance.

'Haider,' Saira snapped a finger in front of her face. 'What's up?'

Faiza shook her head and smiled at Faiza. 'Sorry, sorry.'

'What happened, baba?' Saira repeated.

'Nothing, just that song …'

'What about it? Bad association?' Rubani asked.

Faiza looked a little taken aback, which made Rubani feel like she'd hit close to home.

'Um, more like weird association, really. Made me think of a night I kind of just ... like an important night from when I was in my twenties.'

'Is it triggering?' Saira looked concerned. 'Did someone ... do something?' She reached instinctively for Faiza's fingers, looping them through her own.

'Oh god, no, not weird in that way. Just one of those nights that kind of, like ... oh, Bani, I just realized something,' Faiza said, turning to Rubani. 'Remember when we were talking about how one-night stands can be meaningful?'

Rubani nodded, still a little guilty about her snap judgements on the subject from the start of the holiday.

'This is one of those things.'

'This is a one-night stand story?' Saira asked excitedly. 'Wait, you have to tell us everything. From the beginning!'

'I agree,' Rubani said. 'Who knows, this might be the one that convinces me to ask the cute bartender to come home with me?'

'Really? Tony's your type? He's very un-Kabir, no?' Saira scratched her chin thoughtfully.

'Exactly.' Rubani smiled. 'Maybe I could do with some "un-Kabir". Maybe I need quickie-quickie-bang-bang to be the opposite of my usual type. The anti-type, if you will.'

'Touché. That's a good rule of thumb for a zero-investment policy.' Saira grinned. 'Okay, Haider, come on.'

'Listen, I'm not shouting this story at 3X my normal decibel, okay? I'll tell you later.'

'No, tell us *nowww*,' Saira insisted. 'There's this coastal place down the road that has live music. It'll be much quieter. Let's get a drink there and come back here; this one is open till four in the morning.'

'Sounds like a plan,' Bani agreed.

'And I wouldn't mind some prawn xacuti,' Faiza said. '*Chalo*, let's find Nattu and head.'

They scoured the crowd for Natasha, finally spotting her mint-green skater dress leaning into the frame of a tall, attractive guy in dark blue jeans. She said something in his ear and he laughed. It was clear there was a vibe; the three didn't feel like pulling her away from it.

'Haider,' Saira looked at Faiza knowingly. 'Nattu already knows this story, doesn't she?'

Faiza made a sheepish face and nodded.

'Okay, so we don't need her,' Saira concluded. 'And we definitely don't need to harsh her mellow. Let's just send her a text telling her where to find us.'

'Is this coastal place far?' Rubani looked concerned. 'There are never any streetlights here – can she walk?'

Yeah, yeah, just a two-minute walk,' Saira waved her hand. 'It's still early. And if she wants us to come get her, we will.'

'Fair enough,' Faiza agreed. 'Let's go.'

As they walked out of the club and into the cool night air, Rubani turned to Faiza with puppy eyes.

'What?' Faiza asked.

'Can you just start telling us, like, now, please?'

FAIZA

THE DOORBELL RANG in a quick triple burst and Faiza instantly sprang up. She looked in the mirror and checked her lipstick, the same cherry red she always gravitated to on a night out. They were going out after ages, and she knew Mira would be in one of her floral dresses, her hair long and flowy, her lips painted a soft pink that would break into a smile when they were flirted with at the bar that night. Mira was always a stark, feminine contrast to her own bold mouth, dark dresses and choppy, unruly bob. Together, they were singles' night catnip.

A second bout of aggressive doorbell ringing sounded, signalling Mira's impatience. 'I'm coming, shut the fuck *up!*' Faiza yelled loudly, drawing a third, thick coat of her favourite stick over her pouting lips – the company called it 'Firebrand' – and it felt apt for nights like this one. She fixed the slipping straps of her black slip dress and opened the door to an irritated Mira.

'Were you taking a fucking dump?' she growled. 'It's so hot – you couldn't have opened the door and gone back?' One would never imagine this elfin little girl in the orchid pink dress and teetering Giuseppe Zanotti's – the clothes may be from wherever, but the shoes were *always* designer – could match the gruffness of her tone.

'I was checking my fucking lipstick,' Faiza shot back, one eyebrow raised. 'Was I calling and harassing you when you spent three hours primping?'

They grinned at each other, and Mira walked into the kitchen with the level of ease she would have in her own. 'You want a drink before we go?' she asked, already pulling out tonic from her fridge and opening the cabinet she knew would have gin.

'Yeah, obviously. I don't want tonic though – this dress won't hide a water belly.' She patted the smooth silk over her stomach, tauter by the day as payoff for her gruelling workouts. 'Just give me a shot? I have *nimboo* in the egg tray; just cut half.'

It was an ease they'd found with each other almost instantly when they'd met on the first day of high school. Mira was new, and Faiza had grown up being popular enough to be arrogant at her snooty Bombay school. She was also just old enough to be threatened by the pretty, doe-eyed girl with the long, straight hair, whom her two best male friends suddenly had a crush on.

But when Mira simply came up to her table at lunchtime and offered her half of her Cherry Pop Tart, she was thrown by her confidence. 'My dad travels a lot; he knows these are my favourite, so he brings them back.' She smiled, holding out a broken half, almost exactly equal to the other. Faiza had only tried Cherry Pop Tarts once before, but had decided she loved them. She had often seen them at the fancy, imported foods department store in Colaba but, despite being at a rich-kid school, she came from a middle-class home, with parents who'd responded to her requests for them by steering her towards Britannia Jim Jams instead.

She admitted to herself – and to Mira – years later that she had grudgingly let her sit at her table the first couple of times because of that Pop Tart. She was acceptable, Faiza had thought, and would do as an imported candy supplier, until she bored of her.

Cut to seventeen years later, and she was anything but bored. They'd found a comfort in each other that most people can only dream of, and they had stayed close throughout school, until separated by colleges and jobs in different cities. Eventually, they'd found themselves living in the one city they'd hated most growing up because of the inherent, Bombay-bred bias that came with it – Delhi. Much to their parents' and friends' chagrin.

'Ugh, I'm so glad I don't live with you – your kitchen is a maze,' Mira's voice floated across the room as she rummaged through a cupboard. It had been part of the pact when Mira had moved here two years after Faiza – best friends make terrible roommates. Besides, they now made enough money to be able to afford privacy.

'*Your* kitchen is a fucking mess, okay? If you didn't have Rani didi, there'd be rats and you know it,' Faiza snapped back, picking up her drink and shuffling Mira along with her on her way out of the kitchen.

They settled on Faiza's couch at opposite ends, their legs stretched out, intermingling. Faiza scoffed as she watched Mira make swipe motions on her phone that clearly indicated she was on Tinder. 'Who's around?' Faiza asked, taking a long sip. 'Anyone cute?'

It often proved tricky that they liked the same sort of guy: well-read and well-heeled for the long-term, well-built and gorgeous for the short. But girl code had always been thicker than blood, which dictated a simple rule of thumb – if they both liked him, nobody got him. They'd never know if one of them had lost the love of their lives along the way, but they had the strongest friendship of anyone they knew – it seemed a worthy trade.

'No, man, everyone's paunchy and balding,' she grumbled and cast her phone aside on a neighbouring single-seater. 'There are no men left in Delhi. I think we need to do our trip ASAP. I want some cute Turkish boys.'

Turkey had been on their fantasy to-do list for a while. But with Faiza's demanding hours as a copywriter at the toxic, inherently sexist Moksha and Mira's burgeoning accessories brand, it seemed destined to stay a fantasy.

'You need to get over this Turkish boy fetish,' Faiza said with an eye roll.

'What?' Mira protested. I've never slept with one! I've done pretty much everyone else; is it so wrong to want to check this off my list?'

Faiza sighed. She was glad it was 2015 and Mira was a woman, because she was pretty sure if a man said that aloud, he'd be a sexist pig beyond repair. The irony was that Mira seemed the more emotional of the two; it was a stereotype that came in tow with her delicate demeanour. However, she often treated men like items on a brunch menu – rarely ordering the same thing twice, with exceptions for favourites.

One such favourite, for several months, had been Vikrant, her newly two words ex boyfriend who had broken up with her because his parents wanted him to marry a family friend's daughter. Mira had acted like she'd been relieved, but Faiza knew how much it would've stung that he hadn't stood up to his parents and fought for her.

'Ugh, I'm so glad,' she'd said over the phone the night he'd broken it off. 'As if I would've married a bloody *maru*. Please,' she scoffed, her voice breaking just enough for Faiza to start picking up her stuff and preparing to head over to Mira's. They'd spent the night eating caramel popcorn and watching *90210,* a long-time indulgence of theirs when they wanted 'pure drivel', interspersed with Mira trash-talking Vikrant and crying.

Tonight was the first time since that Mira had sounded genuinely keen on going 'hunting' – their word for finding a man for easy, meaningless sex. They usually chose their prey and split off when things started getting heavy. A good night ended with both of them finding someone, a bad one with only one of them finding a trophy. They cared about and championed each other through everything, but they still had egos.

'I'm sick of my vibrator, my hands, porn, everything – I just want someone now, I've had enough.' Mira sighed.

'Listen, you'll obviously find someone, but I just want to make sure you're ready,' Faiza said, downing the last dregs of her drink. 'Don't just sleep with someone for the fuck of it. It always gets messy with these guys, you know that.'

'It's these *Delhi* boys! I'm so tired of them all. Like, they're all bloody momma's boys and half of them look at me and think "wife, kids, house in Gurgaon near my office in Cybercity". No, thank you,' she said, shaking her head, and Faiza knew she was overcompensating for Vikrant.

'Okay, we're not going to find any boys if you don't hurry *up*.' She moved over and nudged Mira's drink, tipping it into her mouth. 'I want to go.'

'Oh god, it's ten,' Mira said, finishing her drink regardless. 'No one is even *there*. Nothing is going to happen for at least an hour, but fine. *Chalo*.'

They booked an Uber and piled into the back noisily, both on separate phone calls with their mothers, assuring them that they would be fine because 'there are boys with us'. It was a lie they needed to tell to assuage their parents' fears that something might happen in 'big, bad Delhi' – and, to be fair, it was also the eventual goal of the evening.

The cab driver, in an attempt to drown out their voices shouting over the others, switched radio stations and turned the volume up. The autotune and synthetic beats of the song (identifiably part of a recent Bollywood family entertainer) were grating enough to get them both to hang up promptly. '*Bhaiyya*, please station *badal do*,' Faiza asked, annoyed. With an air of silent disdain, the driver switched stations again, this time landing on the only English music station the city still had. A familiar song filled the car, and the minute Faiza recognized it, she saw Mira light up at the same time.

'*There's a fiiiiire starting in my heeeearttt*,' Mira sang out, tone deaf and oblivious, caught up in the music. '*Reaching a fever pitch and it's bringing me out the dark*,' Faiza belted out in unison, her throaty voice somewhat offsetting Mira's scattered notes.

They sang with the abandon they usually reserved for a drunker version of themselves. It was the association the song brought back, when Faiza had come to Greenwich to stay with Mira during her break at Parson's. They'd been at a dive bar close to her school (one they'd chosen because it seemed cheap) and spent the evening listening to the same six songs that were being played on repeat. When they'd finally had enough shots, they'd begun to belt out the Adele hit that was all the rage at the time. They were then politely served with their bill, mid-drink, the barkeep, with a crisp smile, gesturing to the door with his head. It had been a happy, stumbling walk home and the song always brought back the memory.

They finally arrived at the bar, the driver sullen-faced at having to listen to the two girls singing badly all the way instead of the saccharine Bolly ballad he'd have preferred. Faiza stuck out a hundred-rupee note, smiling at him and saying, '*Sorry, hamne itna shor machaya.*' The driver accepted the note with delight, thanking her with feeling.

'Why did you need to give that *sadoo* extra money?' Mira whined as they started climbing the stairway to the bar. 'He was such a grouch. I hate people like that.'

'You hate everyone, Miroo.' Faiza rolled her eyes, employing a nickname she knew her friend hated, that only she could get away with.

Mira made a face at her as they pushed through the crowd, still somewhat sparse compared to what it would be like in an hour. 'Whatever. You're buying me a drink since you have so much money you can throw it at cabbies.'

They pushed past the crowd in the lantern-lit smoking area outside and made their way in, swallowed by the bar's wooden walls, neon signs and throbbing music. They pushed through to the bar, and Mira smiled at the young man flipping a cocktail shaker with a confident smile. 'Hiiiii,' she drawled, flashing a bright grin at him and shrugging her long hair over her shoulder. 'I don't know if you remember me, but I wanted to ask you for a cocktail you'd made for me last time?' She batted her eyes just a little and raised her shoulders to suggest she'd forgotten the name. 'It was something with watermelon and gin …?'

The guy smiled at her in recollection. 'Of course I remember you!' He leaned across the counter. 'Yup, it was a watermelon punch. Coming right up!' Faiza shook her head at Mira, who she was pretty sure had known the name of the drink. Mira made a face at her and then turned her attention back to the bartender, who'd already whipped up her flamingo-pink concoction.

'On the house,' he said, flashing his not-so-pearly whites at Mira, who looked like she was too surprised to understand. 'Oh, no, of course not, I couldn't!' Mira said, scrambling for her wallet in her purse. 'I insist. You can get the next one.' He smiled back, shaking his head. Mira held up her hands and pretended to surrender, taking the glass and raising it to him in thanks. As they moved away from the crowded countertop, Mira lowered her voice (despite the pounding music) and whispered in Faiza's ear, 'Please. For the next one, I'm going to the rooftop bar.'

In anyone else, Faiza would have abhorred such behaviour – she had very different views on feminism than her best friend. But there was something about Mira – for her everything was a game, but a fun one where no one was supposed to get hurt. She realized she maybe forgave it a little more because Mira, in turn, was the one who got hurt the most.

They pushed past a gaggle of stilettoed teenagers teetering dangerously and using each other's interlocked arms to create a web of support. Faiza smiled, remembering when they had run around in a rat pack, safe in their numbers. It had taken them a while to shed the inhibition that had come with being out in this city late at night – and with it, they'd shed their excess acquaintances too.

They had just about made it out through the door and into the muggy July air when Faiza saw a familiar face smile at her. It was her friend Nikhil, from work, and he was motioning madly across the crowd. She turned around and grabbed Mira's arm, steering her in the direction of his table full of friends. 'Ow, what?' Mira yelped, but without trying to free her arm from Faiza's grasp.

'My friend's here; I just want to say hi to him,' Faiza said, her voice getting a little lost in the din.

'Ooh, is he cute?' Mira asked, as Faiza had expected her to. 'You can see for yourself,' Faiza quickly managed to reply before they arrived at his table.

'Hiiiiii,' she said, out of breath, exchanging a hug and smiling politely at his friends.

'Guys, this is Faiza. Faiza, this is Sahil, Daniel and Nidhi,' said Nikhil, gesturing across the rough, beer-sodden wood of the table. 'Faiza is the reason I don't shoot my boss in the face every morning,' he grinned down at Faiza from his 6'1" vantage point, pushing his floppy, straight hair out of his eyes.

'I explained it would also be illegal.' She laughed, shaking their hands. 'This is Mira; Mira—'

'I remember everyone's names,' Mira said through a clipped smile, clearly only interested in learning one. 'But I'm sorry, I didn't get yours?'

'Oh.' He laughed. 'Sorry, hi, I'm Nikhil.' He shook his
head at Faiza and sipped on his drink. 'The guy she's clearly
never mentioned before.'

Mira laughed as Faiza said 'Hey!' and whacked his arm
feebly in protest.

'It's true,' Nikhil said mock-seriously. 'You only talk to me
because I sit next to your work wife.'

'Who is this work wife? I must know all about her,' Mira
said, smiling at him, her eyes staring straight into his. It was a
look Faiza knew, one that indicated she had found her target
and was locked and loaded. Nikhil was nice, but not someone
she'd invoke their code for. She was a touch nervous about
it all getting awkward if they slept together and one of them
vanished. But it wasn't her problem if she played no part
in making it happen. She looked at her phone and feigned
concern over an imaginary text.

'Sorry, guys, I need to make a call,' she said, ducking out
while they talked to each other about Mira's business – a
story Mira loved to tell, and that Faiza could recite by rote.
She slipped out, mumbling 'be right back' under her breath
in case they deigned to listen.

She made her way to the dance floor. It was never high
on Mira's night-out agenda, but Faiza loved dancing. The
allure of it hadn't dimmed over the years – the all-consuming
music, the darkness, the strangers. She could be there by
herself for hours, no friends or man required, and lose herself
in the swirl of alcohol and volume.

It was only when the DJ broke from his console for a
drink that Faiza realized almost forty minutes had passed. She
looked at her phone and saw several missed calls from Mira

and one from Nikhil. She started to hurry back to them. As she quickened her pace towards the door, texting furiously, Faiza bumped into someone and felt a growing circle of wetness on her dress.

'I'm so sorry!' She looked up at the man whose drink she'd spilled – though, luckily, most of it had soaked her own black dress. 'I wasn't looking; this is my—'

'It's completely fine. I saw you barrelling at me; I should've ducked for my life.' The man grinned at her, and when she got a look at him, she swallowed nervously. He was *gorgeous*.

The Man was exactly her type, physically. His broad shoulders and possible six-pack (if the cling of that worn, grey T-shirt was anything to go by) worked well with his crooked smile and warm brown eyes. Eyes that were currently twinkling a little. Or seemed to be twinkling only to her because it was too dark to see them properly and Faiza was filling in the gaps.

'Well, um, anyway, I'm still sorry,' she answered tentatively, because she hadn't been able to decipher if the 'barrelling' comment was a joke or a thinly veiled dig at her.

'It's perfectly fine and I think you got the worst of it.' His tone was warm, and she was inclined to think he meant it. 'Luckily, it works with your dress.'

'Excuse me?' Faiza narrowed her eyes, wondering if it was allusion to the fact that her dress was see-through and therefore more revealing because of the spill. She looked down and realized he'd only meant that it didn't show because her dress was so dark. 'Oh.' She laughed. 'Yeah, that's pretty much why I wear dark things. So I can spill with gay abandon.'

'Is this a regular thing for you? Bumping into people with drinks so much you've tailored your wardrobe to it?' He smirked. He was wittier than the average Delhi Joe she ended up liaising with over mojitos, who were mostly too caught up trying to mention how much they worked out to manage actual humour.

'Ha ha,' she rolled her eyes, but she was smiling. 'Stop crying over spilt gin. Unless you're angling for me to buy you another one, which I suppose is fair ...'

'Actually,' he said. 'I was hoping I could buy you one instead.' Faiza looked up to find an earnestness in his face – and she suddenly had a burst of feeling. Like she wanted to kiss him. That feeling was usually the lock-in moment for her, when she knew she liked a man enough to take him home. He took her silence for hesitation and quickly piped up, 'I mean, I'm already getting myself one ...'

'I'd like that.' Faiza smiled, biting her lip. It was her favourite coy move, and it almost always worked. 'Great, let's go,' he gestured, allowing her to lead the way.

As they reached the crowded bar, her usual method of procuring a drink (being one of the only women at a bar full of men) didn't seem to be yielding results – there were too many women leaning over and shouting their orders. 'Shall I?' The Man asked, but she shook her head. 'Too many people,' she yelled, leaning into his ear so she could be heard above the noise. 'I have an idea,' she said, her voice wafting away amidst the nostalgic notes of remixed Kesha. 'But you'll need to carry me.'

'What?' he yelled back, gesturing to his ear and shaking his hand to indicate he couldn't hear her. She pointed to him, made a baby-carrying motion and then pointed at herself. He instantly began to laugh.

She wondered if she'd lost him. Her zaniness sometimes proved a bit much for lesser men. Luckily, he didn't seem to be one of them.

He set down his empty glass and stooped to the floor, pointing at his back. She used the bar counter to hoist and swing her onto his shoulders with more ease than she'd imagined. Given the nmber of people pushing into them, it should've been clunky and awkward. Instead, it was surprisingly sexy.

As she balanced on those solid shoulders she'd been admiring, she waved at the astounded bartender. Once he'd had a minute to let the comedy of the situation sink in, he too started laughing. 'What can I get you?' the bartender shouted. 'Two G&Ts,' she yelled back, and he signed a thumbs up to know her words had registered.

There was no reason to continue to stay up there, but Faiza liked the warmth of his body on her legs, the feeling of safety his shoulders gave her even though she was in a precarious position. It had been a while since she'd had sex, and her body was zinging from the contact in ways that surprised her. She reluctantly tapped him on his arm to indicate she was ready to be let down, and he lowered himself so she could hop off. They smiled at each other with the familiar awkwardness of two strangers who had been too close too fast.

'So …' he said, as the bartender jerkily slid their drinks at them across the sticky countertop. 'So … thank you for this,' she gestured to her glass. 'And, um, I'll see you around?' she said and edged forward like she was going to walk away, but with some hesitation.

'Could I, um ...' he said, smiling tentatively. *Isn't that the cutest*, thought Faiza, noticing the apprehension. She was more used to the overconfident smirk most Delhi men thought never went out of style.

'Um ...?' she teased, looking at him with a smile. They both broke into a laugh.

'Could I get your number?' he said, more relaxed this time.

She stared at him thoughtfully for a second. 'Who are you here with?' she asked.

'My friends? They're outside, on the terrace.'

'Aaaand how attached are you to them?' she asked. He gave her a questioning half-smile. 'I mean, not attached like, would you care if they burnt down in a garbage fire, but *tonight*,' she grinned.

He laughed, his eyes fixed on hers. 'Not very. Actually,' he amended, 'about as attached as you are to yours. I'm hoping it's friends for you too, right? No boyfriend is going to come out of the woodwork and punch me in the face?'

Oh my god, Mira. She'd completely spaced about going back to her. Noticing her panic-stricken expression, The Man grinned and said, 'You forgot about them, didn't you?'

'Her!' she smacked her forehead. 'Just one. She's outside with a work friend I bumped into. Hopefully she's still with him. Oh god, it's been more than an hour — I'm awful!'

'An hour, ouch.' He grinned. 'I'm sure she's worried. Am I the reason? I couldn't have taken a whole hour ...' he prodded, knowing perfectly well he hadn't.

'No, I just kind of split to da—' she stopped, wondering if the fact that she'd left a group of people to dance by herself would make her come off as extremely strange.

'To?' he said, unrelenting.

'Well, to dance,' she conceded.

'By your ... self?' he said, visibly confused. He looked as though he wanted to ask a follow-up but had thought better of it.

'You're wondering why I wouldn't bring my friend,' she explained. 'Well, for one, I prefer to be alone because it's easier to sort of, um ... get lost in it?' she said, hoping that didn't sound as fruity as she imagined. 'And also, Mira hates it, so she would've ruined it by hurrying me up,' she added.

He smiled and looked at her quizically. 'I'd like to know more about that later. I mean, if you'll tell me ...'

Something about his tone seemed warm enough for Faiza to want to tell him right then. 'It's hard to explain but I like the ... swirl of the whole thing. The darkness and the music, and the bass that's so intense you can feel it under your feet. It's like your senses are heightened because everything's so saturated with volume and flashes of bright lights through the blackness of it ...' she stopped, realizing she probably sounded like a pretentious moron.

'I sound like a pretentious moron.' She laughed. 'It's just ... a nice way to be alone.'

He smiled again. 'I have a thing I feel the same way about, so I get it. And no.' He raised an eyebrow. 'You really don't. Usually because pretentious morons never think they sound that way.'

He grinned and she suddenly felt a weird pang in her stomach, but it was a good weird. The feeling one gets when their middle-school crush accidentally brushes past them in the corridor.

Suddenly her phone rang, something it only did when someone called more than twice in a row, because she perennially had it on Do Not Disturb. Fuck, Mira.

'I'm so sorry, just one second,' she shouted over a mellow remix of 'No Diggity'. 'Mira, I'm texting you. *I'm texting you I can't hear you,*' she screamed into her phone and hung up.

'Just give me one sec,' she signalled to The Man, as she walked away, simultaneously opening Mira's growing text chain. She skimmed through all the annoyed *Where are you?*s and *Faizu wtf!*s and quickly texted her back: *Met someone, talking. Are you okay?* She'd barely sent the text when Mira replied with a thumbs up and a wink. A second text followed in seconds. 'But come up soon.'

Now that she'd checked on Mira (and got her blessing), she felt more at ease. And, she realized as she walked back to The Man, she also felt ridiculous for still not knowing his name.

'All good?' he said, his face furrowed in concern. *He really is cute,* she thought again, feeling that familiar spreading of warmth in her stomach she did when she really liked someone.

'All good,' she assured him, and then, before they could forget again, added, 'And I can't believe it took me this long, but hi, I'm Faiza,' she laughed.

He laughed too, the same thought suddenly occurring to him as well. 'Dev. Nice to meet you.'

He really is so cute, she told herself as he bit his bottom lip.

'So, Faiza,' he said, his half-smile back on his face. 'Will you dance with me?'

Something about the way he said it made her fight her instinct – to laugh at that cheesy line. Instead, she found herself taking his hand and leading him to the dance floor. In a moment of perfect timing, the DJ switched from a throbbing EDM-esque remix to an R&B-disco song by an Australian electro duo she loved. 'Oh my god, I love this song!' she shouted, sure he wouldn't know it but hoping he would like it.

He smiled and nodded at her. 'Me too!'

Please. She cocked an eyebrow and said, 'Oh yeah? Who's it by?'

'Midnight Pool Party,' he replied with easy confidence. 'It's called "Vulnerable". And, before you ask,' he held up his phone that was locked and blank-screened, 'I didn't Shazam it.'

She couldn't explain why she did it. Maybe it was the fact that he loved this song when no one she knew had ever heard of it. Or maybe the lyrics were starting to get to her.

'Do my best to not show you I'm vulnerable.'

Maybe it was the fact that she had wanted to since the first time he'd grinned at her.

She leaned in and kissed him. For a second, she couldn't feel him kiss her back and it made her panic. *Fuck. Fuck fuck fuck*.

And then, surely, he kissed her back. He looped his arm around his waist, drew her close and kissed her again. The music swirled around them as she took in his woody scent, the softness of his lips, the warmth of his body …'

She pulled back. She could feel herself blushing, which was new.

'I should really find my friend,' she said coyly, looking up at him.

He looked almost dizzy, like he'd been spinning in circles and had suddenly stopped.

'Um, yeah, we should,' he agreed. 'But to be honest,' he said, lowering his face to her ear, 'I really wish we didn't have to.'

In lieu of a response, she turned around and grabbed his hand, leading him away from the dance floor and towards the door. As they made their way up the stairs to the roof, she was desperately tempted to turn around, but held back. She wanted to seem cool, in control, and turning back would ruin the effect.

As they pushed through the crowd, she caught sight of Mira's pinkness and headed in her direction. She was still with Nikhil, and evidently another ardent suitor had joined the ranks.

'Hi, hi, I'm *so* sorry, I'll explain,' Faiza said in a rush as she reached Mira, who looked nowhere as distraught as she had sounded via text. Laughing, with what was clearly her an umpteenth cocktail in her hand, she seemed unperturbed by Faiza's disappearance – and completely in her element.

'Where were you?' she asked in a strangled voice, still smiling. She then flipped her hair as she turned to Faiza, a manoeuvre she often used when she wanted to cover her mouth. 'Your friend is extremely boring. When I first saw him, I thought, "Why has she not?", but now I know exactly why not.'

Faiza smiled at the three guys, who introduced themselves uninvited. They had moved on to small talk about how much this bar had changed, so Faiza turned back to Mira.

'Who's the other dude, then? Some rando you found?' Faiza asked, giving him a quick sidelong glance. The preppy guy, with his polo shirt, short-cropped hair and vacant expression, didn't exactly scream excitement. But maybe she was just being judgemental.

'Ugh, he's your Nikhil's friend from school. They saw each other at the bar when he'd gone to get me a drink and it's been all 'Bro? Bro!' ever since.' Mira rolled her eyes. 'Also, you didn't tell me he was a Dosco. Hard pass on Doscos always, you know that.'

'So, what, it's been a total wash?' Faiza suddenly felt wary about telling her about the impulsive kiss. It was always a little awkward when it only worked out for one of them.

'Pretty much,' Mira sighed, but then gestured her head in Faiza's direction. 'But I like what you found,' she grinned.

Faiza rolled her eyes, just as her phone started to buzz. She looked down at the screen, which was flashing her creative director's name.

'Oh fuck.' There was panic in her voice. 'Something is wrong if he's calling at this hour,' she said, as the screen kept flashing angrily. 'I need to take this; I'll just be back,' she said, already on the move.

She had to head all the way out of the bar and onto the road to find a quiet spot to calm her extremely agitated boss's nerves about an angry email from a client. Even though it wasn't her fault, her creative director had found a go-to in her, someone who could be worked into every problem, knowing Faiza would handle it. It took almost half an hour of going through several email trails, cooing and handholding to get her to agree to 'deal with it in the morning, when you're calmer'. It was only when she hung up that she realized she'd been gone for thirty-six minutes and could've very easily lost Dev in that time.

To Mira. It struck her out of the blue, with an uneasy pang, as she walked back in and saw the two of them laughing, her hand on his shoulder. It was irrational, but she suddenly felt very aware that technically Mira had clocked in more time with him. They'd been chatting for over half an hour. But at least she hadn't kissed him. Or had she?

Well, finders keepers, Faiza thought, crossing over to them, her stomach feeling queasy as it might right before a maths exam.

'I'm so, so sorry; that was my boss. Ish.' She shook her head. 'But no more of that tonight.' She held up her phone and made a display of putting it away in her bag.

Mira rolled her eyes at Faiza and looked over at Dev. 'She says that, but just watch her jump when that wretched woman calls again. Girl, you need to set boundaries with that bitch!'

Ordinarily, that kind of comment from Mira wouldn't have bothered her. But today it irked her because it seemed like a put-down.

'Well, we all have our assholes,' she said, snapping back. 'Like that mansplaining investor of yours. I'd have slapped his face off; I don't know how you can stand to smile and nod at that piece of shit. You're enabling him, you know.'

It was a bit further than she'd wanted to go. She almost sounded petty. Clearly, this man would now think she was an unstable sociopath and Mira was, well, Mira. Or at least, the version of Mira she'd created for the opposite sex. Mira for Men.

But Dev surprised her by smiling. 'I know this kind of man.' He nodded in sympathy. 'I just really hope I'm not the type.'

'You're not,' Mira said, sipping on her drink as she locked eyes with him. 'I can tell.'

Her flirting was making Faiza nervous. It simply wasn't fair. They had always had a tacit understanding, one that had served well for years since they liked the same kind of guy. First come, first served – or, if there was no clear timeline – no one served.

Another hour passed, and it became clear with every passing moment that Mira and she were in a contest. Mira clearly wanted him and was barring no holds, as Faiza was trying (without coming off desperate, she hoped) to reclaim what had started out as *her* liaison. As the crowd started to thin out and the lights slowly began to come on, the end of the night stared them in the face – a time for decisions.

'I'm going to the loo. Come with me?' Faiza announced, refusing to give Mira a choice. She dragged her best friend to the ladies' room on the lower floor and shut the door behind them.

'So,' she said, opening up her bag and pulling out her lipstick to refresh it. 'What is this behaviour?'

'What behaviour?' Mira feigned surprise, leaning up against the counter. 'He's really cute – I like him. Is that a crime?'

'Mira, seriously? Fuck off.' She was surprised at how annoyed she sounded. They almost never fought about men.

'Wow, jeez, don't be such a bitch!' Mira clapped back.

'You saw what it was like out there. There were no decent guys. None. And if you hadn't stuck me with that idiot friend of yours, I would've found this boy myself.'

'Well, you didn't fucking find him. *I* found him and I'm not going to fight you for him,' she said, sharply. 'That's why we have our rules. So we don't fight over guys.'

Mira stared at her thoughtfully. When the silence had become too long, Faiza finally snapped. 'So are you getting a cab home, or do you want us to drop you?'

'I have ... an idea,' Mira said slowly, clearly still thinking it through as she said it.

Faiza raised an eyebrow. 'I'm not letting him choose, Mira. We're not meat.'

'No, idiot, as if we'd present ourselves like baboons. I'm thinking, let's ... share him.'

'You want me to send him to yours tomorrow after I take him tonight? Well, that's fucking disgusting.'

'I'm thinking more like ... we *both* take him tonight. Together.'

Faiza stared at her vacantly for a second, and then, when realization hit, she yelped, 'Fuck, no.'

'Just listen for one minute before you go mad—'

Faiza was too busy shaking her head fervently to let her finish. 'Mira, no. *Fuck* no! You cannot be *this* sore a loser. It's actually unhealthy,' she said, almost breathless from talking at warp speed. 'Yes, we like the same man – it's happened before and it'll definitely happen again, but just *no*. In this case, I clearly found him. I ran up to you because I was worried you were alone. And now you're just being a little bitch!'

Mira waited for her to finish and stared at her in exasperation.

'*Ho gaya?*' she asked. Faiza let out a deep breath, saying nothing.

'If you really want him, I'll back off,' Mira said, her voice calm. 'But I actually think this could be really fun. Think about it. You've always wanted to do a threesome—'

'Yeah, but not with *you!*' Faiza interrupted.

'... and I've done it, so I know it can actually, like, not be weird,' Mira finished, ignoring her. 'It can be massively fun, and it will be. You can't deny he's into both of us.'

Well, no, she couldn't, but she'd be damned if she didn't try.

'You're being mental.' She shook her head again. 'Like, forget everything else – you think we'll be fine tomorrow? Just casually fuck each other like we're randos from a bar and go back to having brunch at Olive the next day? It'll change everything, Mira.'

'Not for most people, no, but it would work like that for us, man. We're the only two people in the world who are chill about sex. And we trust each other. We've seen each other naked a zillion times, we've slept together in *chads*, we've made out drunk. If anything, it's the most natural next step.'

'As if,' Faiza scoffed. 'That's the shit the creepy boys joke about. It's not something you'd entertain or is it?'

Mira looked sheepish. Faiza's eyes widened to saucers. '*Is it?*'

'Uff, calm down. Not actively, but in passing, yeah, sure. Like every man we've ever dated has thought about it, so have I.' Mira shrugged. Faiza was about to say something, but Mira quickly cut her off and continued, 'Let me put it this way: I thought my last threesome was fun. Easy. And I think it would be easier with you because I trust you more than anybody, trust you with my body ... you know? I feel like I would be free with you and that would just mean great sex for everyone. Consider it before you just shut it down.'

What happened next was a blur, something that seemed to be happening on a screen in front of her, not actually *to* her. Somewhere after her tentative 'yes', Faiza remembered being whisked away from the bar by Mira and Dev. Then a dazed car ride, the awkward giggles, the heavy flirtation, the upbeat salsa song on the radio interspersing their voices. She didn't even recall asking Dev. Mira must've done it and come off as the coolest girl in the world. By the time they'd stumbled into Mira's house, the two of them were laughing at something and Faiza was still feeling a bit fuzzy. But it was too late to back out.

Shots, Faiza thought, realizing she needed far more liquid courage than she currently had to see this through. 'Shots!' she said aloud this time, and the two heartily agreed. Three measures of discount tequila later, she was fuzzier than ever. But it had worked – she felt braver.

Brave enough, in fact, to push down her anxiety and jump in. While she was mid-sentence, Faiza leaned over Mira, who had (naturally) planted herself next to Dev on the couch, and kissed him. *God, he's a good kisser*, she thought, her body responding to him, leaning into him. Mira leaned back, watching.

And funnily enough, it didn't bother Faiza.

She pulled away from Dev, who looked dishevelled from her hands in his hair and her lipstick on his mouth. She looked at Mira, who just looked back at her and smiled. Faiza leaned in, drew Mira's face close to hers and kissed her.

They'd kissed a million times before: as a joke at parties, as a form of affection, and to Faiza it had always been as natural as a hug. But tonight, something shifted. The kiss changed from its usual familiar shape to something stronger, and she couldn't pull away. She kissed her hard and Mira kissed her back with an intensity that almost threw her. They kissed so long that Dev eventually started stroking her back, begging to be included.

It only made sense, then, for Mira to kiss him. Mira leaned over and pulled him towards her and they kissed long and slow. Faiza felt a little uneasy, like the pang one gets in their stomach the minute one realizes they're getting bad news. She shook it off; Faiza had expected to be jealous, so it shouldn't have surprised her. She wanted back in.

Faiza pulled Dev away gently and gave Mira a look. She put his hands on her waist and moved on top of him, letting her hair fall gently to the side, caressing his face as Mira watched. While they kissed, she pulled Mira in, moving her hands to her breasts.

For a second, Faiza felt a rush. It was unlike anything she'd known. She let go of Mira's hands and let them wander over her body, the rush intensifying until it almost made her dizzy. She had to remind herself about Dev for a moment, that he was there, he was why this was happening.

There was music in the background, and Faiza knew from the slow, erotic beats of the song that it was from Mira's 'Bedroom Jams' playlist. They'd made it together one lazy Saturday afternoon, but Faiza never thought she'd actually hear it again.

She pulled away from Dev and went back to Mira. This time, she felt clearer, less hesitant. She moved over Mira, drawing her body over hers until they were lying flat on the couch together, Faiza on top. It felt like her body was on fire and she kissed her harder than ever because she needed to put that fire somewhere. Mira kissed her back, just as ardently, pulling her so close their skin started to feel like it was melding.

To Faiza, it felt like an out-of-body experience. Like she was watching it happen in a way. But at the same time, it was less cerebral, deeply physical, as if every inch of her body was on edge, responding sharply to every whisker of movement, every soft burst of breath.

Her feelings were floating fragments, never really coming together to make a concrete one. Part of her was in shock. That it was *Mira's* hands that had made their way under her dress and freed her from her sexy, date-night bra. *Mira's* soft tongue was exploring her mouth with soft, furtive pushes. *Mira's* taut stomach was writhing under hers as she felt herself grow more and more aroused. Her best friend, so deeply linked to her life, her childhood, her past. A link that had, until now, been platonic.

It was surreal. It felt like the beats of the perfect song, the kind you become obsessed with and play on loop. It was so instinctive, so thrilling – the kind of moment that gives you goosebumps, except it wasn't a moment. It was every second. It felt so natural to take off Mira's clothes and hold her naked body against her own. It felt so natural to let their fingers slide into each other's, breaking from their furious kiss only to stare into each other's eyes. So natural to come, faster than she ever had, more intensely than she knew she could, as Mira's fingers moved frantically inside her.

When it was over, when they had both brought each other to a more frenetic climax than they had ever described to one another on their sleepovers, the haze cleared. Suddenly it was the two of them again in the cold reality of the dim apartment lights. And it was clear that a line had been crossed. One that could never be crossed back.

Dev, who had been touching himself as he watched, seemed to have thought he'd waited enough. He climbed on top of them, kissing Mira over Faiza's shoulder. But Faiza had snapped out of it. She was no longer there. She pulled away gently and moved over to another couch under the guise of watching them.

They kissed and Mira's fervour was as intense as it had been with Faiza. It stung her unexpectedly hard. She watched Mira moan as Dev looked at Faiza, who was sitting with legs coyly crossed, trying to stay in character. But watching them became more difficult by the minute. He started to kiss her all the way down her body and Mira cried aloud with pleasure.

For a moment, she tossed her head back and looked Faiza in the eye. Faiza suddenly felt a surge of delicious pleasure. He kept kissing Mira but Mira kept watching her. Faiza suddenly found herself aching for her again. But just then, Dev drew himself up to his full height over Mira. He was hard and Mira wanted him, so what was going to happen next was inevitable. Faiza couldn't understand why her eyes were pricking with tears, or why she suddenly felt she might throw up. All she knew was that she needed to leave.

As she walked away towards her room, she could hear Mira suddenly moan, sharply, intensely, and she knew exactly why. It made her nauseous and angry and jealous beyond anything she'd ever felt. But not jealous of Mira. Of the man that was fucking her.

For a moment she couldn't get her head around it. Everything she knew about herself and their friendship, stopped her from understanding it. To be bothered by it seemed alien, like waking up one morning with a deep desire to skydive after disliking heights your whole life. It had come out of left field and she felt like she'd been punched in the gut.

As the sounds from the living room grew louder, Faiza's heart grew heavier. She had never felt this lost. It was like this moment had shaken her world up like a snow globe and now everything was up in the air, unsettled.

She was staring into an abyss, with no idea what it was or where it would leave her. She didn't know if it was love. She didn't know if it had always been love, and that idea was far too terrifying to even think about. She didn't know what it meant, what it would mean, or why it hurt so much to hear Mira's soft cries outside, each one like a knife twisting deeper into her gut. The only thing she knew was that it had turned out exactly as she'd feared at the start. The night had changed *everything*.

TEN

THE GIRLS SAT in silence, the story still sinking in. They had
reached the restaurant soon into the story and, when a menu-
bearing waiter came beaming and proclaiming, 'Welcome
to Rohu, what can I get you?', the three had haphazardly
ordered 'margaritas all around' to get back to Faiza's story
as quickly as possible. Now, with the second round of their
drinks drained, the place finally began to seep in. The
twinkling fairy lights, the woman crooning 'Imik Simik' by
Hindi Zahra, the pinewood tables peppered with candles that
gave off the aroma of cinnamon and warm vanilla sugar –
all finally began to register. It was a beautiful place, open-
air and breezy, but the girls were too enraptured by Faiza's
recollection of her night with Mira to really notice.

'I'm waiving the two-question rule,' Faiza said with
kindness. 'Nattu alone had a hundred, so go ahead. It's okay.'

'Good,' said Rubani. 'Because you know I have a big one.'

'I think I might know what it is.' Faiza smiled.

'I think you might, too.'

'Oh, just ask it already!' Saira was frustrated.

'Are you bi?' It was only natural to ask. Rubani had met
only too many girls who would be only too happy to make

out with her at a party one day, but firmly insist they were 'straight as an arrow' the next. Faiza, though, never seemed the type.

The corners of Faiza's mouth upturned in what might possibly have been a smile. She tucked a lock of hair behind her ear and cleared her throat gently.

'I thought about it a lot after that night. And I decided, most likely not. I tried to recall my growing-up years – had I always been attracted to women? Was I just too fucking stupid to notice until Mira? Then I realized that, sure, there were little things – I always notice women, and I often think they're beautiful – in fact, I was thinking that just the other day on the boat, about you guys.'

'Really?' Rubani was surprised.

'Yeah, I thought that all of you idiots have very little self-esteem for hot girls,' she smiled.

'Speak for yourselves,' Saira complained. 'I've become a complete cow, stuffing my face with prawns at every meal since last week; it's sick, man.'

'Anyway,' Rubani shot her a look.

'Yes, yes, sorry, more important things – but also, prawns reminds me,' Faiza said, waving her arms wildly and catching the attention of one of the cheerful waiters scurrying past with his coconutty-curry-laden tray that left a wonderful fragrance in its wake. She ordered enough for an army and made an exaggerated motion to indicate that her attention had been fully restored to factory settings.

'You were saying you can think women are beautiful without comparing yourself,' Rubani prompted.

'Yeah, that sounds a bit weird, I know,' Faiza said. 'It's

more appreciative than competitive. A few times before that night, but especially after it, I tried to visualize myself with a woman. Kissing her, touching her, going down on her – it didn't repulse me or anything, but it just didn't do anything for me. Not the way thinking about men does.'

Rubani smiled. It had always been her belief that everyone was at least a *little* gay; it seemed unnatural for them *not* to be. In the beginning, she had worked to reconcile herself to the idea of being bi – especially in the years before she'd slept with a woman. She had always dismissed her impulses as mere curiosity. It was only when a straight friend introduced her to Garage84 – which she'd taken her to as a 'fun, Friday night gimmick' – that she realized how at home she felt around other queer people. And then, years of conversations with the friends she started to make there had helped her understand her sexuality – and sexuality in general – better. Over time, it became absurd to her that attraction could be limited to binaries, but she didn't consider herself educated enough on the subject to voice her opinion. It did, however, mean that she completely understood Faiza's attraction.

'Sigh. It's a very sad fate in life to be attracted to men,' Saira tsk-tsked.

'I swear.' Faiza shook her head. 'I also think that's why the Mira thing freaked me out so much. It was an anomaly. I couldn't understand it.'

'Is she that ex-best friend you said you didn't speak to anymore?' Saira asked. 'Is that why you stopped talking?'

'Yeah.' Faiza touched her nose, like a correct guess warranted in a game of charades. 'Not like *right* after that night, but that's what fucked everything up.'

'She's one of those straight girls, isn't she?' Rubani asked, her voice scathing, thinking of her own past. 'Those girls that make you feel like you're disgusting because you're into them.'

'I don't know if that's what it was,' Faiza said. 'I tried telling her one night when we were out, but she acted too drunk to remember the next. I think it was mostly me. I started backing off. I was too afraid of what it meant and of the fallout if I actually tried to make her talk about it. I would've been humiliated if she laughed at me. I mean, she was my best friend, you know?'

'I completely get it, though.' Saira nodded, snapping a stick of lavash from the herb-scented bread basket in half.

'I really do,' Rubani said, meaning it. 'The idea is painful enough. Actually, dealing with—'

She stopped short, suddenly noticing a familiar figure walk into the restaurant. She was flanked by what looked like family members on either side, with a toddler who couldn't have been more than two perched in the crook of her arm. Her formerly tall, athletic body had that touch of extra weight that the years bring upon even the best-intentioned people, and her hair had changed from black with strands of sun-bleached brown to an even-toned salon shade of amber – but it was definitely her. She'd know that husky smoker's voice and that familiar crinkle by the eye anywhere.

Rubani slid down a few inches in her seat, hoping that Saira's mop of curly hair would shield her from view. It was unusually flat today and refused to serve its peripheral vision-blocking purpose.

'Oof, Saira, wash your goddamn hair,' Rubani grumbled.

'Why are you randomly being a bitch?' Saira shot back.

'Asha is here,' Rubani said, her voice deliberately low.

'Who the fuck is ... ooooohhhh,' Saira said, placing the reference.

'Wait, who?' Faiza looked around, confused. 'What's happening?'

'Haider, stop!' Rubani said, her voice strangled. 'I don't want her to see me. I just can't ...'

Rubani's blood had run cold. Now that the woman had turned several times to talk to the man beside her (*Brother? Husband?* she wondered), she'd confirmed it was indeed Asha. The very girl who had spurned her hopeful advance and shut her down hard in college. Having to exchange pleasantries after a decade and a half of absentia, especially one that ended with a mortifying moment like that, was near-unbearable.

'Can we get out of here, please?' Rubani pleaded, her tone frantic.

'Okay, yes, um, of course,' Saira said, quickly springing into action. 'Let me just cancel the order.' She waved her arms wildly again – and caught Asha's eye.

Asha squinted, as if to confirm she was indeed seeing Rubani and smiled when recognition dawned. She leaned over to say something to her husband-slash-brother and handed over the child, waving back in their general direction.

'Oh fuck,' Rubani breathed. 'Fuck fuck fuck, she's coming over. Saira, what the fuck!'

'I was just trying to get us out of here, man!' Saira insisted. 'Ironically, a waiter popped up right then and Saira sent him away with a sheepish grin.

'Baan?' Asha called out, as she reached their table. The familiar nickname was as much a punch to the gut as seeing her face up close again.

'Asha, hey,' Rubani said, desperately hoping she didn't sound as shaken as she felt.

'I can't believe it's you, Baan,' she said, circling the side of the table as her arms reached out for a hug. 'What's it been – ten years?'

Thirteen, Rubani thought, trying to calm her thumping heart. Asha pulled her in for a hug that immediately made Rubani feel like she had fallen back in time. It was first year, and they were on her tacky, floral-printed bedsheet watching *Gossip Girl*. The swirl of scents that was Asha ensconced her: the faint aftermath of the jasmine oil she used on her hair, her cocoa body butter, the woodiness that her skin seemed to emanate unprompted by bottled perfume. She remembered it all too well. Rubani almost recoiled but reined in the instinct.

'This is crazy, though!' Asha exclaimed again, either oblivious to or consciously ignoring Rubani's restrained reception. 'Saira!' she said, her tone a touch overfamiliar for the two brief times they'd interacted 'How are you? You look amazing!'

No comment on me, Rubani registered. *Maybe she's afraid that if she says I look nice, I'll accost her in public.*

'You look great too,' Saira said politely. 'It's good to see you.'

'Hi, I'm Asha,' she said, stretching her hand out to Faiza. Faiza smiled and introduced herself.

'So what are you doing in this neck of the woods?' asked Asha, as they moved a little to the side and away from the table.

'Holiday with the girls.' Rubani smiled, looking over at them.

'Ooh, fun! What's the occasion?'

Rubani considered not telling her, but then decided to.

'I just broke up with my boyfriend.' She shrugged. 'And I needed a break from the city. They dropped everything and came with me,' she said, realizing that they actually had done just that. Her heart was suddenly full of fondness for her friends, for their commitment and ability to prioritize her, despite everything else in their lives. She glanced over at them. They were trying hard not to look like they were spying and pretending to be inordinately interested in one of Faiza's dog memes. She smiled at them, feeling a sweet sense of comfort.

'Oh wow!' Asha exclaimed, surprised, possibly on hearing Rubani say 'boyfriend', a reaction she was hoping for. 'That's so great; it's been donkey's years since I've had a girls' trip, man! We struggle to get together for lunch only once a month, if we can.'

Social protocol demanded that she ask questions in response, so she went with the one she was most curious about.

'So, um, who are you here with?'

'Oh, right! My husband Varun and his parents. And, of course, Vishal. It's his third birthday in two days, so we decided to make a week of it. We try to do a family trip once a year, at least.'

Rubani took in her family. Nearly-three Vishal was picking his nose. Husband Varun had slumped just enough for his paunch to be the centrepiece of the table. The in-laws looked comfortably disinterested in the place that seemed perhaps a touch too young and lively for their dinnertime tastes. And then she looked at Asha. Really looked.

She may not be unrecognizable, but time *had* changed her. Her once-smooth skin, which Rubani had fantasized about running her fingers down on many a night huddled in front of the laptop, was now giving way to fine lines, crinkled more at the corners than before. Her eyes, sparkling in her memory, had lost a little of their teasing glint and sat on a bed of soft shadows. Her posture, which had been stately in her mind's eye, had bent slightly with weariness. Her mouth was probably just the same, but it no longer made her lose her train of thought as she vividly imagined kissing it.

Rubani smiled. 'That's great, Asha. I'm so happy for you.'

'Thanks, Baan,' Asha said 'And you seem to be doing so great! I mean, I'm sorry to hear about the break-up, of course …'

Asha trailed off in a manner deliberate enough to imply she'd like details. Details Rubani didn't feel inclined to give.

'I think it was for the best,' she said and realized that while it still hurt too much to feel like that right now, it probably was.

'Oh, okay, of course, I just assumed …' Asha said, a little flustered.

'That's okay.' Rubani smirked, resisting the urge to use the old adage about 'ass'uming.

'But it's really great to see you,' Asha tried to recover. 'You look amazing.'

'Thanks! Changed the hair.' She grinned, revelling in the deliciousness of not returning her compliment. A fact that registered, if Asha's face was anything to go by.

'Well, it suits you,' Asha said.

The words hung in the air just a fraction of a second

too long to pass for normal. Rubani felt strangely free, like she'd been terrified of seeing a ghost every time she looked up in the mirror, and now that she actually had, there was nothing scary about it. The Asha she'd built up over years of ruminating, amidst self-flagellation for her impulsiveness, was but a whisper lost in the cool Bangalore air of thirteen years ago. The woman standing in front of her had, on paper, the life Rubani thought she'd wanted: the partner, the child. And yet, seeing it waiting at a table across from her, it made her realize it was exactly where Asha had believed she was destined to end up. And where *she* no longer needed to be. She looked over at her phone, where Natasha had texted saying she was *running to them, because how is it suddenly cold now?* and smiled.

'Well, good running into you,' Rubani said. It was time to return to her friends.

'Oh my god, yes, I'm so glad we did,' Asha said with enthusiasm. 'Message me if you're ever in Cal? We'll get lunch. It'll be good to properly catch up.'

'Sure, sounds like a plan,' Rubani said, her tone overly sweet.

Asha insisted on taking Rubani's number, saying that she would text, and finally hugged her and went back to her Norman Rockwell table. Rubani came and sat back down at her own table, letting out a long, exaggerated sigh.

'Fucking A, man,' Saira said, with a low whistle. 'Asha of all people.'

'Saira caught me up,' Faiza said. 'It must be hard to see her after so long, *na*? Are you okay?' she asked gently, placing a hand on Rubani's shoulder.

'Funnily enough, yeah,' she said, a slow smile spreading across her face. 'I mean, honestly, I've been afraid of running into her for years. I had this very *Music and Lyrics* speech also, about what I'd say if I saw her again.'

'What was the speech?' Saira asked.

'Well, um, mostly fuck off,' Rubani grinned. 'With a couple of extras like "You're a presumptuous bitch" and "I can't believe I cared so much about you," etc.'

'Did you say any of it? Did you legit tell her to fuck off?'

God knows she had thought about it, when she'd visualized her own version of Charlotte's 'I curse the day you were born' speech to Big from *Sex and the City*. She had thought about running into Asha for years, at different stages of her life; the film-diploma cinema-nerd phase at Xavier's, the partying edit intern at Horizon Productions, the only-girl-creator-at-Boys-Club phase, and in her 'now' phase; the calmest, most collected version of herself she'd ever known. Each time, she tacked on a new addendum: about assumptions, about having power over her, about the cruelty of her reaction. But in the moment today, caught off guard, she realized she'd transitioned to a different phase altogether.

'No, weirdly, I didn't want to,' Rubani said. 'I guess … I don't think I feel angry at her now.'

'*Really*?' Saira frowned in disbelief, remembering the broken pieces of Rubani from thirteen years ago clear as day.

'Eh, I mean, not as much as … I don't know, pity sounds condescending. Y'all will call me judgemental again.' She rolled her eyes.

'What did I miss, friends?' A breathless Natasha sat down, tossing her bag onto the table and sloughing off her heels like dead skin. 'And, *vaise*, why did you all just ditch me? By the way, there's a bread-omelette guy on the road behind – smells *divine*.'

'You were practically halfway down that dude's throat,' Saira said, waving her off. 'And we needed a quiet place for Faiza to tell her story. But bro, you missed a shit tonne ...'

Saira quickly recapped the events of the night while Rubani tuned out of the conversation and into the moment. The woman singing had just come back from a break and her rendition of 'Don't Know Why' by Norah Jones was hauntingly beautiful. The buzz of quiet chatter laced through it, and everywhere she looked she saw various versions of holiday faces: the always mildly stressed-out families trying to manage their offspring, the couple that had run out of things to say, the couple that was not interested in talking, the bevy of boys celebrating their friend's last moments of freedom before he tied the knot, the solo traveller, in this case an older ash-blonde man with a bun scraped high and a multi-coloured kurta she'd seen versions of at the roadside stalls. He caught Rubani's eye and smiled at her warmly. She smiled back, enjoying the moment of familiarity with a stranger.

'So anyway, that was the point at which you burst in with all your noise and drama,' Saira summarized. 'Now we'll go back to Rubani, please, okay?'

'Sorry, Bani, oh my god, tell me everything, baba. I don't even know how you're still sitting here,' Natasha said, reaching over and squeezing Rubani's hand.

'You were saying we'd call you judgemental?' Faiza gently prompted.

'Yeah,' Rubani said. 'I think I just felt a little ... I don't know ... sad for her. Like, it doesn't seem as if her life is unhappy – and who am I to say in any case, but it just seems ... so normal. And not in an enviable way. I'm sure her husband is nice, she has a great kid and all, but is that all there is? Is that what I would've been in some years if I'd married Kabir? If so, I guess I'm glad I didn't. I don't know what life I want exactly, but it's not that.'

Saira was smiling from ear to ear. Rubani was afraid to probe.

'What? I'm a terrible person?' she asked.

'No, I mean, it's uncanny, because I was saying something spookily similar to Haider when you were talking to her.'

'As in?'

'As in, the whole thing looks so ... ordinary. It's like all the boxes of life have been checked and – now what? You know?'

'*Please*, you were not saying that,' Rubani scoffed.

'No, she was,' Faiza said, in defence. 'Which actually was nicer than what I was saying.'

'And what was that?' Rubani asked, curious.

'That she's like a four at best,' Faiza smirked. 'Sorry, I can be an asshole; I don't know her, I don't care about her. But Bani, you are way out of her league. You either have very little self-esteem or terrible eyesight.'

The three girls laughed.

'You *are* an asshole,' Rubani said. 'And I love it.'

'Was she hotter in college or what?' Natasha tried to recall. 'I just remember not liking her weird, printed kurtas.'

'You just never liked her in general because of what

happened,' Rubani said with fondness, suddenly feeling very lucky. She had the urge to look over at Asha's table again, but stopped herself. Her eyes settled instead on a beautiful woman, in a flowing white kurta and printed pants, sitting by herself and drinking a glass of red wine. There was something incredibly attractive about her, something graceful in her movement as she sipped on a glass of Rioja with her blush-pink mouth, the warm colour in her slim face that didn't seem store-bought, the way the wisps of hair that escaped her low braid fell softly across her almond-shaped eyes.

The woman caught her eye, and Rubani instinctively felt the urge to avert them; it had become second nature to her as a bisexual that every look – however innocuous – could be misinterpreted. But the woman only smiled, raising her glass slightly in Rubani's direction. Rubani smiled back, nodding in acknowledgement. She wondered what the woman was doing alone at such a pretty restaurant.

'Well, it's hard to like anyone whose closet's staple colour is muddy brown,' Natasha said, snapping Rubani out of her trance as she tossed her hair for additional 'bitchy' effect.

'Stop it, you guys!' Rubani said, blushing, but laughing at the same time. 'She's right there!'

Rubani's eyes moved involuntarily to Asha's table, where she saw the former love of her life sneaking glances over the tall, bamboo-spined menu and quickly looking away.

'Fine, whatever, don't let us bitch about her,' Saira said. 'But one thing is clear, okay? Sorry, it's petty, and I don't give a shit, but you won at life. You're hotter, practically famous, smarter, everything-er. You owned this bitch.'

Rubani looked at the three girls in her corner, her three best friends who had come through for her so spectacularly, and who she knew would do it all over again if she asked.

'Yup,' Rubani smiled, pulling them into a group hug. 'I did.'

ELEVEN

'I CAN'T BELIEVE we only have three days left, ya!' Natasha said, neatly folding a dress from a slightly askew pile of pastels on the bed. Last-minute packing wasn't for her; she preferred to have things in order so that everything just needed a quick pulling together as the holiday ebbed.

Faiza, who preferred never to unpack in the first place, pulled out a pair of raven-black wayfarers from the side pouch of her mammoth duffel and plonked it on the bridge of her nose. 'It has really fucking flown by, no?'

There was a knock on the door. Natasha pulled it open to find Rubani and Saira mid-conversation.

'Can we go, please?' Saira asked, tapping her foot impatiently.

'We really should,' Rubani pressed. 'Traffic is already looking bad.'

'Okay, yes, just hand me my sneakers and we'll bounce,' said Faiza.

Forty-five minutes later, the girls walked into The Goa Collective, a weekly flea market that every local friend of theirs had recommended. 'Tourists love it,' they had said with a smirk, and the girls had decided to believe them instead of taking offence. Saira had been a few times – and had witnessed its descent into wholly mainstream, piece by piece, over the years – but she still enjoyed going. She had texted both Warren and Maxime to meet them there. She'd wanted to spend time with Warren to compensate for the terse atmosphere the fight had created – they had guised it well, but Rubani's storming off had tipped him off that the afternoon had turned sour. Maxime she simply wanted to see again, and though nonchalance was great, she was on the clock.

The girls all had friends in the city, so the group decided to spend a day apart to meet them; they didn't want to risk a clumsy group dynamic that quartered off into awkward factions. Of the segmented drinks and lunches, only one had spilled over into today – Faiza's ex – now friend, Ishaan. Natasha knew him, and the others had met him before, heartily encouraging her to invite her chilled-out, gin-brand-owning former beau to hang out with them, 'provided he brings gifts', Saira had suggested with a wink.

I will come bearing bottles of my finest libations, he'd texted back with a martini glass emoji when Faiza relayed the conditions.

'Ugh, we're hanging out with boys today. I don't want to see boys anymore,' Rubani complained.

'What is this, middle school?' Faiza grinned.

'*Girls are best, jaan lo, baat yeh maan lo*,' Natasha sang. Pulling out a number from her endless repertoire of Bollywood songs was a gift only she herself appreciated.

'Speaking of "girls are best",' Saira said, rolling her eyes and turning to Rubani. 'How's it going with your Tinder girl?'

'Honestly, quite well!' Rubani answered, her eyes brightening. 'She's fun to talk to. She likes a lot of the same things – R&B music, my kind of TV – except *One Tree Hill*; she hates that for some reason. She's even seen a bunch of my videos on Goddess and, apparently, always thought I was cute. But, like, I don't know if she's just saying that.'

'Bani, don't have her babies just yet,' Faiza said wryly, as they wandered into a stall with S&M-esque leather jewellery on display. 'Shall I get this for Zaden?' she asked, holding up a dog-collar choker with metal spikes. 'Very him, don't you think?'

'Totally.' Natasha smiled. 'Goes perfectly with his perfectly pressed white shirts, *na*?'

'But this is all very relationship-y,' Saira complained. 'You were supposed to have fun with the next person, remember?'

'I know, I know!' Rubani protested. 'But to be fair, she hasn't asked me any, like, "serious" questions. It's mostly just pop culture things, and we send each other memes and stuff.'

'Have you sexted at all?' Faiza asked. 'You might want to do it quickly, establish that vibe.'

'Before it goes into *shaadi* zone,' Natasha teased, as Saira's phone started to buzz.

'Hello?' Saira answered, stepping away to hear clearly. The girls wandered around the store, thumbing through studded harnesses and bondage handcuffs. Saira returned with Warren in tow.

'Look who I found!' she announced happily.

'Warren! It's so good to see you again!' Natasha said warmly, giving him a hug. Faiza followed suit, proclaiming she loved his Gone Fishing T-shirt.

'Hi Warren,' Rubani said, a touch shy. 'I'm so, so sorry about that day. I was really badly behaved, but in my defence, it was just … a bad day.'

She really had been mortified. She had probably come across as a manic hothead, the kind of person for whom a dramatic storming off mid-meal was second nature. As someone who usually tucked her desire for confrontation neatly into her lapels in order to present as good-natured; incendiary was the last thing she wanted to seem. Especially to him.

'We all have them.' Warren flashed her a kind smile. 'On mine, I turn into the Hulk and start crashing around madly, throwing spices. So your reaction is much more relaxed in comparison.'

'I promise I almost Hulked out, but I didn't want to take it out on those beautiful prawns either,' Rubani teased.

'Oh, my prawns can handle it.' He laughed. 'And besides, at least we have a chance to make up for it now.'

Rubani laughed back, her cheeks turning just the slightest shade of pink.

Saira looked at them thoughtfully for a second. *Am I imagining things, or is there a vibe here?*

She glanced over at Faiza and Natasha for confirmation, and found the two caught up in the conundrum of whether or not to go through with the gag purchase of a tight-laced BDSM corset. She rolled her eyes.

Now Faiza's phone buzzed. 'Oh, Ishaan's here,' she said, checking her texts. 'Where should I ask him to meet us? Not here – he'd have a field day and complain about how we never did kinky shit when we were together.' She sighed.

'I take it we're meeting an ... ex?' Warren ventured tentatively.

'Unfortunately, yes.' Faiza laughed. 'I haven't been able to shake him off for a decade.'

'Maxime is also here,' Saira said, opening a notification. 'Should we just go and get them?'

They walked up to the entrance and collected the two. Ishaan and Faiza looked surprisingly organic together, Rubani thought; she could see them as a couple. Both tall and lean, his dark hair shorter than hers and curling at the ear. She seemed sleeker than him, though; there was a relaxed air to his body language that Zaden's powerful frame had likely never known. Introductions were made, and a trip to the makeshift cocktail bar ensued, its counter laden with premixed pitchers of margaritas and cosmopolitans, coated in sheens of moisture. When every member of the group had a drink in hand, a decision was made to split up in order to do the different things that everyone felt like doing. Faiza and Ishaan headed towards the live music arena to see the band in action up close; Saira and Maxime left to wander through the shopping stalls; and Rubani, who'd had her eye on the big, blazing barbecue in a corner of the market, took Natasha and Warren with her.

'So,' Ishaan said, turning to Faiza as they made their way past a group of dreadlocked men speaking French and eating cotton candy, 'how's the Z-man?'

Faiza rolled her eyes again, this time on hearing him employ a nickname for Zaden she'd always hated.

'He's good!' Faiza said. 'He's just opened up another place in Lodhi Market – sushi, sashimi, the whole nine. Got a fantastic chef in from Osaka whose negiyaki is to die for.'

'Henh?' Ishaan said, making a confused face. 'What are these words? What is Nagasaki?'

'Negiyaki, you philistine.' Faiza laughed. 'It's this pancake-type thing – really good. Come visit one day and I'll give you a discount.' Her eyes sparkled.

'Discount! What a *cheapdi* you are. You better give me free meals, being married to the boss and all.'

'Who says *cheapdi* anymore? Been a while since you left Delhi, no, you fucker? Don't know the cool slang anymore?'

'But thank god, man. Imagine. I was always miserable there, you know it. I mean, except for …'

Ishaan trailed off, but Faiza knew what he was implying. Their time together had been good – the one thing that had saved them from the tedium of the jobs they'd hated at the time and fractured family dynamics. Sex had always been at the core of their relationship – beginning with casual hook-ups that led to a year of seriousness and eventually devolved into a comfortable, friends-with-benefits dynamic that had served them well until he jumped ship to Goa to start his distillery. Several years and other relationships later, they were still in each other's lives. And while those lives had carried on, the intimacy remained.

They walked into the crowd, parting it as they made their way right to the front of the stage. A Queen cover band was playing – a dismally pale imitation, so they drifted away, choosing seats at the back in order to talk.

'Yeah, yeah, I know. I really was the best fucking thing to happen to you,' Faiza said, fluffing her hair.

'Um, hello,' he said, brandishing the bottle of gin he was holding and waving a hand over it. 'Award-winning gin brand? Voted best craft gin in the country in 2020? Ahem, ahem?'

'It's been three years – get over it,' Faiza laughed.

'But really,' Ishaan said, his tone serious. 'You were. No one was ever ... you know ...'

His words pulled at a thread Faiza had always known was there – she'd just never let herself tug at it. But something about this moment, the ease of it, the familiarity of his space, the warmth of his touch as he looped his hand in hers, let her go there.

'Do you ever wonder ...' Faiza began, then stopped.

'All the time.' Ishaan smiled wistfully, squeezing her fingers. 'Do you?'

'Not all the time,' Faiza said, avoiding his eyes.

'But ... sometimes?' he pressed.

'Yeah, sometimes. Everyone wonders sometimes. What we had was pretty brilliant. It was just ... timing, I guess.'

'I guess ...' he sounded unconvinced. 'I didn't think you wanted "serious" at the time. I think maybe I didn't push hard enough.'

'Oh, you pushed pretty fucking hard at first.' Faiza exhaled a whoosh of air. 'I just wasn't ready. I was too young and unhappy about so many things. It wasn't something you could've fixed. I think you started to understand that later.'

'Would you have moved to Goa?' he ventured suddenly. 'If I had asked?'

'Well,' Faiza said quietly, 'you never asked.'

Their silence would have been tersely loaded had it not been disrupted by a blaring, unambitious rendition of

'Bohemian Rhapsody'. The moment was at a crossroads and Faiza wasn't sure which way she wanted it to turn.

'Plus, you had to meet the Z-man,' he joked, steering the moment back to a safer track.

'That I did,' she said, a smile playing on her lips.

'You're happy with him,' he said, almost as a statement, as if meant to be a reminder to himself to keep his feelings in check.

'I am,' Faiza said, with feeling. 'Very happy.'

'Much happier than you would've been with me. I mean, it's no fun being with a distiller, I'm sure. The hours are long and slightly nuts ...'

'Yeah, because life with a restaurateur is so predictable.' Faiza smiled. 'But, um, are you single? You haven't really mentioned anyone lately.'

'There is no one to mention, man.' Ishaan clucked, shaking his head. 'I was seeing this girl, Samira, which lasted a few months and then got weird as shit, but no one since.'

'Samira, I remember, but that was almost a year ago. No one since? Really?' Faiza realized her tone might be bordering on pity, so she quickly reset. 'You want to end up an old maid?'

'I'm ready for Bharat Matrimony, buddy; leave it to mumma,' he said, with comical effect.

'So, I'm guessing just casual shit since then,' Faiza said, with a touch of jealousy she was working overtime to camouflage with feigned insouciance. 'It's not like you to be celibate for a year.'

'Oh, you got that right.' He laughed, his familiar dimples reminding her of how attracted she once was to him. And startling her with the effect they still had.

'It's just,' he started, shifting in his seat, 'I haven't really found anyone else I wanted a future with. Someday, maybe,' he said, averting his eyes.

She saw an opportunity to investigate the term 'anyone else' light up like a glowstick, but looked away on purpose.

'Absolutely,' Faiza said. 'We'll have her over for negiyaki.'

A few yards away, Saira and Maxime were strolling through a stall full of vibrant tie-and-dye clothing. She marvelled at how comfortable it had felt to speak to him; conversation flowed from art to Goa nightlife to her job with the ease of a current that knew its path; no snagging, no sudden crashes. She regretted not calling him sooner, not seeing him on her day apart from the girls and filling the space with the group of young designers she hung out with every time she was in Goa. *It's good networking*, was the excuse she always gave herself, but in contest with the way she felt around Maxime, it didn't pass muster.

'Would you really wear this?' Maxime held up a bandana with a fuschia and indigo mandala. 'Is this what fashion people wear?'

'Well, "fashion people" don't appreciate being reduced to a type,' Saira scolded.

'Fair point,' he said, putting the bandana back. 'I'm guessing you get that a lot.'

'A lot,' she sighed. '*Devil Wears Prada* was a curse. God bless that movie, though,' she said, kissing an imaginary cross and pointing it up to the sky. 'Great movie. Best movie. Best Meryl Streep. But the number of people who thought my job was frivolous because of it was exhausting. Fashion has history; it's art in the most interesting way because it ties into everything – politics, culture, queer history, self-expression, feminism, religion. I guess it was one of those movies that was seminal for fashion, but the protagonist leaves it because she is too "smart" for it. That irritates me, because it adds fuel to the "fashion-is-for-idiots" fire, you know?'

'So, basically, it's not accurate?'

'It is, in a way, for American fashion magazines and *that* culture – although not entirely for them either. But Indian fashion mags are very different. We don't have that closet, for one. And we *definitely* don't all eat fucking six-calorie salads.' She gestured to her own figure. 'As you can tell.'

'Whatever you're eating is working, so please don't stop,' he smiled. *A good response*, Saira thought. It met her exacting standards, which would've been irritated if he had said he hated salad-eating women, or even that he liked women who really *ate*. Women and their relationships with food were always layered and complicated, in her opinion, and whatever they might be, a man's take on it didn't need to factor in.

'I mean, anyway, it's a subject I have a lot of feelings for,' she joked. 'A story for another time.'

'I'd like that.' He smiled warmly. 'We'll get pizza and watch *Devil Wears Prada* and you can point out everything objectionable about it.'

Regret dug its heels in deeper.

'Listen, what are you doing tomorrow night?' she asked on an impulse.

'Packing for a bit, because I'm flying out the day after, but nothing else,' he shrugged. Deeper and deeper they went.

'Why, what do you have in mind?' he pursued.

'I was wondering if you'd want to have dinner with me?' she asked.

'Hundred per cent,' he said. 'I've been wanting to ask since that night at Silent Noise, but I was afraid you'd say it was a girls' trip and you couldn't.'

'I didn't take you for such a chicken,' she teased, whacking his arm and moving closer.

'Oh, I'm absolutely a little chicken when I really like a girl.' He grinned. He was close to her now, so close that she could feel his body breathing hers in.

'Well, lucky for you, I'm not afraid of anything,' she said, looking up so her lips were just inches away from his.

'Then I guess I should stop being afraid to do this.' He smiled, as he leaned in and kissed her.

It was the kind of kiss that jolted her out of time. She'd felt it maybe once before in her life, but it had been so long ago that she'd forgotten its impact. It was all-consuming; every part of her body and mind was caught up in the spiral. The scent of tobacco in his cologne, the clearly identifiable traces of Dove shampoo in his hair, the taste of his mouth, a whirl of gin, lemon and cotton candy. It was heady and delicious enough to make her forget that she was standing in a flea market in India, with strangers gawking at their locked lips and walking past with hurried feet. It was intoxicating enough for none of that to matter.

'Are those two … seriously? *Sabke saamne?*' Natasha said, watching Saira being tipped over by Maxime as they kissed furiously outside a colorful stall behind which stood a slightly perplexed owner. 'Bani, look. *Look!*'

Rubani, vexed at being pulled away from a conversation with Warren about collaborating on a food video for Goddess, looked over only to be taken aback. Saira was kissing Maxime like they were at the end of a hardship-filled romcom and had found their way back to each other, and she immediately felt jealous. Not about Maxime – she really liked him for Saira. But of the gay abandon with which Saira was kissing him. With Kabir, and everyone before him, she'd always been so cautious about PDA. Hand-holding was just about okay, but the one time a liquored-up Kabir had planted a very French kiss on her at a party, she'd been mortified. It had dissolved into a fight, one of the many they'd begun to have. She glanced at Natasha and, from the expression on her face, knew her friend felt pretty much the same way.

'Oh Saira.' Warren shook his head sagely. 'I hope that French guy's a decent bloke.'

Rubani was surprised to feel a tinge of jealousy, now very much about Saira.

'You're worried about her?' she asked gently.

'I guess I'm protective of her,' he said with a fond smile. 'Especially in Goa, because guys are always hitting on her. But she hates that, of course. Me being protective, I mean. I don't think she minds the guys.' He chuckled.

Rubani's chest tightened a little. She'd spent most of the last hour talking to him about everything, from her career to why he'd given up working at Nobu to come back here – enough for Natasha to maintain some distance, like she was now. She hadn't really noticed him at his house through the haze of anger about the fight, but she was really enjoying his company. That he was just being nice to her as the friend of a friend – a friend he was probably attracted to – hadn't occurred to her.

And why wouldn't he be? Saira was stunning six ways to Sunday. Full-figured Saira, with breasts that a B-cupped Rubani would have killed for, beautiful curly hair that was longer than her own would ever grow, and a Scarlett Johansson-esque mouth that was blush-pink without lipstick. When you partnered it with her personality, that somehow managed to be effortlessly cutting and life-of-the-party at the same time, she was so much more instantly desirable. It only seemed natural that he was harbouring feelings for Saira; she'd been stupid not to see it.

'I was wondering why that hadn't happened,' Rubani said cautiously.

'Why *what* hadn't happened?' Warren asked, looking mildly confused.

'You and Saira,' she tried to keep her tone even. 'Must be the protective thing,' she said with a forced laugh.

'Oh god, no,' Warren moved his hands in a crossing motion. 'Saira? That would be like hooking up with my baby sister. We've known each other too long, man. And besides, it's just not that type of vibe with us. I love her to death and all, but she's like family. Sometimes like a child too, because she's such a brat.' He laughed.

Relief coarsed through Rubani's body like the first stream of a perfectly hot shower. She couldn't quite explain why this felt like such good news – she'd barely known the man a minute – but it did. And it felt like news that had to be celebrated.

'Duly noted,' she said, her eyes sparkling as she looked

directly at him. It was an aberration for her; she always preferred it when the other person made the first move.

'Nattu?' she called out to her friend, who was pretending to be extremely interested in a batch of plastic-wrapped cookies. 'Do you want to go karaoke?'

'Oh my god, *yes!*' Natasha, who was clearly bored, exclaimed. They had done it on their girls' trip all those years ago, and she knew she could count on Natasha to be drawn to anything with the faintest trace of nostalgia.

'I'm texting these guys to meet us at the gelato stall,' Rubani said, her fingers already zipping furiously across her screen. 'Warren, come with us?' She looked up at him, a mix of attempted coyness and genuine earnestness.

'Well, I'm a really, really bad singer ...' Warren said. But then he grinned. 'So, yes, absolutely.'

TWELVE

THE BAR WAS a lot seedier than she remembered. Granted, they had never come in sobriety, but surely alcohol could only cloak a place in so much fond reminiscence, Natasha thought to herself. It didn't seem like the place had been bursting with a plethora of shifty-eyed men who stared unabashedly at the girls as they walked in wearing shorts and dresses. She suddenly felt very glad that they had the three men with them, each somewhat intimidating in their own way, to serve as a shield.

'Shall we get a table outside? *Far* outside?' Rubani urged, mirroring Natasha's hesitation.

'Yes, please,' Natasha said gratefully. They cut across the sticky, beer-soaked floors of the restaurant, throbbing with the sounds of clattering plates and running children. Perhaps it had changed immensely, but if memory served, it had once had lots of chipper tourists and locals who had sung with them as they bawled out tone-deaf versions of 'Wonderful Tonight' and other forgotten relics from their parents' generation. It certainly did not have this lethal blend of noisy families and leering men that created a vortex of palpable discomfort.

Once they made it outside, the tables on the beach weren't as bad – a reprieve from the uneasiness of the indoor space, but connected enough for them to be served. Because of its slightly unsexy location – far from the maddening metropolitan-traveller crowd – the people at this karaoke bar, except for the diners, were a mixture of locals and tourists who were looking more for a fun evening than a 'conceptual experience'. It was a touch grimy, but easy in a way Goa only used to be about ten or twelve years ago, Saira mused.

'And the reason is … *youuuu*,' yelled a group of inebriated thirtysomethings, revelling in the throwback song every millennial knew almost by rote.

'Why does everyone sing the same five songs at karaoke, I wonder,' Warren mused.

'I know, right?' Rubani shook her head. 'This one, always. And "Wonderful Tonight". And "Don't Stop Believin'". Oh, oh, and "Livin' on a Prayer".'

'Also, anything by fucking Nickelback,' Faiza scoffed.

'*Fuck* Nickelback,' said Saira, who was a few drinks ahead of the rest, owing to her flask and a bottle of Coke they'd picked up en route. 'I want to sing some pop. You can't judge me! I'm gonna sing Britney.'

Maxime smiled at her, bemused. 'You simply must. I'll sing with you – I know all the Britney songs.'

'Really?' she said, her eyes hopeful.

'No, not really.' He laughed.

'Bastard,' Saira pouted. 'You men are all bastards. Even the good ones.'

'Hear, hear!' Faiza and Rubani raised their glasses in solidarity.

'Hey!' the three men protested in a chorus of hurt tones.

'Not all men, right?' Natasha said defensively. 'Not Alex, or Zaden.'

'That's nice.' Ishaan grinned. 'Don't worry about us, we're just chopped liver.'

'Nope,' Faiza disagreed, ignoring Ishaan. 'All men. Even them. Maybe they're like thirty–forty per cent less bastards, but men are *born* bastards. It comes with the privilege of being a man – they don't experience the world like we do. They have this fucking entitlement that comes free with having a dick, and that makes them insensitive. Can't explain it.'

'Haider, I fucking love you,' Saira said, reaching over and hugging Faiza. 'Only this girl understands me!'

'That's not fair, though,' Warren protested. 'Would it be okay to generalize all women?'

'Oh, like that's ever stopped you "bros"?' Saira said defiantly. 'You guys generalize us all the time! Women are needy, they're emotional, oversensitive. They're PMSing – that one's my favourite.'

'My favourite is "You're not like other girls,"' Rubani smirked. 'You have no idea how much I hear that from guys on dating apps. All you need is to have short hair and be bisexual and suddenly "you're not like other girls".'

'Damn. All through my teens I thought that was a compliment,' Ishaan said softly to Maxime, who was shaking his head.

'I had an older sister,' Maxime said in response, smiling. 'She knocked a lot of sense into my head.'

'Mine is, "She's asking for it." Men love that one, don't they? Anything goes awry and, "Man, she was wearing such a short skirt, she was asking for it."' Faiza clucked her tongue.

'All men don't say that! They don't believe that!' Warren protested again.

'No, it's true,' Natasha said, a bit subdued. 'I grew up with a lot of that. Papa always had a problem with me wearing anything that exposed my legs. If I wore a slightly low-cut top even, he'd say "*Beta*, take a jacket."'

'It's one of those things – like, Faizoo, we say whatever, but it's our job to protect ourselves, no? I can only wear this,' she gestured at her thin silk sundress with a neckline that plunged deeper than the Titanic, 'when I'm here. Even then I have my shawl.'

'That's awful,' Maxime said. 'That's not how it should be.'

'Most guys don't get that, though,' Rubani said softly. 'Like, there's this fear I feel every time I enter an elevator alone and there's even one man. If there's more than one, and no women, I feel so nervous till I get to my floor. I can't explain it …'

'I know that one.' Saira nodded in agreement. 'I once got into a fight with a marketing guy because he was like, "Oh babe, same! If I was in an elevator full of women, I'd be terrified! Women are so intimidating, they'd probably judge my outfit and make me cry."'

'These men *toh* I can slap till their faces crack,' Faiza said, shaking her head.

'Men don't *really* say oblivious shit like that?' Warren looked aghast.

'Oh, you'd be surprised,' Faiza said. 'It's everywhere. And honestly, it's very often the little things – things men say with a disclaimer of "I'm totally a feminist, but …"'

'Fuck yes!' Rubani pointed excitedly at Faiza. 'It happens

to me at work all the time. If I'm in a bad mood, I must be on my period. And once, I wore this T-shirt dress to work – which was a bit short, but oversized – and this guy who makes these awful videos appropriating queer content all the time but he's actually straight – looked me up and down, sighed and said, "I shouldn't; you have a boyfriend."'

'UGH.' Saira shook her head, taking a large sip.

'The minute they know you're bi, of course, you're *extra* easy. You're the girl that's probably at bars kissing girls to the left and seducing their boyfriends to the right, who's had more threesomes than lunches, who flirts with everyone and their uncle – and aunt! I sometimes think I'm quite boring in comparison to whatever the fuck straight boys think I am.' She laughed, and Faiza sniggered in unison.

The three men seemed visibly upset – partly at the character assassination of their gender at large, and partly at the experiences the women had had.

'Okay, sorry, sorry,' Rubani said. 'I didn't mean to make it a "men are bastards" rant. I guess we all have this conversation often, just not usually in front of men.'

'I mean, I don't mind talking about it at all,' Ishaan offered. 'It's just … kind of messed up. I think I speak for all the men at this table when I say that we try to be good guys. I suppose there's always so much involved. Stuff we don't really account for.'

'The elevator thing, for instance,' Maxime added. 'I legitimately had no idea that was a thing. I've been in so many elevators with women, and I smile to be nice. I didn't think *that* was what was running through their heads.'

'Do all women feel this way?' Warren asked.

'Um, you can never say all,' Natasha treaded with caution. 'Some women might feel differently about some aspects. But then, for a lot of other women, things are far worse – we come from undoubtable privilege and it's *still* scary, so I can't even imagine what it's like for …'

'But the bottomline,' said a slurring Saira, sipping on her fifth G&T, 'is that men are bastards.'

'Men are bastards,' the men at the table said in unison, laughing.

'Sorry on behalf of my sex,' Warren said, leaning into Rubani's ear. 'We'll try to do better.'

'Good,' Rubani smiled back. 'I can start by giving you individual lessons. First class: Don't tell us to smile more.'

'Noted.' Warren grinned. 'I think we should pencil in the next lesson for tomorrow? Over dinner, before you go?'

'We'll see,' Rubani said with a demure smirk. 'I might have a PTA. But let me tell you tomorrow morning?'

'I'm happy to wait,' he said, his eyes twinkling.

'Ey! You two! Stop your *khusur-pusur*,' Natasha said, taking Rubani by the hand, and tugging at Saira's with the other. 'Let's go. We're up.'

'What do you mean?' Rubani looked alarmed. 'We're singing?'

'We're *singing*!' Saira declared, an inch away from a 'whoo'. She grinned at Natasha, trying her best to make a serious face. 'It had better be Britney, bitch.'

'Next up are Natasha, Saira and Rubni with "Baby One More Time",' the emcee's voice cut through.

'It *is* Britney, bitch!' Saira threw her arms around Natasha, planting a sloppy kiss on her cheek. 'I love you, Nattu. Let's *go*, Bani!'

'Yeah, go on, *Rubni*,' Faiza smirked.

'Rubni! Oh my god, I'm dying,' Saira snorted with laughter.

The three made their way up to the stage, struggling through the sand. The others followed suit, keen to see the performance up close. They positioned themselves near the bar, for easy access to the shots that Faiza made them promise to do every time Saira said 'whoo'.

'I'm ordering two rounds, but I know we'll need more.' She laughed.

'You're still an asshole, eh?' Ishaan smiled fondly, finding her hand and looping his own through it.

Faiza's heart quickened just a little, but she did a phenomenal job hiding it. 'Always and forever, baby.' And she didn't pull her hand away.

The girls belted out a chaotic rendition, too bestrewn with giggles and off-timed starts on each new verse, to be anything remotely close to an enjoyable listen. After Saira's first three whoos, Faiza had hastily declared the drinking game a misstep – but Maxime and Ishaan wouldn't let her cop out. Saira finished with five whoos altogether, and the results were a set of people now visibly more inebriated than the singing contingent.

'What the hell happened to you lot?' Rubani asked, walking over to the belly-laughing foursome who were terribly amused by Warren's budding moustache.

'These three think I can't grow a moustache,' Warren said, pouting. 'But you see it, don't you?'

Rubani pretended to make a careful study of Warren's upper lip, which was as smooth as a teak desk in an army general's office. His mouth, though – just full enough with a tiny black dot on his upper lip – looked infinitely kissable. She cleared her throat with feigned importance.

'Um, yes, very good moustache,' she nodded sagely.

'It's getting there!' Warren protested.

'Bani prefers clean-shaven guys, don't you, Bani?' Natasha teased, bumping her shoulder playfully. Rubani turned seven shades of red in quick succession.

'Oh, well, in that case,' Warren grinned, 'I don't think it's really getting there.'

Rubani smiled. It felt like seventh grade – that rush of liking a boy in class and looking for little clues that he might like you back. Pretending to be bashful when your friends teased you about it, but secretly lapping up the simple tensions it created with the person you had a crush on. *I do have a crush on him*, she realized, to her surprise. It was a nice feeling, like climbing the rungs into a pool and finding the water warm and welcoming. She let herself sink in and be immersed in it.

A little ways away, Saira was humming the bars of another Britney number and stirring her cocktail, which was eighty per cent ice water at this point. Maxime walked up to her, brandishing a fresh caprioska, making Saira's face light up.

'A man after my own liver,' Saira said, leaning back and lauding him with gentle applause.

'I figured you'd want a new one. This is essentially *paani*.' Maxime smiled.

'Ugh, it's so weird. You sound so Indian when you say *paani*. And then you say Paris and it's like I'm in a Goddard film. Say "Paris",' she commanded.

'Paris?' Maxime looked confused. He pronounced it *'pahree'* as he had the first time, and Saira could swear she felt her nether regions skip a beat.

'See? *Paani, pahree, paani, pahree.*' She rotated between exaggerated accents. 'What is this sorcery, Maximus?'

'All the better to get a second date with you, my dear.' Maxime grinned, baring his teeth.

'Why do you want a second date with me, huh, Maximus? You're only going to go back to Colaba. And I'm definitely not going to Colaba.'

'That Delhi–Bombay animosity again, huh?' Maxime smiled.

'No, no, I like Bombay. It has great bars. And cute boys.' She waved a hand in his direction, and Maxime took a mock bow.

'But I don't live there …' she trailed off.

'True,' Maxime circled the rim of his whisky with his fingertips. 'But I don't think that should be a reason for us not to see each other again. At least, it isn't for me.'

Something about the way the dim bar lights cast a warm glow over him as he said that made Saira's heart melt. His beautiful skin which, if one looked closely, was ever-so-slightly freckled across the nose. His cavalierly tousled hair that looked like it could use the running through of a comb – but would survive just fine without it. And his eyes – always the first thing Saira sought out – that forever danced between two colours, playful in their duet. They were a soft, deep blue right now, and filled with sincerity.

'Maximus?' Saira said, feeling suddenly vulnerable, and too hazy with alcohol to curb it. 'Why me? Why do you like me?'

'I don't understand,' Maxime frowned.

'Like, why me, out of the four of us? Is it because you met me first? Like is it a "dibs" thing and you think it would be rude to hit on my hotter friends? Because I know Natasha said she was married but it's an open marriage, so like, I get it if—'

She was stopped suddenly by a kiss. It felt as if someone had spun her around for five minutes – like that game she'd played as a child – and then released her. Everything was spinning – the only difference was that she didn't want it to stop.

'You,' Maxime said, his voice low and intense, 'are the hotter friend.'

'I am *not*,' Saira said, her face hot with delighted embarrassment.

'You are. You're completely out of my league, and if you let me take you on a second, sober, date, I will list out all the reasons why.'

For a writer who never found herself at a loss for them, Saira had no words. She leaned in and kissed him, this time intense and unabashed. She had no idea how long they'd been kissing when Natasha broke them up and jokingly asked if they would like to come up for air.

'Uh … sorry,' Saira said, flushed and extremely turned on. She held on to Maxime, unwilling to let him go. He clearly had no desire to either.

When Natasha turned her back to get them a fresh round of drinks, Saira pulled him close and lowered her voice so as to be out of her earshot. 'Come home with me,' she said with a slight slur in her speech. 'I'll tell Rubani – she and Warren can go hang somewhere.'

'Nope,' Maxime shook his head with conviction.

'What?' Saira exclaimed, a little louder than she had intended. She cleared her throat. 'So after all that, you're going to reject me?'

'I'm not going home with you when you're drunk. Let me take you out tomorrow. And if you want me to go home with you then, I will.'

'Ugh, please don't be a gentleman tonight – I am *saying* I want you,' Saira almost growled. 'You have my consent!'

'Yeah, your drunken consent,' Maxime said, kissing the top of her head and pulling her close.

'Well, you're drunk too! So then it counts, doesn't it?'

'No,' Maxime said fondly. 'But tomorrow I will be a slave for you, Britney.'

Saira squealed at the reference, kissing him again.

Faiza looked back at them as she and Ishaan made their way back to the table. She felt happy for Saira. She had liked Maxime from the moment she met him. Catching a quick burst of their conversation as they'd passed them by – a randy Saira trying to convince Maxime to come home with her as he gently turned her down – had only made her like him more.

'Saira's definitely kidnapping that boy, eh?' Ishaan grinned, as they settled into the unravelling cane chairs at their table. The distinction between the old Goa restaurants and the sleek new ones that had sprung up for the bougie urban tourist was often most apparent in elements like these: furniture sourced from neighborhood markets often on its last leg versus pieces flown down especially from some architect's studio in southern Spain.

'Not if he has anything to say about it. He's currently trying to persuade her into going out with him tomorrow.'

'Decent dude – I like his vibe.'

'Same,' Faiza agreed. 'Turning down the drunk girl when you're also drunk is a good-guy move.'

'Ouch, that hits me right here.' Ishaan thumped a hand over his chest.

'Oh, please, that was different,' Faiza scoffed. 'We were together. We both wanted it.'

'Our drunk sex was amazing, wasn't it?'

It had been. He'd set a bar many carnal passers-by had almost never managed to cross, both with and without spirits involved. Faiza had missed the sex for a long time after they had split, scouring the apps for men that looked like him only to find them a pale imitation of the original. They hadn't slept together in almost ten years, except for the one time she'd been in Bombay for work, just after she'd met Zaden, but before she started dating him. It was a wild night, a celebration of all the marathon sex they could have only with each other, barely stopping for water every so often to replenish their thirsty bodies through the night. The sex with Zaden was sublime, but with Ishaan it had been raw and unfettered. Borderline animal on certain days. It was enough to make her think about him sometimes even as Zaden's body moved against hers, and enough to make her feel a stomach-turning guilt every once in a while.

'It was.' Faiza smiled politely, in a tone akin to agreeing that someone 'had a lovely home'.

'Can I tell you something?' His voice dropped a few notches.

Faiza, suddenly feeling the impact of her multiple shots, stared at him weakly as if to say, 'Go ahead.'

'I think about it a lot. The way we used to fuck.'

It was as if a flash of heat suddenly seared her entire body. Just hearing him say the words had a visceral effect; she didn't even notice that her body arched slightly as she felt his breath on her ear. It was a dangerous moment.

'You two just abandoned me!' Natasha came shuffling up through the sand, one hand bearing her impractical heels while the other carefully balanced a margarita.

'Sorry, man, I was dizzy from the shots.' Faiza had never been more glad to see her best friend. She looked so chipper and breezy, with no idea that she had just pulled her from the cusp of a game-changing mistake.

Ishaan, looking visibly thrown by the interruption, cleared his throat. 'Can I get you guys your next round?'

'I'm good!' said a tipsy, oblivious Natasha.

'Jack and Coke?' said Faiza, her voice breaking nervously at the last syllable, unable to meet his gaze.

'Faizoo! I love you!' Natasha said with glee, wrapping her arms around her neck.

'I love you too, Nattu,' Faiza smiled. And by god she meant it.

THIRTEEN

THE SADNESS OF the holiday ending felt like the close of summer vacation. The final night they'd been dreading had arrived. By this time tomorrow, Saira would be back home, prepping for her usual Monday morning meeting with her team instead of putting on her make-up for a night out. It was so bleak to think that in twenty-four hours they would be back amidst the smog and cold of a late-November Delhi, and the soft beach breeze and palm trees would be but a memory. It felt like a bit of a gut punch to Saira every time a trip came to an end – and this time the impact was worse because of Maxime.

She loved how his name had rolled off her tongue when they had made love last night. It had been as close to perfect as a second 'first' date could get, by her very specific standards. He'd taken her to dinner at a restaurant she loved and had mentioned in passing the night they'd met. Then they'd gone for a drink to a hole-in-the-wall local bar – the kind of easy, unpretentious place Saira usually ferreted out herself when she travelled. They'd ended the evening with gelato from a patisserie by Sweet Water Lake, talking for hours until Saira decided she didn't want to talk anymore.

They'd stumbled into his room so hard she'd hit her head on the TV-bearing mantel. They flowed in the opposite direction of romance-novel sex, beginning hard and rough the first time, slowing to soft and sensual by the third or fourth – she lost track as the night wore on in one intoxicating blur. She rushed out in the morning under the guise of being late for brunch with the girls, because she had no idea how to say goodbye to him. It was usually quite easy to sneak off without explanation as daylight hit. The difference this time was that she didn't want to.

So? Can I see you tonight? Even for a little bit? Maxime's last text glowed at her from her overbright phone screen, unanswered. She put the finishing touches on her winged liner and adjusted her sleek, mulberry boilersuit, torn between the deliciousness of seeing him one last time and avoiding the angst of having to part ways. She tapped her phone, thinking, but put it aside. This was a problem for later.

'You like?' she said, appearing with a little twirl before the girls who were waiting at the entrance of Paralía.

'Ooh, very nice,' Rubani remarked. 'I'm borrowing this.'

'Sure, but you'll swim in it,' Saira said, sizing up Rubani's tiny frame. '*And* you'll have to fold up the pants,' she said, squeezing Rubani's cheeks as the girls laughed.

'Asshole,' Rubani smiled. 'Okay, shall we head?'

They drove to the beautiful Anjuna restaurant that Ishaan had told them would be perfect for their final dinner. 'It's suspended over the sea and their xacuti is unreal,' had been his summation, and the burst of ocean views and local fare it offered seemed a fitting end to their adventure. The air had a particular scent that usually only wafted through the palms after a fresh August rain; except it was November and bone-dry. As they walked into the place, which was about eighty percent creaking wood and ceiling lanterns, they found their expectations satisfied. The space was charming, full of character and ideal for their last night.

'Such a pretty place, *na*?' Natasha remarked, as they settled into the ladderback chairs sinking into the sand.

'Reminds me of the places I used to go to with my parents when we were here,' Rubani added. 'In a good way, though.'

'Simpler times.' She sighed. 'I miss that feeling – hanging with your parents is different now.'

'At that time I was super irritated, man,' Saira said, shaking her head. 'I hated being a kid; all I wanted to do was be a grown-up. I used to keep telling myself I'll come back here without them and really have fun.'

Saira's parents, well-meaning but overprotective, had inadvertently meted out the kind of stifling diktats that an only child usually felt smothered under – and it only enhanced Saira's unfettered personality. The result had been years of sometimes successful (but often foiled) attempts to sneak out, constant conflict and a persistent desire to leave home the first chance she got. When she had, she'd wasted no time making up for the years she'd been kept on a leash – a trait that often shepherded her to recklessness.

'Which you did,' Faiza pointed out. 'Several times, if I'm not wrong?'

'Oh yes,' Saira wiggled her eyebrows suggestively. 'But now I think it was so nice to have someone pay for dinner.'

Rubani looked at her and shook her head in disbelief.

'I'm kidding – wow, Jesus,' Saira said. 'I miss lots of things.

Like, when Baga was actually chilled out and eating the alpine mousse at Britto's. Or the Infanteria bakery that my father and I discovered on one of our walks. And those older night markets! Man, those hippies who ran the stalls were so awesome. I barely ever go that side now because it's become disgusting – but I miss how it used to be.'

'I don't really miss the family stuff,' Faiza added softly. 'Family dinners were quiet. Always a little tense. Even on holiday. They still are every time I go home. I'd much rather have dinner with you guys,' she smiled.

After putting an order in place for as much crab xacuti and fish curry as they could humanly digest (and a rib-eye for Rubani, who'd not had her fill of red meat yet), the girls dove deep into conversation, probing each other on details about Ishaan, Maxime and Warren. Rubani was just finishing telling them about Warren, and how they had exchanged numbers with a promise to meet when he came to Delhi next month, when a familiar face caught her eye. It was the woman she'd seen at Bombil the same night they'd run into Asha.

The woman smiled at Rubani in recognition. Just like last time, she looked beautiful in that delicate, very chic Indian way that Rubani had always wished she could pull off. In a cream ikat-print dress that flowed softly down to the middle of her calves and a curtain of jet-black hair that went well past her narrow shoulders, she had the aura of easy grace that Maybelline couldn't manufacture – you had to be born with it. Her smile was open and friendly, sheathed in a coat of plum-hued lipstick, and made her pierced nose crinkle. Just like last time, she was drinking a glass of red wine. And just like last time, she was alone.

Rubani suddenly felt an urge to check on her. *It's Goa*, she thought. *No one should be eating alone.*

'Guys, this is random, I know, but would you mind if I asked that lady to join us?' Rubani asked. 'The one sitting by herself in the nice Anokhi dress?'

'Um, sure. But why? Do you know her?' Natasha asked, confused.

'No, I saw her at the restaurant that night we ran into Asha, and we just, like, smiled at each other. It sounds stupid, I'm sure, but she seems sweet. And even last time she was alone, so …'

'I mean, she could just want to be alone,' Faiza pointed out. 'Some of us are quite happy eating in our own company.'

'I know, yeah, that occurred to me but …'

'Go for it,' Saira offered, 'if you feel like it. It'd be nice to meet another fun person on the trip.'

Rubani walked over to the woman and introduced herself. A few short moments of chatter later, she indicated to the waiter to bring her new friend's order over to their table, and the two walked back to the girls.

'Everyone, this is Ahana,' Rubani introduced the woman as she smiled and held out her hand to each girl.

'I hope I'm not disturbing you,' Ahana said apologetically. 'Rubani was kind enough to ask me to join you, but I'm sure you must want some privacy.'

'Oh, no, no, we're very public people.' Saira grinned. 'And it's lovely to meet you.'

'Absolutely,' Natasha agreed. 'The more the merrier.'

'Besides,' Faiza said, 'We've had a lot of time alone together. So you're definitely not disturbing anything.'

Ahana smiled, sitting down between Rubani and Faiza. 'Still, it's very nice of you to have me.'

'Not at all,' Rubani pooh-poohed.

'So, Ahana, are you travelling by yourself?' Faiza asked.

'I am! My second time actually – I'm still getting used to it. I never really did it much when I was younger. But finally on my fortieth birthday, my daughter booked us tickets to Dubai as a present but ended up not being able to make it because of her exams. So, I decided to just go by myself. It was a little frightening, but I had fun.'

'That's so lovely!' said Natasha, who was surprised at the revelation that she was over forty. She wouldn't have put her anywhere above her mid-thirties, at a stretch. *She must have a fantastic skincare routine*, Natasha thought.

'I'm so glad you did!' said Saira, who one could always count on to be instantly personable. 'Travelling alone is my second favourite way to do it – the first being with friends, of course.'

'I still haven't done it, except for work, which doesn't count,' Natasha said wistfully. 'I think I'm just too daunted by the idea.'

'To be honest I would've preferred to have Alia – my daughter – with me,' Ahana said, tucking her hair behind her ear. 'But travelling solo can be quite nice.'

'How old is your daughter, if you don't mind my asking?' Faiza enquired.

'Twenty-two this Jan,' Ahana said, her voice ringing with pride. 'She's finishing her programme at the University of Edinburgh.'

'Ahana, let me say this on behalf of everyone at the table – you do not look nearly old enough to have a twenty-two-year-old child,' Saira declared with her usual candour.

'I have to agree,' Rubani nodded. 'You must have had her at twelve!'

'You girls have made my day!' Ahana blushed. 'I did have her young, at twenty-three. We got married at twenty-one. Well, *I* was twenty-one; Pratap was older, of course.'

'This one here also got married very young,' Saira gestured at Natasha.

'Too young by their standards, definitely.' Natasha smiled. 'I think none of them want to settle down till they're sixty.'

'I wouldn't say sixty.' Rubani grinned. 'But I certainly wouldn't have done it at twenty-four, Nattu. I thought you were mad at the time.'

For all her love for commitment, Rubani had still not seen reason in Natasha's early wedding. It wasn't Natasha's choice of partner she questioned – she had always liked Alex – but the quickness of it bothered her. In retrospect, all Rubani thought she'd known about herself at twenty-four was that she found it easier with men than women, but liked them the same. With men, there was little to no chance of being shut down; and few she'd seen an 'ever after' with at that point. With women, however, she always felt that she was risking rejection. She often found herself just a smidge unworthy of them – especially the ones she particularly liked. But even when she found a woman who reciprocated her feelings, the idea of being tied down at that uncertain age, in so permanent a way, seemed terrifying. It was, perhaps, she had thought shamefully, a luxury that the law didn't allow for it; a convenience she could hide behind if things came to that boiling point.

'I think it's so lovely that you girls have that freedom now,' Ahana mused. 'I often thought about whether it would have been better if I'd got married later, and had a few more relationships before Pratap.'

'Well, I'd personally advocate having less serious relationships and more, um, fun,' Faiza said delicately. 'That's one of those things you miss a little when you're in a long-term relationship.'

'Oh, I am all for it.' Saira raised a toast and a clink of glasses followed suit. 'I'm still doing it. Serious relationships are just …' she shuddered a little. 'Unless it's the right person, of course – but I just don't think I've really met him yet.'

'Yeah, I get it.' Faiza smiled. 'I used to be like that.'

'And then the right person came along,' Natasha cupped her face in her hands and fluttered her eyelashes.

'Faiza's been with her partner for – six? – *six*,' Rubani confirmed, 'years now. They live together,' she told Ahana.

'That's wonderful,' Ahana smiled at Faiza encouragingly. 'And I do think you're right. Having fun is important. It's something I often wished I had done more of! I felt guilty thinking about it after my husband passed, but …'

Ahana suddenly realized that she had given out a startling piece of information. The girls looked sombre and just the tiniest bit uncomfortable. There was a staggered chorus of 'I'm so sorry' and she felt like an idiot for bringing it up.

'It's been some time now, girls, but thank you,' Ahana said.

'You don't have to talk about it if you don't want to,' Rubani offered gently.

'I don't talk about it often, but it's easier to do it now. When I'd just lost him, my whole family would be very careful not to bring it up. We were just trying to get by, and thinking about it was very painful, so we thought it'd be better this way – focus on the good things in life.'

This resonated with Natasha, who had adopted that same approach after her mother's passing. People had thought twenty-one was the age where you could become mature through the process of dealing with the grief of losing a loved one with the suddenness of an eight-on-the-Richter earthquake. But Natasha had realized in retrospect that she had still been a bit of a child, one that needed her mother. The loss had shaken her, causing an all-systems shutdown, making her go into autopilot for two years. That is, until she had met Alex. He had held her hand and provided a certain peace with his quiet company on nights she couldn't stop crying. The days turned into months, and soon she had been able to think of her mother with fondness, and not through a wellspring of uncried tears.

'It was hard at first,' Ahana said, 'but over time I managed to find ways to get by. And I'm still learning,' she said with a wistful smile.

Dinner soon arrived, and Ahana passed her plate around the table like a generous parent, insisting that they should all try some. The conversation eventually shifted from the grimness of loss, due in part to Ahana's firm effort to row away from it. It now began to flow easily and soon glided into the experiences the girls had been having on this trip. Recommendations for restaurants were exchanged (Ahana had three more days in town), and the concept of Silent

Noise was explained to an incredulous Ahana, who eventually declared it 'too young' for her taste. Saira had taken a fast liking to her – Ahana didn't seem conservative or stuffy. She debated whether it would be okay to talk about the idea of Rubani having her first one-night stand with her – the vibe certainly felt comfortable enough. She texted the three on their group for their opinion, and while Natasha wasn't a hundred per cent, the other two gave her their blessing. *I don't think she'll judge*, Rubani texted back. *I don't think so either*, Saira replied and proceeded to fill Ahana in. Her response, to their delight, was promising.

'I say it should be Wags,' Saira declared. 'You two are flirting like highschoolers in heat.'

'Sai-*ra*!' Rubani was aghast, but Ahana just laughed warmly.

'I take it this is the main mission for the holiday, girls?' she asked, smiling.

'Well, it's more Saira than the rest of us,' Faiza said, spearing a prawn with her fork. 'But we all agreed fairly early on in the trip that it was a good idea.'

'I mean, only if she meets someone she *wants* to do it with,' Natasha said, careful not to offend Rubani again.

'And you think that should be, um, this Wags person?' Ahana said, looking confused by the name.

'Warren, yes, sorry – Wags is a nickname. *I* think so, but Rubani refuses to do anything about it. This is our last night, and madam has made *zero* moves,' she said, chomping on a piece of fish.

'She believes she's not a one-night-stand kind of girl, you see,' Faiza said, pointing her fork at Rubani. 'Not her style to have 'meaningless sex'.

'Well, I don't believe that's always true,' Ahana said with some hesitation.

'As in?' Rubani asked.

'As in, I don't think a one-night stand is meaningless,' Ahana suggested, making the girls like her even more. 'I'm not an expert, of course,' she added hastily, but was met with another staggered chorus of 'That's exactly what we've been saying!' Rubani shook her head and laughed.

'*You've* had them as well?' Rubani groaned. 'Am I the last woman on earth who hasn't?'

'Well, to be honest, I've only had the one – after Pratap passed. And I know this sounds exaggerated, but I would say *that* one night actually changed my life.'

Natasha nodded vigorously and Rubani playfully smacked her hand across the table.

'It changed your life?' Faiza asked, her curiosity piquing. 'That's a big statement.'

'I know I'm making it sound very dramatic, but I had never been with anyone but Pratap, you see. He was everything to me, the only person I had ever shared my, um, body with. This other person helped me understand those things a little better. You girls are lucky that you have been with more than one person. When you haven't, it's the only way you know how to look at yourself.'

For Ahana, marrying young had been a regret in her later life that surfaced every time she hit a tempestuous patch in her marriage. Sometimes she felt it when she heard stories of her friend Priya's post-divorce escapades – 'exclusively with younger men because men our age are too bloody selfish'. Other times, she felt it first-hand when she and Pratap made love; every now and then realization would dawn anew that she knew most of her husband's moves by rote, and how they would often end in an anticlimax.

It wracked her with guilt — she hadn't been taught to prioritize her pleasure, and it took a long time for her to realize she could even ask. But even when she did, it was within the confines of comfort, ricocheting between the two or three positions that Pratap didn't seem unnerved by. Her only recourse for wild sex was vicarious, through risqué video clips she watched on her phone in the shadows of night, as she touched herself gently afterwards, afraid of the awkwardness that would arise from him waking up and catching her out.

'Oh, please tell us the story!' Saira pleaded, knowing she was the only one with the guts to ask. 'I absolutely promise not a soul at this table will judge.'

'I'm not worried about that.' Ahana smiled. 'But it's a long story, with some sad parts.'

'I apologize for Saira,' Faiza said. 'She has no boundaries. Please don't feel like you have to revisit a sad story to entertain us.'

'It's not a *sad* story, per se; just some moments in it are sad,' Ahana clarified. 'Well, it does have a happy ending … I think.'

'Only if you're comfortable then,' Natasha offered.

Ahana paused thoughtfully for a moment, and then a smile spread across her face.

'On one condition,' Ahana said. 'We get dessert after this.'

AHANA

IT HAD BEEN almost three years, but it still felt like weeks. So much had happened in her life since then: Alia had graduated; they had moved house after nearly two decades in their beautiful, three-bedroom apartment in the heart of Bangalore; she'd even started drinking green tea after all those years fighting Pratap's lectures about its 'amazing antioxidants'. Three years, and she still had the same dull ache she'd felt right at the start, still felt like she'd been slapped in the face, her cheeks smarting even now.

She got up to make dinner, just for herself tonight, because Alia was in Gokarna with her friends for the long weekend. She'd have to get used to it – another couple of months and her only child would be off to Edinburgh to study Linguistics, and she'd only get her for the big holidays because 'It's too expensive, Amma, I can't fly back every time I get a break. Plus, I want to take the train and travel around Europe during the short ones.' She'd agreed – it *was* expensive – but she would have been happy to bear the fare if it meant seeing her daughter more.

She looked around the kitchen and suddenly felt

overcome by the wave of extreme tiredness she had known every day since the moment she'd got the call about Pratap. The moment that had changed her life for the first time. Suddenly everything that seemed easy the day before now felt too overwhelming and it made no sense to carry on. It was in those moments that she would want to collapse to the floor or lie on the couch for the rest of the day – but she had to force herself to stay active. She simply hadn't been allowed to indulge her emotions. Her parents would have had none of it. So she coaxed the feeling to ebb and returned to the business of life.

If Alia had been here, Ahana would have made her a shepherd's pie or a quiche, or any of the sinful desserts her daughter loved, calories be damned. But it was just her now, and she didn't feel like doing anything elaborate in the kitchen. She opened the freezer and stood in front of it, debating whether to pull out the mutton she'd marinated last week. She could make a basic curry. Or just fix a quick sandwich with the cheese in the fridge.

Her phone rang just as her freezer started to beep angrily because the door had been open too long. She shut it in a hurry and scrambled for her phone. Alia used to laugh that she even had a ringtone. 'It's 2019, Amma, everyone's phones are on silent.' But if her phone didn't ring, Ahana would never find it. Hell, she couldn't even find it now as it loudly played a Sinatra song Alia had programmed in for her.

By the time she finally recovered it from the bottom of a couch cushion, the caller had hung up. She smiled fondly on instinct as she saw the name on display. It was Pranay,

Pratap's younger brother, calling to check up on her from
Bombay like he often did. She had always liked Pranay. The
trouble-making sibling of the Rao family had driven her
husband mad since they were children, but she could never
bring herself to be angry at him for too long. He was simply
too charming and good-hearted, and since he never took
himself seriously, she never had as well. That meant he often
got away with murder, because he knew she would take up
for him with Pratap.

He answered on the second ring. 'Too busy to pick up, ah?'
he said warmly, his voice laced with that familiar southern
drawl typical of 'the Bangalore accent'. A decade of living
in Bombay hadn't erased the biggest marker of his born-
and-bred Bangalore personality. 'I'm not important enough
anymore?' he teased.

'Exactly. I prefer to screen people like you. Who knows
why you're calling?' she retorted mischievously. Their banter
was always easy, and it had been a comforting go-to in the
years after Pratap's death. The only thing that sometimes
left her with a twinge in the stomach was how much he
reminded her of his brother.

'Oh! *Achha?*' he said, emphasizing the '*ch*' and laughing. 'I
was actually calling to say that I'm in town and brought you
that slimy mithai shit from Bombay, but if you're going to be
mean, I'll just eat it by myself in my room.'

'What now? You're in Bangalore? I just spoke to you and
you didn't say anything!' she said, all at once, excited. 'And
what room? You're in a hotel? Do you want a slap?' she added
in a scolding tone.

'Okay, okay, relax, *ma*. I'm here for work, it was last
minute, they told me just day before. Bloody weekend also

got ruined, man. All for one stupid meeting in Marathahalli of all places,' he groaned.

'Is that why you're staying in Marathahalli?' she prodded. She wasn't letting up on the hotel thing, firmly from the school of thought that family members should stay with family when in the same city. 'Early morning meeting? You have to wake up at six or something?'

'*Baabs*, they booked a room, ya,' he protested, employing an abbreviation of the mispronounced 'bhaabiji', his nickname for her, that always got her riled up. 'They book it for other cities, no? Along with the flights? Anyway, let's have coffee tomorrow? My meeting is only day after; I just need to get here early to pick some things up from the Bangalore office.'

'Let's have coffee?' she exclaimed. 'I'm not some friend of yours from college. I was just about to make dinner; pack your things and come. You can go back tomorrow night,' she said with the authority of a sister-in-law – firm and uncontradictable.

'Ay, it's eight already! And I have to—' he started but she cut him off, 'Sounds like you want that slap I offered earlier.'

'Oof, okay, fine, but it will take me an hour. And what are you making for dinner?'

She smiled. 'Mutton curry and rice. But if you want something else, just tell me.'

'I love your mutton curry-rice; make, make. I'll stop somewhere and bring some dessert.'

'Aren't you bringing my *singar ki mithai*? Did you eat it already? Really, Pranay, shame on you.'

'*Chi*, never. That's why I'll stop, no? Only you eat that cakey yellow shit; normal people need actual dessert. Okay, bye, I have to pack now – my sister-in-law is damn mean when I'm late.'

The doorbell rang twice, a marker of Pranay's usual aura of impatience. In the hour since he'd called, Ahana had sprung into action. After putting dinner on, she pulled out a bottle of whisky (for him) and gin (for her), quickly filled the ice bucket with perfect rounds of ice and freshened up the linens in the guest room. She chose delicate peach sheets because she knew the feminine hue would get a reaction from him, and she smiled at the thought.

After an additional few minutes of clutter-clearing and cushion-fluffing, the house was ready. The only trouble was that *she* wasn't. He'd be here any minute and she was a full mess – hair bound back the way she always had it when she cooked, in an old T-shirt and some comfortable shorts she'd stolen from Alia's closet. That she managed to fit into her daughter's size S clothes was a point of pride for her, one she celebrated by occasionally nicking things from Alia's closet. Maybe she could steal something now that would make her look halfway presentable.

She didn't know exactly why she felt she had to look presentable. It was only Pranay, who had spent many short vacations at their home wearing nothing but a pair of boxers in desperate need of darning. He'd seen her in face masks, with oil in her hair and Alia's old SpongeBob slippers on her feet. But, as she caught a glimpse of her reflection, she suddenly felt ten years older than her forty-four – and was determined to not look the way she felt.

She quickly weighed how much time she had, and decided she could swing a shower, but her long, wavy hair would have to forgo a wash. She had barely stepped out of the bathroom when the doorbell rang – in a burst of doubles after the patient first set while she scrambled to fix herself up. There wasn't enough time to actually put her clothes on properly, so she threw on Pratap's old robe in a mad rush and tied it tightly at her waist. She hurtled to the door and opened it, feeling out of breath and faced with a big grin, a bag from Glen's Bakehouse and Pranay's open arms.

'Baabijeeeeee!' he mocked in his thick Bangalore accent and stood grinning, poised for a hug. The pieces of Pratap in his thicket of dark, wavy hair and aquiline nose would've been almost too hard to look at if they weren't distinguished by Pranay's distinctly un-Pratap half-smile and the caramel eyes he'd inherited from her mother-in-law that her husband hadn't.

She greeted him with a gentler version of the slap she'd threatened him with earlier. 'You have NO patience. It's such nice weather also – you couldn't have waited five minutes for me to wear clothes?'

'*Arey*, what is this formality of clothes, like we're strangers. Give me a hug!'

She laughed and wrapped her arms about him. The familiar oud and vanilla of his Tom Ford Noir – she knew because a bottle was always perched on the guest bathroom counter during his visits – hit her as they embraced. Such a contrast that scent was to him, too intense and layered for someone who had never thought to take anything seriously.

'Okay, come in, come in,' she said, breaking away less because she wanted to and more because she thought she should, and reached out for his bags.

'Stop trying to steal my brownies!' he said. 'I have your dirty mithai; the brownies are for me.' He held the boxes out of reach. 'Besides, you should go and change – *log kya kahenge*, etc.'

She rolled her eyes. 'Fine. You know where the guest room is; I'll come in a minute,' she said, already walking to her room. She had just shut her door and opened her closet when she heard a faint yelp: 'Pink sheets!' She laughed quietly to herself, vacillating between a long, black cotton dress that had just come back from the wash, and sat at the top of a neat pile and a shell-pink floral dress that always made her feel particularly feminine when she wore it. After staring at her options for a while, she chose the black. *Safer*, she thought.

When she came back out, having run a comb through her hair and slicked on some nude lipstick, Pranay was already at the table, ladling curry atop a mound of rice. It made her happy to see him enjoying the way Pratap would have. The two might have been different in many respects, but the way they tucked into her cooking like hungry children was something they had always had in common.

'You're such a *bhukkad*,' she teased, as she helped herself to half the amount on his plate – her metabolism wasn't what it once was, and she had to save space for her mithai. He held up his finger to imply that he would retort when he was done chewing, but she didn't give him a chance.

'So, how's Bombay? What flash floods and cyclones are happening next? What's it like living in a small box for a ridiculous amount of rent? Too much space after that sweet, Bengali girl moved out to have two full rooms?' she mocked.

He was through with his mouthful. 'Excuse me, that ended almost a year ago. And it's better to live in that box than in this village, okay? You know how much traffic I got stuck in? I landed at bloody three, ya. This airport also is so bloody far away – why do you still live here?'

For a second she was quiet. She had contemplated moving after the accident. The house, the city, everything was too full of memories, mostly happy ones. But it seemed unfair to uproot Alia right in the middle of her board years – and all her friends were here; she had some semblance of stability. So she'd stayed – the moving on would have to wait.

She smiled softly at Pranay. 'The weather.'

He put his non-eating hand up, grudgingly conceding. 'Okay, fine, the weather is beautiful. It's always *so* nice. Bombay turns to shit after the rains, but here the air turns amazing.' The downpour outside, as if on cue, picked up a little as he said that. 'Ooh, I know! We should go and get cake fudge from Corner House at Airlines! We can sit on the wet swings and irritate the owner,' he said, a glint in his eye.

'You *just* went and got brownies, no? You're such a child,' she chided, wondering why she always had to gravitate to this mother role when she was around him. Why couldn't she just be spontaneous? Go and sit on the swings and eat a decadent, nostalgic dessert?

'Hmm okay, buzzkill. Anyway, I'm already too full to move and I really want a drink so, *chalo*, another time.'

She gestured at the small trolley parked in the corner of the room, beaming with booze and its fixings. He made an impressed face.

'Wow, what a hostess you are, mm? Ice bucket and all, like I'm the ambassador of France or something.' He chuckled.

Something about the comment made her blush inordinately, like maybe she'd made too much of an effort. 'This is just good hosting, okay? I'm not some bachelor boy who will pull out warm beer from a cupboard and pop its cap with his teeth,' she huffed.

'Please. It's extremely cool to be able to open a bottle with your teeth and you know it.'

She would never admit that she thought it was cool. It was the kind of easy indicator of strength she found sexy, but she'd never let herself think that about Pranay, of course.

'Yeah, yeah. Put your plate in the sink; I'll make you a drink.'

He smiled and, whisking his plate off the table, stood up. 'She's a poet and she doesn't even know it,' he hummed as he disappeared into the kitchen.

She stood at the bar trolley and fixed him a dram. Another thing the brothers had in common was the way they drank their whisky – Chivas 18 over exactly one large, round cube of ice. It was always easy to fix them both a drink at parties, or when Pranay was over. She was the one who would mix the drinks because Pratap could never quite get her gin fizz right, and it was simpler than giving him a tutorial.

As they sat down, glasses in hand, Pranay gently swirled his. He took a sip and said, 'Still keep Chivas in the house? You've become a whisky girl now, ah?'

'It's Pratap's only,' she responded, her voice quiet. 'He had brought back a few bottles from the duty free before …' There was a moment of discomfort – neither could find an appropriate segue. Then she smiled brightly and held up her glass, ice cubes clinking as she shook it, and said, 'And clearly I'm still a gin girl. I don't know how you drink that stuff, it's *too* strong.'

'Excuse me, this is bloody good scotch! How can you not appreciate it? Try one sip; you'll find notes of toffee and dark chocolate if you really pay attention,' he said, swirling and inhaling the scent of his drink.

'You sound like one of those insufferable sommeliers at a tasting.' She laughed, screwing up her nose. She put on a haughty expression and a drawl intended to sound snobbish. 'You'll find layers of earthy dirt in the texture, with a touch of burnt toast and a smidge of oaky oak.'

Pranay looked at her and laughed. 'Joke's on you – it *does* have an oaky oak finish.'

She narrowed her eyes. 'Not my point. Whisky tastes like whisky, not apples and rainbows and sunshine; you both are so strange …'

They went quiet again. They often did, whenever there was mention of him – like a fragment of a moment of silence for his departed soul, like a weight that needed to be heaved off the conversation to allow it to breathe again. This time, she decided against it.

'I miss him,' she said, pushing back tears and trying to let her voice ring only with fondness. 'We should be able to talk about him. Normally,' she added, looking up at Pranay. 'Without this … awful silence.'

'Or crying,' he said, gesturing to a tear that had rolled down her nose despite her best efforts, splitting her face clean in half. Her choked voice turned to an involuntary giggle as he cracked a smile. 'I know. I always turn into a blithering fool when I think about him.'

'It's okay, it's more than okay.' His tone was gentle. 'I feel like crying too. I do, sometimes, when I'm alone at home, or in one of these hotel rooms. There's nothing to do but think, and then I think about him …'

His eyes were suddenly full, glistening. He tilted his head back, as if to roll the tears in limbo back into his head, but they spilled over. He quickly raised his hands and brushed them away violently, almost as if he was trying to erase them from his face. She, too, softly swiped away the last remnants of her tears that had already started to meld with her skin.

'We're pathetic, both of us,' she said, with a different energy now. 'It's been three years, and we have so many happy memories. We should be able to talk about him like that – happily. He would want that, wouldn't he?'

Pranay smiled, weakly at first, and then with a glimmer of his regular aura of mischief. '*Arey*, he loved it when people cried over him. I remember when he left for college and Ma was non-stop wailing, he was smiling and goading her, you know? Like, "Oh, Ma, you won't even miss me that much, I'm sure," just so she could go, "How can you say that? I'll miss you so much!" and then cry more. He had no shame!' By this time, his smile was a full-fledged grin.

She laughed at the visual in her head – a young Pratap, all of eighteen, heading off to college, and her overprotective mother-in-law being her usual, clingy self. 'I'm sure that's not what happened!' she protested in Pratap's defence. 'You also exaggerate so much. *You* have no shame.' She threw a cushion at him.

He caught it just short of his face. 'Please. You just don't want to believe he was such an ass. Okay, now your turn.'

She tried hard to think of a story she could recount without tearing up. She mentally rifled through her memories like they were a stack of photographs, catching quick glimpses and shuffling past. She finally paused at the visual of the Family Picnic Disaster of 2004. 'I've got one, I've got one,' she said, like a child in class who knew the answer. 'We had gone to Cubbon Park. Alia was four-ish, I think, and you remember how she was as a child. Always running around; she could never sit still.' She smiled, as Pranay nodded in agreement. 'So she decided to run away while I was still setting things up and went to this random girl who was settling down on the grass with her boyfriend. Alia just decided to sit with them and refused to come back to our spot. She started eating their food too!' Ahana was laughing now, as Pranay chimed in, 'Shameless, just like her *appa*.'

'She kept talking to them and eating their sandwiches. Every time I picked her up to move her, she would start to scream. What a brat! Pratap was furious with her – I think it's the only time I've seen him go completely red. And she just kept saying, "Appa, bring our cake, *na*? We'll share with aunty." The poor girl. She would've been twenty-one–twenty-two at best, and here was some sandwich-stealing toddler calling her aunty in broad daylight!'

'Oof, I remember that scream of Alia's! Pratap used to go crazy, ya. How did y'all ever get her to stop?' Pranay mused.

It hadn't been a happy experience. Her view was that they

should sit with her, address her concerns and calm her down. Pratap had been less 'spare-the-rod', wanting to Ferberize his daughter and lock her in a room till she stopped. Finally, to his chagrin, her approach held sway, and while it took her nearly a year, she got Alia to stop her tantrums.

'Oh, a little of this and that,' she said, glossing over it. 'Kids also grow out of these things. Anyway, you want that dessert now or what?'

'No, ya,' he said, shaking his head. 'Now that I've started this whisky, I don't want to change the taste.'

She agreed. She didn't normally feel like more than one drink, but today she was enjoying hers enough to want to have another. She made them both a second round and put on some music in the background. Def Leppard. She was feeling nostalgic.

'Why are you playing Pecos music?' he asked, naming an old Bangalore bar they all used to frequent, best known for its diluted beer, chilli beef and only having strictly classic rock on the menu.

'This is *my* music, okay?' she explained to her thirty-eight-year-old brother-in-law, who had escaped the eighties' glam-metal era altogether by growing up in the nineties. 'And it's good, so just enjoy it.' She closed her eyes and tuned into the easy guitar riffs of 'Hysteria' as she sipped on her drink, swaying slightly.

She opened her eyes to find him smiling at her, with a look she couldn't quite place. There was fondness in it, but also something else. He lifted his drink quickly to his lips, as if to cover the smile, and cleared his throat. 'At least play their famous song, ya,' he complained.

She rolled her eyes and scrolled through her playlist. The

catchy, instantly recognizable notes of 'Pour Some Sugar on Me' filled the room, and she looked at him as if to say, 'Happy?'

The evening moved with easy comfort, through several more artists and nearly as many drinks. By the time he was also swaying gently and pouring them a sloppy sixth each, she realized exactly how long it had been since she'd got this drunk. It had been with Radhika, her best friend, who had dragged her out to a bar nearly a year after Pratap's passing because she'd believed Ahana needed to drown her sorrows in endless GinTos. They had – and all she remembered after a point was a lot of giggling, and Alia having to practically carry her up the stairs. The experience wasn't an encouraging predecessor.

'We should stop,' she said, making a colossal effort not to slur.

'Okay, teacher,' Pranay teased, setting her drink down in front of her. He seemed more in control of his words – he had always been able to drink her and Pratap under the table. She resented how much clearer he sounded. That, and being called 'teacher'.

You think I'm just some gross old aunty, don't you? she thought, with a pang of hurt. *I wasn't always like this. I used to be fun. I used to be attractive enough to get drinks for free.* That her being beautiful seemed like a distant memory made her sad.

After a short silence, Pranay looked directly at her and said, 'You're still attractive, Ahana. You're still very … And I would never think of you as old or gross, or an aunty – ever.'

Her hands flew to her mouth. Had she said her thoughts out loud? Like in some tacky sitcom? It felt like she had sent a bitchy text about her boss *to* her boss by mistake – and there was no way to recover.

The music was still going, now travelling down a John Mayer playlist he had stolen her phone to put on. The melodic song was luckily just loud enough to compensate for the awkwardness, but also soft enough to allow her to think about how stupid she felt.

'I'm, um … sorry,' she said, at a loss. She didn't know where to go from here. It seemed like the smartest move would be to abandon her drink in favour of her bed and leave the room before saying anything more embarrassing.

'You don't really think that, do you?' Pranay asked, his tone even softer now. 'You don't think that's what I think about you? That you're some frumpy aunty?'

She felt trapped by his question. Because, yes, sometimes she thought he saw her as this parental figure, forever chiding and taking care of him. But she wasn't much older, and it didn't feel good to be in that role. It would have been nice if sometimes …

'It doesn't matter; I'm being silly. You have these silly thoughts sometimes – when you get as old as me.' She laughed, trying to shrug it off with a joke.

He was quiet again, looking right into her eyes. Then, without warning, he got up and moved to the couch to sit next to her. And he sat down very close. She'd never had this kind of physical proximity to him before; it unnerved her.

'Ahana, you're my sister-in-law. You realize that, right?'

She felt herself going hot with anger. It was bad enough that she'd slipped up and said what she did; on top of that there was this insult to injury.

'I know that, Pranay,' she snapped. 'It wasn't like I—'

He put his hand over her mouth, gently, to stop her. She could feel the warmth of his fingers on her lips. It was the most intimate form of touch she'd felt in years.

'You're my sister-in-law,' he repeated, his tone lower this time. 'And that's why I have never said anything. I haven't been *allowed* to say it.'

He moved his hand away, and that was when she realized his other hand was holding hers. She sat there, speechless.

'Do you know how it would've sounded if I ever said it? If I'd told you how beautiful you are? I didn't want to be that sleazy brother of Pratap's, whom you felt you had to avoid because he hit on you and creeped you out. You and Pratap both trusted … It wasn't right.' He was talking a little faster, as if trying to gather the myriad thoughts that had scattered onto the floor like marbles.

She knew she should say something to calm him down. He looked so flustered that she wanted to help, but she felt nailed to the couch.

He took a long gulp of his drink, as if to stop himself. When he'd drained the glass dry, he smiled an almost sad smile.

'Even if I had said it, you would've just laughed at me. You always laugh at me,' he said, slumping back in his chair. 'You never take me seriously.'

She sat there in silence. His words hung in the air, waiting to waft in some direction to either be encouraged or dismissed. She knew what the right thing to do would be. But …

'I don't laugh at you,' she said gingerly, easing his fingers out of hers. She took his hand and willed herself to look him in the eye, but something stopped her. 'I thought that's just ... how we were.'

He gently squeezed her hand. 'I know. It's just tough when ... I mean ... It's okay ...'

'When?' she prompted him. Some unknown force seemed to be pulling her down this rabbit hole. And part of her wanted it.

'Ahana ...' She shifted uncomfortably. She still had an out. 'When?' she repeated.

He took a couple of seconds, then caught her gaze and looked her straight in the eye.

'When I know how much you've gone through, how much you've suffered, I just want to be there. I want to see you laugh; I wanted so much to hold you every time you cried. I wanted to ...' He left the thought incomplete. 'But I always thought about Pratap. I owed it to him to now be your family, to be around like a ... a brother. But I don't feel like one.'

It was a lot – *a lot* more than she ever thought he'd say.

'Ahana, I try to be good. If I hadn't had all this whisky, I *would* have been good. But it shouldn't be this hard to see you, man. I shouldn't feel like this and I shouldn't be here. That's why I don't come home anymore, okay? I shouldn't have come today either.'

Suddenly the hotel made a lot more sense.

He seemed to have taken her silence for disdain, as he cleared his throat and started to get up in order to move away.

And before she knew it, she was stopping him from leaving. She didn't even realize how or when her mouth had moved close to his. Suddenly she felt its softness, and the bittersweet tang of whisky. The taste reminded her of Saturday nights early in her marriage when Pratap would go over his usual two pegs and kiss her boldly in the car on the way back from whatever dinner or family gathering they'd been at.

She pulled back at that thought, and this time her eyes met Pranay's. Something had shifted within her, and the surrealness of what was happening gave her a confidence she didn't recognize. She could tell he was about to start speaking, so she stopped him again, this time more urgently than the last. She went with her instinct to press her body into his, and she heard him utter a small groan of pleasure.

When she looked back on that night, she realized that was the moment she had really felt him let go. Until that point, there was an uncertainty in his kisses, a sense of disbelief. When she chose to kiss him again, and with more intensity, it was as if that was when he truly allowed himself to believe that this was real. He pulled her close and kissed her back with a deep fervour, sinking into it with no rescue tube.

He pulled himself away and looked at her. Her body was saying yes, but it seemed he needed her to as well. 'Ahana, is this …'

'Yes,' she breathed, her eyes closed. 'Yes, it is.'

He picked her up, her legs wrapping around his waist as they kissed almost furiously all the way to her bed.

It had been so long since she'd been touched that her body was reacting like it was the first time, with a sense of déjà vu. To have someone's lips on hers, someone's hands running across the length of her torso with that kind of undisguised ferocity seemed alien, but in the best way possible. His urgency was nothing like Pratap's languorous touches, always studied because he knew her body.

Pratap had been this urgent only two or three times in his life, and something about the way Pranay struggled to hike up her dress brought the memory of one of those times back with a searing flash. It had been Alia's first sleepover, at her nani's – the first time they'd truly had the house to themselves in the three and a half years since their daughter had been born. Ahana had thought the evening would involve some candles and a lot of foreplay. Pratap's near-neanderthal stripping of her had been completely unexpected – and incredibly exciting.

He'd taken her against the kitchen counter, fumbling with her dress and grabbing her like he couldn't get enough of her body, of the taste of her. It had been one of their wildest moments of lovemaking, and she still went weak when she thought of it.

Except now. Now she felt a sudden flare of white-hot sadness. The guilt, the shame, the excess of what she was doing hit her and she didn't even fully realize it until a tear slipped from her eye.

But he did. The minute her eyes had glazed over, Pranay had stopped, and looked at her as a single teardrop rolled down the side of her face haphazardly.

'Ahana, are you okay?' His voice was so concerned it only made her want to cry more. 'I'm so sorry,' he said, starting to get up. 'I'll stop; I'm so sorry. I don't want to …'

She stopped him, her arms pulling him back to her, as she put her mouth on his. She shook her head against his lips, pulling him tighter. 'Don't stop,' she murmured against his chest. 'Please, don't stop.'

The way he kissed her changed. The urgency had been replaced by a tenderness, just like the heat of the moment had been replaced by tacit assurance that they both wanted this to happen.

She had never known she could feel this way about him. If there had been signs, she must have driven past them. She had never felt jealous when he spoke of the women in his life, nor had she ever found him attractive in the same way she did about Pratap, and even her first boyfriend. She had never thought of him as ugly either; she'd just … never thought of him like that at all.

But now, in this moment, it all seemed like an unlocking of something. She was turned on by that hit of oud in his scent, by the strength of his arms as they tightened around her, by the softness of his mouth that pressed into hers so fully. It was like he was a different man entirely, and yet one she had always thought of as a little bit her own.

He pulled back from the kiss and started to raise her dress over her head, and it jolted her back to reality. No one except her husband had seen her naked in decades, and she'd never really thought about the next time someone would. There were the logistical nightmares – no waxes, no trims. Plus her stretch marks and stomach were not things she cared to bare – not to a man who'd never had a girlfriend over thirty. It was stupid, she knew, but she wasn't up to the comparison. She stopped him, hiking up only her skirt and tugging at him, pushing herself against him.

'What's wrong?' he said, clearly not distracted. 'Did I do something?'

'No, no, I just … don't want us to be naked,' she said, under her breath, and then quickly amended it by saying, 'I mean, *you* can be, I just … I don't …'

'But why?' he said, still kissing her neck, unable to keep his hands off her.

'I don't want you to see me …'

'Ahana,' he said, in a soft but firm tone, 'I won't push you. But you should just know that … my god,' he stopped and kissed her furiously, 'I really fucking want to.'

Something about the way he said that had an instant effect on her. No man had ever spoken to her like that before, with unrestrained want. She almost didn't believe it, but the pressure of his fingers on her waist indicated that he was holding back much more. He either meant it, or was a terrific actor.

'Okay,' she consented, with some hesitation, and he looked at her once again to make sure. She nodded a bit more confidently, and the minute she did, he yanked her dress off before she could realize what was happening. The sudden movement threw her; she was practically naked in front of someone that was not the only man she had ever truly been naked with.

'Oh my god,' he said, taking her in. 'You're … fucking insane.'

His mouth moved from her lips to the sensitive little nook between her collarbones, her neck, her chest, the chasm between her breasts. He reached behind her back and unhooked her bra with an ease that made her unexpectedly jealous. *How many girls had he done this with?* she thought. Then another thought came so close on its heels they nearly crashed into each other. *This isn't going to mean anything to him, is it?*

Self-preservation almost made her stop, but everything he was doing felt too good to fight. His hungry hands, his warm mouth, his impatient body against hers – everything about it was surreal and glorious, like an amazing dream you'd hate to be roused from.

'Oh god,' she moaned softly, and knowing she was turned on seemed to spur him on too. He was kissing every inch of her body, which started to wake up in little jolts and bursts. Nerve endings she never knew she had stood up like little soldiers, each getting her more ready than the one before it. She was so caught up in his kisses that she wasn't prepared when his mouth was suddenly on her, warm and wet. Her eyes flew open, and she looked down to see his buried head, his own closed in concentration.

Pratap had never been inclined, and she'd never liked pushing him. He hadn't expected her to return the favour either, which she supposed was his way of being fair, but that didn't change the fact that it was something she'd always wondered about, but tucked away into a corner of her mind – a lost tin in a dusty storeroom.

Watching him now was almost as arousing as the way his mouth felt on her. His tongue darted in and out, almost expertly (Again that pang of envy arrived: *How many women had he done this with?* She pushed the thought out as quickly as it had come.), and it felt so good. But watching him down there, unbridled and consumed by the act, put her in a wholly new realm of pleasure. That a man could want her in such an intense, unchecked way was enough to make her come.

She did, twice in quick succession, because he'd opened up her body in a way she had either never known, or couldn't remember. The first time it felt like she was mid-air for a split second. Her eyes flew open on instinct as she came, but all she saw was a pool of swirling light, like a bright camera flash. The second time was languid, absorbing, though she was still reeling from the aftershock of the last.

She was exhausted, and still didn't want to stop, and the dual-edged feeling overwhelmed her. She stopped and withdrew a bit. She was almost giddy, but still that sense of quid pro quo held sway.

As she bent down over him, he suddenly grabbed hold of her shoulders and stopped her. 'No,' he said firmly, in a move that was a complete antonym to the gratefulness she was expecting.

'But ... why?'

'Because that's not why I did it. And that's not what I want. I want it to be about you this time. Just indulge me?' he begged.

This time. The words almost stung her. *One of many times. He was assuming there would be a next time.*

He laid her back and started kissing her gently. She was surprised at how safe she felt with him. His arms enveloped around her, his warm skin on hers, his soft breath on her lips when they parted from their kisses – it all felt too natural to fight.

He looked at her for reassurance, and she gave it to him,

by pulling his head into a kiss. There was a duality about that kiss – the end of something, the start of something. She pushed back that feeling of guilt, tried to force away the words that kept haunting her. *Pratap. Alia. Shouldn't. Don't. Fucking everything up.* She tried to clear out the clutter through her liquor-induced haze and focus. There was no point to this moment if she couldn't be in it.

You shouldn't be in it, the words came back, breaking from their stream-of-consciousness flow to make a whole, unforgiving sentence. The visual of a smiling Pratap at Agonda beach in Goa, one of their happiest holidays, kept flashing in front of her, slightly marred and crumbling, like the burnt edges of a photograph.

'Ahana,' he said, questioning, sensing her distance.

'Just … kiss me, please.' She knew the tears were there, burning at the back of her eyes, and she couldn't think of a better way to stop him from seeing them roll down her face.

He kissed her, and she kissed back hard enough to let him know it was okay. It was all okay. It was okay for him to make love to her. It was okay for her to feel him against her, to enjoy it, to want it. It was okay for her heart to break a thousand times as he moved inside her because it felt like a betrayal to the man who loved her. It was okay for him to say *he* loved her, in that moment, and know it would never be brought up again, because it couldn't be.

It was okay. And she would be okay. For the first time since Pratap had died, she felt like she could really believe that.

They lay there after, their breathing short and unmatched, catching up to their levels of normal. The haze of alcohol had cleared significantly, and she felt a little focused at last. She had expected a rush of shame when the drink wore off but, funnily enough, she felt calm, like she'd just put down a heavy bag of groceries, and the feeling was creeping back into her worn limbs.

For a long time, they said nothing, but there was something heavy about their silence. She could hear the faint strains of a meandering Spotify playlist that seemed to have led them to some melodic French music, and it filled the quiet just enough. She looked over at him to check if he had fallen asleep. But he was staring at the ceiling.

'Ahana ...' he began, his voice low, hesitant.

'It's okay, Pranay,' she said, cutting him off. 'Tomorrow.' She surprised herself by moving over to his chest and resting her head on it. He masked his surprise well, and pulled her close, taking the moment in instead of questioning it.

As she started to drift off, she pushed back the thought of that tomorrow. The tomorrow that lay in wait beyond the blanket of the night; foreboding. Tomorrow, with the promise of a conversation she didn't want to have, a heart she didn't want to break. He was Pratap's brother – her husband's brother – and so it couldn't become real. But it could remain a moment. The beautiful moment that had given her back more than she even knew she'd lost. The moment that changed her life – again.

FOURTEEN

NATASHA WAS SURPRISED to find a tear slipping down her left cheek. She was reminded of that deep feeling of loss, that haunting desperation to find normalcy again. It made her instantly afraid of losing Alex – a thought that hadn't really bothered her until that moment. The idea that some terrible, unforeseen incident could take away the man she had grown so inextricably linked to over so many years was too awful to bear.

She thought of the last time she had seen him – at the threshold of their two-bedroom house, as she dashed out the door, twenty minutes later than she should've been for her flight. The rush had left no time for languorous parting kisses; all she managed was a quick peck on his pursed lips before making a run for it. The assumption had always been that there would be more – more intimate moments, more kisses, more togetherness for the rest of their whole lives. But hearing Ahana's story about grappling with the suddenness of her husband's loss long after he had left hit Natasha hard – she realized there was no preparing for it. She shot Alex a quick text under the table with the words 'I love you', out of context, as a reply to his last text asking where the louder set of their two speakers were.

'You were right,' said Rubani, who mirrored Natasha's reaction and dabbed at her eyes with a paper napkin. 'That was sad. Beautiful, but still sad.'

'Beautiful,' Faiza agreed. 'But not sad. Not if it gave you back a sense of self.'

'So,' Saira said, clearing her throat, 'would it be okay if I asked you something?'

'Saira!' Rubani hissed in apprehension.

'Please, of course,' Ahana offered kindly, slicing off a forkful of apple pie and sliding it through the now-melted ice cream. 'Anything you like.'

'Why didn't it ever happen again? With Pranay?' she asked, a little hesitant. 'I mean, it just seemed like there was so much chemistry, and I can understand why not, but also … why not?'

Ahana smiled. 'I thought about it a few times when I was feeling especially lonely. And I realized that if it had become … something more, I wouldn't have been able to handle it. Not to mention Alia, my parents, his parents …'

For a moment, she looked wistful. The future had flashed in her weaker moments, and she could see a life with him – simple things, like reading near each other, or sitting at a cafe across from each other. Him infecting her with his endless energy, her anchoring his whirlwind ways. But the idea had the whiff of fantasy – warm, faint and unrecognizable, unable to face up to the rigours of reality. And that very idea ruined even the beauty of what they'd had. Of what he'd given her.

'I will not lie to you,' Ahana said, focusing on her crumb-encrusted spoon as she swirled it in the pool of molten vanilla. 'There were moments when I wondered. But I think it would have put everything in too much danger. And if it had not worked, *aiyo*,' she pulled at her ears. 'I would have lost one of my closest friends, and it wasn't worth that.'

'I think this is the very definition,' Saira said, looking pointedly at Rubani, 'of a meaningful one-night stand.'

Rubani ignored Saira's directness and, on instinct, reached out for Ahana's hand, which Ahana took as if it were the most natural thing in the world. It was something Bani had always loved about women – when the need arose, they offered comfort and warmth to each other freely. They could be physical and intimate without being sexual, and it was beautiful. If men had the same dynamic with each other, she was yet to see proof of it.

'Thank you,' Rubani said, her voice almost breaking. She cleared her throat. 'Thank you for telling us your story. It really means a lot to me that you did.'

Ahana felt herself tearing up a little and tried hard to blink the threatening spillover back into her eyes – to no avail. It was moments like these she was grateful for, and she owed so much of it to both Alia and Pranay. Her daughter had always been her biggest cheerleader, pushing her to do things that made her happy. The confidence to do them had come from Pranay, who had unlocked her ability to surprise herself. To choose herself. That she was sitting here, leaning into this sublime, chance bonding was due in no small part to who they had encouraged her to be.

'*Arey*, I should be thanking you girls,' Ahana said, wiping her cheek. 'This has been the nicest evening of my holiday.

It was so sweet of you girls to call me over – you have big hearts.'

'We have loved having you,' Faiza said, meaning it. 'I only wish we had had more time on the holiday, so that we could hang out again.'

'Oh, in all of this we forgot to check – are you still based in Bangalore?' Natasha asked.

'I am, but I keep going to Delhi for projects.' Ahana smiled. 'Usually at least once or twice a year.'

'Yay,' Natasha clapped. 'We'll have to take you out, *dilli* style.'

'Ah dear, I hope that doesn't mean butter chicken and Punjabi music?' Ahana made a face, which cracked into a laugh.

'Yes, it does,' Saira said through a friendly evil grin. 'But don't worry, we'll do some cool, Bangalore-approved things also.'

'That sounds wonderful,' Ahana said. 'I would really like that.'

Rubani, who had not let go of her hand, squeezed it once more.

'So, Bani,' Faiza turned to her friend with purpose, 'are you finally convinced, or do we need to keep at it?'

She knew Faiza was asking in jest, but she was starting to feel convinced. She had already been feeling inclined – Faiza's story had been a tipping point, but Ahana's had sealed the proverbial deal. To learn that a night with somebody had the potential to revive a part of you that had been quieted with grief, and also tap into parts of you you didn't know existed, was enough. Hearing Ahana talk about that night was moving – how it had had gone beyond being just sex and into something she didn't even know she needed in order to move on. Their situations weren't comparable, she knew, but, as corny as it seemed, maybe it was something she, too, needed to find lost parts of herself.

'Ya, babu, how many more life-changing stories you want to hear?' Natasha complained.

'Okay, okay.' Rubani grinned. 'I'll do it. I promise you,' she turned to Ahana, and then to her friends, 'and all of you that I'll do it. But on one condition. Not tonight. Soon,' she added before anyone could object.

'Not tonight,' Natasha agreed. 'Tonight is about us.'

'To us!' Saira raised a toast. 'For sex is good but sisterhood's better.'

'Ugh, look outside,' Saira said, nudging Rubani in the airplane seat next to her.

Beyond Saira's window lay some semblance of the city they called home, cloaked in the dark veil of smog that November had taught them to expect. Somewhere beyond the thickness of the grey were the city's lights, just about starting to come on as the last streaks of sunlight evanesced. She looked over at the aisle across, where Natasha was sleeping angelically while Faiza flipped through the in-flight magazine, stopping every so often to smirk.

The plane hit the ground with an unfinessed thud, causing both girls to lurch forward as they grabbed each other's arms for support. As it taxied to a halt, it struck Rubani that the holiday was well and truly over. They would emerge from the bubble and into acrid reality in a matter of minutes.

As the familiar ding before the landing announcement sounded, Rubani felt reluctant to leave. It wasn't just that the holiday had been far better than she had imagined – when she'd left heartbroken, her mind too full of cataclysmic thoughts about life without Kabir. She had expected to drown her sorrows in alcohol and long crying sessions on the laps of her indulgent friends, who had made it clear this trip was primarily about her. What she hadn't expected was coming back feeling better than she had in a long time.

It wasn't the cannonade of cocktails that started in the a.m., or the feel-good food she'd scarfed down without her usual careful deliberation about how it would translate onto the camera. It wasn't the sun and the sea, which often had the power to heal infinitely, but not her broken heart. It wasn't even the people she'd met – though she knew she would definitely remain in touch with Warren and Ahana. It was ultimately that feeling of closeness with her friends, the sense that their connection was now unbreakable. It was an intimacy deeper than many other past relationships – including romantic ones – and she would never take their open hearts for granted again.

'I love you, S.' She leaned over and hugged Saira, who was struggling to untangle her seatbelt from the headphone cord.

'End-of-holiday feels are happening?' Saira said, squished against her shoulder.

'No, just like that.' Rubani smiled. 'I can't say it every once in a while?'

'You totally should,' Saira said, finally freeing her wires. 'Especially to me – I'm extremely lovable.'

Rubani's instinct was always to roll her eyes, but today she just chuckled. 'Yes, you are.'

'But I'm still upset about one thing,' Saira continued, making Rubani feel something strange in the pit of her stomach. Saira was fully capable of uttering words that could ruin her fuzzy mood, and she didn't like the thought of it.

'You never had your "meaningless sex", yaar!' she complained. 'After all my effort.'

Rubani grinned. 'I've promised you, haven't I?' she said. 'Is this weekend too soon?'

'Oh my *god* – Mila Kunis girl? I thought you were feeling marriage vibes with her – what happened?'

'I pinky swear.' She held out her little finger and hooked it through Saira's. 'You will be the first person I call.'

'You'd better,' Saira said, linking her finger with Rubani's tightly. 'We clearly have to be each other's best friends – those two don't give a shit about us,' she joked, cocking her head in an attempt to check in on Faiza and Natasha a few rows over, where they were laughing and unloading their luggage.

The four stuck together at the airport, going through the motions of collecting their bags from the conveyor with an air of post-holiday melancholy. They pushed their loaded trolleys to the gate slowly, revelling in the last moments of chatter before the exit doors flew open to officially mark the end of the trip. The brisk pea-soup air hit them as they stepped out, and the girls sighed, turning to each other.

'Well,' Rubani said, her heart full.

'Here's where I leave you, babies,' Natasha said. 'Alex just texted. He's waiting for me at the car park.'

'We could share a cab?' Saira looked at Faiza. 'I'll drop you – Def Col is on my way. Bani, I can drop you too.'

'No, no, it's close enough – I'll just get my own. I want to stop at Modern – there's nothing to eat in the house.'

'Okay, so … see you guys next week?' Faiza ventured.

'Most def!' Saira said. 'My place. Girls' night.'

'And I promise I'll stay over,' Natasha offered, her eyes sparkling.

The four friends hugged, a clumsy, haphazard hug as their limbs interwove around each other, dodging bulky handbags. For some reason, Rubani felt like crying, but she held herself back. It was not a sad moment, not really. They had to return to their lives at some point, but it was how they had returned that mattered. Holidays had the potential to shatter the most iron-clad friendships; that they had returned with theirs strengthened was a beautiful, fortuitous anomaly.

Rubani slid into her Uber, and the familiar gravelly voice of Badshah rapping about his multiple penthouses and women filled the car. It was the truest marker of being back in her city, one that filled her with a weirdly wonderful warmth. As she settled in for the forty-five-minute ride home, she scrolled down her phone's home screen and clicked on the Tinder icon. The page automatically opened to her last chat – a days-long conversation with Alisha, aka 'Mila Kunis girl', about how creepy it was that men fetishized the school uniform so much.

She scrolled up on their conversation, right to the start, which coincided with the beginning of her trip. She noticed the scroll took longer than she'd anticipated – they had been in touch more than she had realized. There were memes, hearts and late-night 'You up?'s aplenty and, to a layperson, it would look like they'd been chatting for weeks at least. Rubani wondered if she should just bite the bullet and ask her to come over.

Her phone pinged mid-mental debate as a text from Warren set her screen aglow. *If I haven't said it yet, I'm so glad you came to Goa.* Rubani smiled, reading the message on her home screen without clicking on it. Another text rolled in, asking if he could call her when he came to Delhi. She didn't feel the need to reply immediately, but she knew she would say yes.

She liked them both in different ways – Warren had the edge because they'd met and had a moment. But she had spent more time talking to Alisha and enjoyed doing it. Their conversations were easy, non-committal, and yet, somehow, never frivolous. Plus, while Warren was an attractive man, the big biceps weren't her go-to – she had always had a predilection for tall, even gangly men. Perhaps that was the allure of the 'anti-type'. Alisha, on the other hand, was the sort of woman she instantly found attractive – petite, with big round eyes and a toothy smile. Her fingers drummed across the glass screen.

She swiped away from Alisha's profile and onto the new list of fresh catch Tinder had curated during her absence from the city. As usual, the process of swiping left became almost robotic when a sea of men in flashy Gucci belts and mirrored sunglasses interspersed themselves with orange-lipped women pouting in washed-out selfies. It was terribly hard to come upon someone interesting, and she was tempted to switch back to the girl she had found and thank her stars.

It was in the limbo between giving up and giving it 'five more minutes' that she saw a profile that caught her interest mere milliseconds before she swiped away on autopilot. She stopped quickly and scrolled through the images. No editing, no pretension, no tacky clothes – and great body. Bonus: just exactly her type.

It was a match! – Tinder announced proudly the moment Rubani swiped right. Two signals and one song later, a text bubble popped up on the app.

Hi Rubani, it's nice to meet you.

Rubani's fingers hovered over the response bar in thought. The second-guessing set in, and it hit her that this unfamiliar person, attractive as they were, had not even the smallest ounce of history with her. The part of Saira's story that had frightened her the most came back in a vivid flash. *I could be murdered*, she thought in a slight panic. *It happens to so many people; how can I know for sure it's not going to happen to me?*

Hi, she replied tentatively. The response to it, and the ones after, came quickly.

Half an hour into getting home and settling in, Rubani realized she had been involved enough in her Tinder texting to completely miss the moment she'd been dreading – walking into a house with no sign of Kabir. They had arranged for him to pick up his things while she was away; it had seemed the most painless way to close their chapter. She had been working overtime not to let her mind concoct a visual of a hollow, bare house awaiting her return.

As she looked around, it was hard to see what exactly had

been removed. All her favourite things were in place – the ones she looked for whenever she came home from a trip: her framed print of Lichtenstein's 'Girl in Mirror', her Katz painting coasters, her borderline-gaudy fuchsia beanbag and the row of *Gossip Girl* bobbleheads she'd picked up on a trip to LA. She gave Serena's head a bop and smiled as it wiggled furiously.

Study the apartment as she might, she noticed practically nothing missing – nothing that had left a dent or a white, dust-encircled space on the floor. The only real sign that something was askew was a spot on the wall, a slightly softer shade of eggshell than the wall around it that had formerly borne a gargantuan *Fight Club* poster. *His* gargantuan *Fight Club* poster. Saira had always scoffed at it, calling it 'proof of his plebeianism'. She chuckled at the memory and realized it was nice not to have it there. The garish pink font had always been jarring to her, something Kabir had never understood because 'you have pink furniture, for fuck's sake', but it now felt like the wall could breathe.

Her phone pinged from across the room. She grabbed a cold beer from the fridge and sank into the beanbag, opening the text from her new Tinder interest. *When would you like to meet?* it read, tentative, water-testing. On instinct, she texted back. *Now? You could come over?*

As soon as she pressed send, her heartbeat picked up to three times its usual rhythm. The sudden risks and terrifying implications of her invitation sent her into a near-spiral of panic, one which she contemplated easing by deleting the text. When she realized she couldn't, her anxiety heightened. She was just about to send another text attempting to take it back when a response came in. *I'd love to. I'd also be happy to meet you for a coffee somewhere, if that's more comfortable?*

Just the offer itself was enough to put her mind at ease. It was also enough to spur her into action. *Come over,* she typed, with a full stop for finality. *But there's something I should tell you …*

A ping came in record time. *Tell me?*

I just got out of something serious, and extremely chaotic, Rubani continued. *I feel like I should mention that.* As she pummelled the words into her keypad with passion, she wondered if she ought to say that she didn't want a relationship. It was true in the here and now, but she knew a part of her always would. Still, it was probably smart to manage expectations.

Taking a deep breath, she carefully typed in the words: *I'd love to see you, but I'm not looking for anything long-term. I'm in this for one night only.*

The cursor blinked. Her fingers hovered over the keypad. Rubani's heart started to race a little.

All she had to do was hit 'send'.

ACKNOWLEDGEMENTS

WHEN I STARTED writing *One Night Only*, we were in the grips of the pandemic's second wave. It was a turbulent time and it terrified me, but it also gave me something special — time to write my book. Writing it allowed for a conversation with myself about friendship and sexuality. Putting it all down on paper — these characters I saw so clearly, the way their stories rolled out — was an escape I needed from the world as it was. I grew to love my writing hours (sometimes mere minutes in a day) and could hardly believe it had all come together the way it had once I typed that final sentence. Even as I saw the book come to life, moments away from being immortalized on paper, it still seemed incredibly surreal.

They say writing is a lonely business, but I've been lucky. My husband Nandan Rosario was part of every chapter, every character direction. He wasn't just my sounding board, he was my Plymouth, unwavering in his confidence on the most trying of days. I am thankful for his faith in me, and our many conversations that have shaped this book. It really helps to be married to a brilliant writer who helps me be a better one.

I owe a great deal of thanks to my agent, Ambar Sahil Chatterjee, who got what my book was trying to say without me ever having to explain it. For all the hand-holding, the long coffees about everything but work, for being my guiding star through the myriad difficult decisions from day one to publication and beyond, I can't thank him enough.

I want to thank Teesta Guha Sarkar for being the kind of supportive, sharp publisher a debut author can only dream of. From getting me the cover I wanted to making me feel truly heard as an author, she subverted every stress-inducing expectation that publishing horror stories had left me with. In her, I found not only a great editor, but a great friend.

A few other editors deserve a mention, not only for offering to publish my book but also for believing in it. I hope they will recognize themselves in this note and know how much their vote of confidence means to me.

I owe a great debt to Rijuta Agarwal – not just one of my closest friends but the designer of the book's fabulous cover, one that was in terrible trouble before she rescued it on a manically tight timeline! Not only did our aesthetic and vision align perfectly from the get-go, she brought the characters in my heart to life in a way only someone as talented and perceptive as her could have.

A special shoutout to the Pan Macmillan India team who, all through editing, proofing, marketing, gave this book so much love that I felt like their favourite author (I'm not saying I *am*, though, pshaw).

Thank you, Belinder Dhanoa, my creative writing professor who taught me in the two years of my master's programme that to be a writer means to write every day, no matter what. It is because of her that I have learnt two cardinal rules of writing: not everything you write is gold, and you can *always* be better at it.

Thanks also to Shreya Punj for encouraging me to write this book in the first place, and for always believing in it. It was over a late April phone call with Tarini Uppal that the idea for the book first blossomed. And she has given me pivotal advice about it ever since. Thanks to my closest friends who read the book when it was but a typo-riddled Word doc, and convinced me that I had something special.

My family: my mother Milan Vohra; my nani Hira Kartar, from whom I inherited a love of literature; my father Vidur Vohra, who never pushed me to be good at science instead of English; and my brother Krishna Vohra. My father-in-law Rupert Rosario, who has been so excited to know that I was writing a book and has since been eagerly waiting to read it. My mother-in-law Annie Rosario, whom I miss deeply.

There are many more to thank that I cannot name, because word counts are real. But it takes a village to turn raw, heartfelt prose into the beautifully bound paperback in your hands right now. Thank you to everyone who has been a part of that village. I can only hope this book has made you proud.